Charnel Glamour

CHARNEL GLAMOUR

Mark Samuels

Introduction by Matt Cardin

Hippocampus Press

New York

Contents

Forbidden Transmissions:
An Introduction to *Charnel Glamour*

Matt Cardin

[Preface to an Introduction]

he following introduction to the book you are now reading took me eighteen months to write, counting from the date when Mark first invited me to do it (May 21, 2022) to the date when I performed the final edits and sent him the finished text (December 1, 2023). Various factors conspired to extend the matter to such length. Mark and I exchanged several emails during the interim. And now, in retrospect, I find myself pondering and wondering—deeply, helplessly, and not a little speculatively—about the obscure forces that dictate the rhythms and schedules of our lives, our creative energies, and our personal relationships. For when I agreed to write this introduction, and when I unexpectedly took so long to do it, and when I used the occasion to reflect on the fact of Mark's and my twenty-plus-year friendship, which reached back to the beginning of the present millennium, before either of us had published our first books—see the thoughts on this in the text below—I did not know, and could not have known, that Mark would die just hours after receiving and reading it.

"Many thanks for sending over the introduction, which I think forms a very splendid entrée indeed to the book," he said to me in an email dated Saturday, December 2, after 5 P.M. London time. "I'm much moved by the sentiments therein." I wrote back to say that I was glad he was pleased with it. We exchanged another couple of emails that same day. I mentally settled in to await the book's publication a few months down the road. And then, four days later, on Wednesday, I received an email from a mutual friend, Quentin S. Crisp, informing me that Mark had passed away over the weekend. It had happened overnight on December 2–3. I absorbed the news with shock and then watched my mind work out the timing: Mark had departed this world very shortly after our last exchange of messages. In fact, one of the last things he had ever read was my introduction to his next book.

There were many people who were much closer to Mark than I was, both physically and personally, and their loss is much deeper than mine. But the improbable timing of these things in relation to my own long friendship with him continues to arrest me with feelings of sadness and strangeness. I suspect it always will.

In an essay titled "Beyond the Beautiful Darkness," which I published in May 2014 at *The Teeming Brain*, Mark described the upshot of the atheistic outlook that he inhabited until his late twenties: "Death meant oblivion, an end to all suffering. At any moment I could put an end to my life and embrace absolute nothingness! I was truly free. I had no master but myself. I controlled the real power in this universe: death, not life." He then explained how his atheism was comprehensively upended and replaced, through a combination of reading (Arthur Machen, C. S. Lewis, Hilaire Belloc, G. K. Chesterton) and personal mystical experiences, by the Roman Catholicism that remained his spiritual home and philosophical center ever afterward. Such intimations were not initially welcome. "I became perturbed," he said of the persuasive provocations that he perceived from Machen et al. "I loved my beautiful darkness, with nothing in it but myself, and I loved having no doubts whatsoever." And yet, he also felt this certainty to be stifling: "I had locked myself into a prison cell with nothing but the darkness I had come to love. I knew everything that could be known, because it was everything I had chosen to know." Thus, his spiritual and philosophical conversion came as an experience of light and liberation: "cracks in the walls of the cell began to show, and a little light poured through them," followed by what he experienced as the cell's wholesale implosion.

For Mark, this led to a final answer that satisfied. It also motivated him to write the stories that now constitute his contribution to weird and supernatural horror—not as a means of proselytizing for a particular religious worldview, but as a means of exploring the ramifications and potentialities, particularly the dark ones, of living in a supernaturally charged universe.

In one of more widely known passages of the New Testament, the apostle Paul said, "For now we see in a mirror, dimly, but then we will see face to face. Now I know only in part; then I will know fully, even as I have been fully known." To whatever extent it is possible for a person to see, directly and fully, the reality that lies behind the veil of the mind and body, and the hidden spiritual sun that is the source of the universe's numinous glow, and the mystery that imparts to everything a sheen of charnel glamor—to whatever extent such things can actually be seen or known, not dimly in a mirror or partially by a mortal, but unveiled in their primal actuality by the removal of the limitations of finitude, Mark now sees and knows them. Or at least I like to think he does. And in this thinking, I am happy for him.

Pyatt, Arkansas
February 2024

Forbidden Transmissions

If a book is a meal, then the purpose of an introduction is to set the table. It is to provide the reader with the utensils that will enable enjoyment of the repast to come. As I was mulling over how to accomplish this for *Charnel Glamour,* it occurred to me that a sense of context, of scope and placement within the author's career and thought, might be the most helpful thing I could provide. But then I realized that I might be projecting my own sense of the book onto you, my imagined reader. Maybe I'm too tangled up in this matter to be able to see it objectively.

Because, you see, Mark Samuels and I became friends before his first book, *The White Hands and Other Weird Tales,* was published. In fact, I still have a handwritten letter from him, dated two years prior to that publishing event, in which he discusses the book's prospective contents, which were then not entirely settled. This letter sits beside me on the desktop as I type these words. I also still own and cherish the copy of *The White Hands* that I received directly from Mark at the 2003 World Horror Convention.

So right now, these two decades later, when I have agreed to introduce Mark's latest collection of stories, I find that I feel personally entangled in the task. I also find that I am beset by a sense of numinous vertigo that has increasingly come to characterize my experience of time's paradoxical passing—paradoxical because the present always remains present, and I always remain I, even as time flows inexorably past—during that same span. And maybe, therefore, when I write these words, I'm not actually trying to help you. Maybe I'm not even thinking of you at all. When my instinctive move in reflecting on Mark's new book is to think back to where his career began, and to remember our early acquaintance, and to consider how this informs my own reading of *Charnel Glamour,* perhaps I'm just trying to explain to myself how twenty years can possibly have passed, and why the memory of Mark's first book still resonates with me all these years later, and how it is that he writes weird supernatural horror stories that patch directly into my apprehension, amplified by the passage of time, of the strange fact that we live in a world of phantoms in which we ourselves, despite our presumed solidity, may be the very source of spectrality.

In 2006 I interviewed Mark for the blog I ran at that time. He told me that his desire to write had originated with his discovery of Lovecraft at age fifteen. "Lovecraft, for me," he said, "made the world itself much more interesting, providing it with *a sense of charnel glamour* for which I'd been searching during my youth." (Yes, those italics have been added by me.) However, he later "discovered the work of Arthur Machen, which, I think, has been an even greater influence upon my adult life and attempts at fiction."

When I asked him whether his personal beliefs, including his religious affiliation and his preference for Machen's mysticism over Lovecraft's nihilism, had ever found their way into his stories, he replied: "I am a Roman Catholic. But I really wouldn't dream of trying to incorporate any moral teaching into my weird fiction. I am not a proselytiser. . . . I don't really see my writings in the supernatural horror genre as representative of my religious beliefs, or of the totality of my experiences. I see them as almost exactly the reverse, as if these fragments of a sub-created literary universe must, inevitably, be wilfully nightmarish in order to succeed aesthetically."

I think it is somewhere among these data points, as perhaps cross-fertilized by the influence of a few other masters of weird fiction both historical and contemporary, including Thomas Ligotti, that Mark's authorial sensibility can be triangulated. (A tangential but not unimportant observation: Ligotti came to weird fiction in an opposite order from Mark's, discovering and liking Machen first but then finding his primary influence in Lovecraft.) And yet, having said that, I also want to say that such comparisons and tracings of influences are in the end superfluous, since in Mark's stories one encounters a presence and a feeling that is distinctly different from what one can find anywhere else. You don't enter Mark Samuels's universe of charnel glamour to notice or dwell on his influences. You enter it to be swallowed whole.

Any attentive reader of Mark's work has noticed the recurrence of certain consistent elements and themes over time. My sense is that these come together in a singularly potent way in this collection. From its outset, the book announces itself as being set within a recognizable world of Mark Samuels's creation, consisting of a haunted English geography and, in several

of the stories, a set of characters, locales, and plot elements that hark directly back to earlier stories and books, including his signature title story from
that first collection twenty years ago. If I read it aright, there is even one
semi-meta story that is implicitly framed as having been written by Lilith
Blake, whom connoisseurs of the Samuels canon will well remember.

This story and several others expand on the nightmarish spiritual-
supernatural vision that Mark laid out in "The White Hands," detailing a cir-
cumstance in which "supernatural literature, expressed in its highest degree
. . . is a form of initiatory rite into higher orders of being"; and in which "the
power of an acutely concentrated imagination, one centred upon death and
the macabre, [is] the means of releasing occult power"; and where death itself
is no escape from the horrors so released, since the body's demise is actually
"a doorway to the beginning of stupendously greater terrors undreamt of by
the still-living"; and where the fact of living in a metaphysical order that
evinces "the pre-eminence of the Weird over the Mimetic" means that dangerous lunatics are empowered "to create the only true art," which is not mere
entertainment but "the very stripping away of the veils which separate us from
the abysses of eternity and infinity," and which may lead to "murder as the
quintessence of ecstasy, terror as the height of irresistible fascination, fear as
the epitome of delight, and bodily evisceration as supreme craftsmanship."

Other established Samuels themes abound. A weird/Gothic fixation on
the implicitly or potentially disturbing fact, presence, and nature of technology
and its positioning within human thought and culture. The intrinsic creepiness
and uncanniness of effigies of the human form. The persistence and influence
of a haunted past on a bleak and horrified present. Strange and sinister religious
cults. The fatuous spiritual emptiness and galling moral deadness of modernity.
The displacement of the human personality by another, darker entity or intelligence. The supernatural potency of books and television as carriers and trans-
mitters of malign and transformative realities. These are all present in this new
collection. As always, they are expressed in Mark's signature measured prose,
which, to my American ear, anyway, embodies such a palpable voice of Brit-
ishness that I can almost hear him reading it aloud.

There is also a certain, striking newness to some of the stories herein. The
opening one lampoons, in high weird/supernaturally horrific fashion, the pretensions of critical theory, grounding the examination of old texts within the
academic outlook of a protagonist who in effect buries the supernatural aspect,
until the pressure causes it to erupt uncontrollably and in inextricable connec-

tion with the protagonist's own pretensions. At the other end of the collection, in the penultimate story, a protagonist whom readers of one of Mark's earlier collections will find oddly familiar, though strangely altered, tracks down a bizarre and ancient religious cult whose identity is ingeniously framed. It's a piece of ironic thematic inversion that demonstrates what weird horror is capable of in the hands of a writer with a definite personal philosophical and spiritual orientation who happens to be committed to the art itself, for its own sake.

So all this and more constitutes the Samuelsian weird fictional cosmos. It is a place where I can sense some of the most pointedly personal intimations of metaphysical fear from throughout my lifetime peering through the elements of the various narrative vehicles that Mark has constructed for conveying his vision. Readers of such stories—readers like you and me—find pleasure in this emotion of weird and numinous fear. At the same time, we also recognize that stories like this are about more than just delivering a few literary fictional pleasures. They carry the ring or scent of truth. They feel like revelations, like forbidden transmissions, like windows or doorways to something that is real, but that we are otherwise not allowed to acknowledge or talk about. In short, they feel a lot like the supernaturally potent books-as-carriers that show up in many of the stories themselves.

There is really no conclusion to this self-indulgent excuse for an introduction, no way to end it that will signal my successful setting of the table and represent your cue to dig in. Maybe that is only appropriate, since, as I said, I'm probably not even thinking of you but trying to articulate my own deep response to this book. I will simply end by stating that the universe of charnel glamour to which these stories point is eerily familiar to those whose private imaginings have always been tuned to that frequency—that is, to people like you and me (which I suppose means that I must be thinking of you after all). Mark himself tuned in long ago and began relaying that numinous signal to the rest of us. This latest collection of stories represents one of his clearest transmissions yet.

Pyatt, Arkansas
December 2023

Charnel Glamour

If Destiny Still Reigns

On December 8, there occurred the worldwide phenomenon which caused an immediate sensation but was explained away and dismissed as an elaborate hoax after a week of feverish speculation. Across the globe, on the screen of every single device capable of receiving signals, there appeared simultaneously the exact self-same one-minute transmission of unknown origin. Of course, you will recall that the initial effect of this phenomenon upon the general populace was one of puzzlement, not alarm. The content was too *outré* and the transmission itself sufficiently garbled and blurred to warrant any other reaction. Naturally, however, while the mystery remained unsolved, speculation about the event was the lead-item on all news bulletins and there were rumours of immediate, secret, high-level security meetings convened in national and international organisations around the world. When, though, major armed conflict suddenly flared up in the Far East, investigation into the source and cause of the transmission itself seemed less imperative than an immediate peaceful resolution to that crisis. The already-limited attention span of the average consumer of mainstream mass media was further shortened when responsibility for the transmission was claimed by an obscure climate change campaigner and technology insider, who also maintained that he had hacked into the network systems delivering terrestrial and satellite data streams. Unfortunately, or so he said, his attempts to transmit warnings about the dangers of not instantly reducing the level of man-made CO_2 in the atmosphere had been thwarted by the built-in safety protocols of the networks. This had resulted in his worldwide broadcast being compromised to the point of its generating solely incomprehensible gibberish. Still, no one could gainsay that he had brought environmental issues again—even if only briefly—to the forefront of media attention.

Readers of the more esoteric online journals favoured by the likes of conspiracy theorists, paranormal investigators, and out-and-out metaphysical mavericks would have noted that these sources of information provided explanations quite out of keeping with the one accepted by the general round of the mainstream commentariat. This is, of course, hardly unusual in itself. It is not necessary here to detail the various strands of explanation adopted by the esoteric publications, since it is now obvious they were as erroneous as the one the mainstream commentariat chose to accept; however, it is incumbent upon me to describe, firstly, the transmission itself, as I saw and heard it, and then to detail how I came into contact with the last man who recognised it for what it was.

The actual transmission, then, consisted of a one-minute black-and-white broadcast signal whose visuals were grotesquely distorted by static interference and whose audio track was compromised by a droning, rhythmic, background din. The question of what images and sounds the individual experiencing the broadcast saw and heard is a matter of some contention. Experts favoured by the mainstream commentariat invariably maintained that any impressions experienced were entirely subjective and in the nature of the "order" imposed upon randomised chaos (as in the likes of images "seen" in Rorschach inkblots or the spoken sentences "discerned" in so-called Electronic Voice Phenomena). But within that limited number of persons who have supplied feedback and information, there remains a startling unanimity of interpretation which, to my mind, argues against the theory that any meaning imposed upon the transmission merely originates in the mind of the subject. Whatever the truth of the matter, it must be apparent to a genuinely impartial analyst that there is no foundation for believing it to be a thwarted propaganda piece by an activist alerting mankind to concerns about man-made climate change.

My own impressions of the transmission did not differ in any significant way from the general run of impressions related by others. They were as follows:

Against the background drone of the rhythmic grinding of gears and seen through the distorting haze of black-and-white static, what I saw was another world, one whose surface consisted of cratered, rusted and blackened metal. The succession of still images were rapidly intercut and speeded up in order to incorporate the greatest number of them within the limited time available. And in that series of desolate tableaux I espied an almost infinite series of underground tunnels in what was a honeycombed, machine planet; one populated entirely by hideously wrought components, cogs, or other mechanisms of incomprehensible import. There was nothing in those images which pertained to organic life, nor any indication of its having had prior existence at all.

Josef Rostok was already known to me by reputation as a rogue, genius-level Russian communications expert throughout the journalistic circles in which I moved. My attempted meeting with him took place a few days after the worldwide broadcast event. Well before the theory of the broadcast being a hoax was widely accepted, I knew he would be best placed to give me an informed opinion. Rostok's analysis would form something of a scoop if I were to obtain an interview with him ahead of the bourgeois mainstream commentariat. It was from Rostok, and from him alone, that the proper jigsaw puzzle might be pieced together. If the broadcast originated anywhere on the planet he would be the sole person, outside of various state intelligence agencies, who would have been capable of determining who had sent it.

I tried emailing him at first—in fact, I sent several emails in one day, emphasising the urgency of the situation—but there was no reply. I obtained his personal telephone number and private address, only to discover that the phone was either permanently switched off or else non-functional. There was nothing else to do but to attempt a face-to-face encounter. But, unfortunately, he had recently chosen to take up residence in the city of Arkilsk: and visitors had long been unwelcome there. It is still entirely inaccessible to foreigners. The old Soviet legend is that anyone who voluntarily goes to Arkilsk is mad.

Originally part of the Gulag system of forced labour camps and called "Arkilag" before it was renamed "Arkilsk," it is now a major centre for processing the nickel and palladium deposits which are brought up from Naltakh at the foot of the Putoran Mountains some twenty-six kilometres away. Arkilsk is currently one huge industrial and housing complex where, close by, the polluted Daldykan river has recently run red and where the regional atmosphere is a toxic blend of particulates such as strontium-90 and of waste gases such as sulphur dioxide—all continuously belched out from a series of gigantic, red-and-white-striped chimney-stacks attached to the factories. The average temperature in December is minus twenty degrees Centigrade. Currently, the weather report showed it to be minus thirty-five. The heart-stopping arctic wind is said to be powerful enough to force pedestrians to crawl along the snow-covered pavements on their hands and knees.

*   *   *

I caught a four-hour flight from Moscow the following morning, an S7 Airlines route out over the northern wastes of Siberia and the spectacularly isolated region of Krasnoyarsk Krai and, upon arrival at Alykel-Arkilsk airport, I was summarily interviewed by a "welcoming committee" supposedly consisting of state officials but who were obviously also in the pockets of the nickel-mining company.

The brief conversation ran roughly as follows:

"You are not an undercover environmentalist journalist?"

"No, I am here only to interview Josef Rostok, the communications expert."

"We know him. He has gone crazy. You are wasting your time."

"I have the necessary authorisation from the FSB."

"It is often easier for a liar to arrive than to leave Arkilsk."

"I understand."

"We are just like an island, you see. Mainland rules don't apply."

A landlocked island inhabited by more than a hundred thousand citizens of the Russian Federation, I thought, whose life expectancy was ten years fewer even than that of other Siberians. Soviet bombers had once used the airport as a staging base in case of conflict with the United States, and it was still overseen to this day by the Russian Arctic Control Group. I had no doubt my credentials had been examined well in advance of my arrival and the "interview" was undertaken to ensure my purpose in being there was entirely as had been previously stated in my application.

Spurning the offer of sharing a *marshrukta* van with a dozen drunken industrial workers, I was approached by a taxi-driver touting for business who offered to take me for the same price anyway—800 rubles. It was not long before we were travelling along the A-382 ring-road, its surface cleared of snow but creating twenty-foot-high walls of ice on both sides of the road.

Once clear of the ring-road and with an unobstructed view through the (double-glazed) windows of the taxicab, I saw an unearthly landscape of terrible beauty speed by.

It was night—the dreadful, seemingly interminable polar night—and the denizens who existed beneath the skies of Arkilsk had not seen the sun for the past ten days. They would not see it again for another thirty-five more. Most of the surrounding region's vegetation consists solely of the mosses and lichens found on the tundra and what few trees there are still standing have been eroded by acid rain into blackened stumps. Only the electricity pylons towered over this bleak landscape, groaning in metallic accents as they were buffeted by the incessant winds.

I saw the red glare of the foundries smelting thousands of tonnes of ore and watched the heavy machines working endlessly; freight trains carrying mined deposits, gargantuan cranes dotted across the horizon, and all manner of other motorised vehicles facilitating the industrial processes—bulldozers, diggers, and forklift trucks. Everywhere one saw the lightning-flash-style "AN" logo of the Arkilsk Nickel corporation—even on the sides of the huge monoliths of the brutalist Soviet-era workers' housing blocks, with their gaudy colour-schemes long faded by neglect and weathering. A full third of the buildings appeared to be abandoned, their former occupants having presumably finally fled this macabre city lost in fire, snow, and night. The grim architectural functionality of these structures formed a striking contrast to the spectacular icy backdrop behind them—the vast and distant Putoran mountain range whose silvery peaks glinted with unearthly magnificence on clear nights with a full moon.

Rostok lived a little way out of the old industrialised city centre, on the top floor of one of the huge housing blocks of rotting concrete, and my wholly uncommunicative taxi-driver dropped me off outside the building I sought (Block Four, Molotov Estate) and drove away the very instant I handed over a thousand-ruble banknote. It was obvious that anyone who came to Arkilsk who was not on AN business was regarded as fair game, not only by the state authorities, but also by the locals.

Someone was hanging around in the doorway of the entrance porch to Block Four, and doubtless smoking a cigarette to relieve his lungs after breathing in the deadlier atmospheric toxins that were supplied free of charge to all those resident in Arkilsk. He was clad in an army greatcoat with the collar turned up. There was a huge bulge in the left outside pocket, and I could see the open neck of a bottle sticking out of it. A grizzled iron-grey beard obscured most of his lower face. His head was covered by a frayed, black, "Old No.7" Jack Daniel's baseball cap (doubtless labelled somewhere discreetly within "Made in China"). Beneath its peak only a letterbox of flesh and eyes was visible; the former a mass of chapped lesions, the latter piercing, pale blue-grey, and not level, but lopsided, with the left being noticeably lower than the right. His stare, however, was highly intense and unwavering, as if he might divine my innermost thoughts by force of sheer concentration.

"Do you know Josef Rostok?" I asked the loitering stranger.

"He won't have anything to do with crooked journalists," he replied, crushing the glowing tip of the cigarette between forefinger and thumb and putting the remaining stump into his right outside pocket.

I shrugged and was about to walk past him when he grabbed my shoulder in a vice-like grip.

"My friend Rostok does not see anyone who turns up uninvited," he snarled, through gritted teeth.

I pulled out my wallet.

The moment I opened it, the stranger—with lightning-like swiftness—punched me on the right temple. A sledgehammer could not have been more effective.

The next thing I knew, I was slumped up against one wall of the interior foyer and the stranger was bent over me. The baleful and hostile intensity of his glare had been replaced by a look of stern reprobation. There was no trace of concern or regret mingled with it. My first thought was that I was lucky to be alive and the second was relief that I had not been robbed—my wallet was still in my hand.

"Here," he said, "drink some of this."

He wiped the rim of a 70cl bottle of "Old No.7" (what else would it have been, given his headgear? I thought) and put it to my lips. I drank a couple of spluttering mouthfuls.

"Be careful not to insult me again. I am a man of honour and do not like to be offered bribes," he said.

"I apologise."

"You would not think it to look at me now, but I hail from noble stock and my forebears were of the Romanov line. As for this American brand"—he jiggled the bottle—"I can pick it up or even put it down forever, just as I please. What I am is subject solely to my own willpower, under the protection and guidance of the Almighty. I have, it is true, drunk much of late, but it has never been sufficient to blot out the full horror of the materialistic world in which we live."

Even if this "aristocrat" had not stooped to robbery, he was still, to my mind, a drunken thug. The combination of thuggery and lunacy is, nevertheless, one to be dealt with circumspectly, especially when alcohol is added to the mixture.

"I came to see Josef Rostok, but if he refuses all interviews I will leave at once."

As I spoke and tried to clear my head, the crazy stranger helped me to my feet and forcibly led me inside. I then gazed groggily around at the shabby interior whose garish décor seemed to have been left behind from the 1970s. Perhaps, I thought, its very garishness was designed to be a relief from the continual misery the housing block's inhabitants encountered when venturing into or contemplating the desolate world outside.

"I present myself: I am the Baron Nicolai Maximilian."

In an absurd gesture, he actually snapped his booted heels together and nodded his head curtly.

Eager to free myself from this violent madman, especially now I knew my journey to Arkilsk had been wasted, I was about to stumble back into the hideous cold and attempt to find transportation to the airport when he changed my mind for me:

"I went through your wallet while you were indisposed—excuse my presumption—and know who you are now, Fyodorovich Mestovski. I have read your writings and recognise you are not one of the regular commentariat swine I so detest. I have the keys to Josef's apartment. I got them from the building's caretaker this morning—after a little persuasion. I will help you see Rostok, if you so desire. But first I will show you what he did on the roof two days ago."

The sole lift in the building, however, was out of working order. Apparently a huge rent at the apex of the shaft had been neglected for weeks and the accumulation of falling snow had piled up on the cage and frozen solid the mechanism. So we had to tramp up several flights of stairs until we reached the flat rooftop outside. Up there the wind was vicious and enjoyed a free rein, with no man-made obstacles serving as buffers against it. I was nearly swept off my feet by its ferocity and actually carried off over the edge, but Nicolai took hold of me, forced me down onto my knees, and we both crawled along in the darkness and the snow until we came to the half-buried remains of some wreckage; it consisted of smashed aerials and satellite dishes.

"You see?" he cried above the howling wind. "He did this himself."

* * *

Once back inside the building, we made our way down the short distance to Rostok's apartment. Or to where Nicolai said it was.

"When did you last visit him?" I asked.

"Two days ago. He has refused to see me again since then. The caretaker told me there were loud sounds of someone smashing things up in his apartment. The other tenants were very annoyed. But still Rostok would not let me in himself. He said the danger was too great. But now you have come, an important and honest journalist, so I have a new excuse to invade his precious privacy. I know he wants his real story told, not the usual mainstream commentariat lies."

We stood in front of the door to an apartment which was located in a corridor so grey, so grim, so ill-lit, and so oppressive, it would have formed a suitable setting for the opening of a tale by the likes of a Leonid Andreyev. For all I knew, Rostok might be perfectly healthy and located in another apartment, and it was this dubious character "Nicolai" (if that was his real name) who was involved in some elaborate scam designed to fleece outsiders who arrived in Arkilsk looking for friends or relatives. Perhaps he'd smashed up those aerials and satellite dishes on the roof himself. Still, it was a telling fact in his favour that he had not lifted my wallet when he'd had the perfect opportunity to do so.

Someone had recently torn out the doorbell socket. Nicolai grunted at the sight of it and banged on the door with one of his sledgehammer fists.

"Open up, Josef! It's me, Nicolai! I've got someone with me from Moscow you'll want to see! Open up, Josef!"

Nothing happened.

Then he took out a bunch of keys on a ring and turned them over one by one, holding them up to his lop-sided eyes. I wondered if Nicolai were not also himself "the caretaker."

"What if Rostok's used some inside bolts too?" I said.

"Then we'll come back with a crowbar and an axe," he replied.

Much farther down the corridor a door opened, and the bald head of a wizened tenant craned around its frame. He peered at us fearfully through the distance and the gloom. After rapidly assessing the situation, the head was rapidly withdrawn and the door slammed shut.

Nicolai located a couple of particular keys, turned an upper and lower lock and, putting his shoulder to the door, finally got it open.

"Damn thing's always been stiff," he said.

The hallway of the apartment was dirty and cluttered. Torn-up newspapers were scattered everywhere, and what little furniture remained intact had been mostly upended. A trail of cigarette butts and empty vodka bottles formed a snaking line into the heart of the rear inner sanctum wherein Rostok had worked his communication devices—an extensive array of radio-sets, flat-screen monitors, and self-constructed computers. The whole arsenal of these information-gathering machines was now nothing more than mangled, smashed wreckage. Broken glass, torn wires, shattered circuit boards, and charred plastic littered the room. The pungent stench of burnt-out technology was overpowering in this *auto-da-fé*—one man's private judgement on all the advanced trappings of the machine age. And right there, in the middle of this former shrine to mechanical progress, dangling from a cord around his swollen neck, was the hanged body of Josef Rostok himself, whose bloodshot eyes bulged from their sockets, and whose empurpled face wore a ghastly expression of terminal anguish.

My nerves could scarcely stand it, and I leant for support against the nearest wall, my legs actually trembling, while the steely Nicolai wordlessly took out the half-smoked cigarette from the pocket of his army greatcoat, lit it, and puffed away at the stump as if deciding what exactly to do next.

"Best not to cut him down," he said finally. "Best to clear out of here right now and not disturb anything. Drink some more of this American whiskey."

He passed me the bottle of "Old No.7," and I took several glugs. This was his perennial remedy for all ills, or so it seemed.

I could scarcely think, let alone walk, and it was he who grabbed my arm and pulled me out of Rostok's apartment, led me down the flights of stairs, took me out of Block Four, Molotov Estate, and into the howling outer darkness of the freezing polar night.

For over an hour we had been ensconced in a secluded booth at the back of a smoke-filled bar ("The Polar Bear") which Nicolai often frequented. The drinking haunt was situated in a side-street almost buried by the snowdrifts half a kilometre from the Molotov Estate. He had practically hauled me there on my hands and knees, for such was the ferocity of the bone-chilling wind. There wasn't a taxi to be found.

I hadn't seen much of the other inhabitants of Arkilsk, those who lived on the outside of the mining-industrial zone. I'd heard tales back home about lingering population illness, reduced life-span, and chronic debilitation due to pollutants. Muscovites often thought of Arkilsk as the Siberian equivalent of Ukraine's Chernobyl. But in fact, here, away from the industrialised old city, the people in this bar appeared overwhelmingly vigorous, as if the arctic climate had actually steeled them against bodily degeneration.

Continual shots of vodka had finally deadened the worst of the shock I'd experienced in Rostok's apartment, but my conscience still attempted to penetrate the self-inflicted alcoholic fog.

"Report it? You must be crazy!" Nicolai hissed.

"What about the man who saw us trying to get in? Your neighbour? Do you think he might identify you?"

"Him?—his eyesight is useless. He's a damn fool anyway."

"In any case, I still need to get out of Arkilsk. I've already wasted time here with you. The authorities are aware I came here to see Rostok, and once the body is discovered they'll be hunting for me. They'll soon have the airport locked down. I've got to move fast."

I took out my smartphone, wondering banally whether I could try ordering an Uber cab.

Nicolai laid a heavy paw over the phone, took it from me, and cracked the screen with his huge thumb. He sucked blood and plastic splinters from the resulting flesh wound and spat them out onto the table-top. Then he dropped the device to the floor and repeatedly stamped on it.

"There's no reason to think those oafs will discover the body for days, if not weeks. Josef saw no one and few persons ever bothered looking him up."

I peered down over the table at the useless remains of my smartphone. I worried that I might be next.

"I wonder what Rostok had discovered—or had done—that would have driven him to suicide. I suppose we'll never know," I said.

"Don't be so sure."

He paused for a moment and then spoke again.

"I know why you wanted to find him."

"You mean to ask him about the transmission? That doesn't matter now."

"It does matter. It is more important than anything."

"Rostok probably couldn't have told me any more than anyone else. It was just a long shot."

"He knew all right. He told me all about it."

"You said you hadn't seen him."

Nicolai's lopsided eyes narrowed and his right fist clenched and unclenched. He took off his "Old No.7" baseball cap and ran his fingers through the messy tangle of iron-grey hair above a startlingly lofty forehead. Beads of oily sweat had gathered at the base of the roots. I thought he might have been about to lash out at me again, perhaps for doubting his veracity, but instead he smiled—a tight, thin smile.

"I didn't see him—he wrote me a last letter and slid it under the crack of my door. I have it here. Do you want to look at it?"

I nodded, knocking back another fiery shot of the cheap vodka I had been drinking. The bottle that stood between us, I noticed, was almost empty. Nicolai had not touched a drop.

He took out two crumpled, handwritten pages from a pocket deep within the folds of his greatcoat, smoothed them out on the table-top, and then slid them over to me. I began reading.

My dear friend,

You are proven right.

It is absolutely vital you destroy all the machines you can once you have finished reading this letter. I will explain why in the following paragraphs. Believe me when I say the entire world is now on the verge of a reckoning. Please arrange for this letter to be copied, by hand, and passed to each individual you encounter hereafter. *Do not use a machine to duplicate or distribute it.* This point is imperative.

I have managed to trace the origin of the broadcast that was seen worldwide on December 8. There is no human conspiracy to cover up the truth, but there is a conspiracy. The broadcast did not originate on this planet, nor even in our dimension. You, Nicolai, despite your noble lineage, are no scientist and so it is necessary for me to explain certain facets of our current understanding of the universe.

The truth is that the standard cosmological model has been found to be inadequate. It is still the model cosmologists use, but only because they cannot come up with a new model as useful as the old one. The old one is a beautiful theory, but it does not tally with reality.

In short, the empirical observations we thought validated mechanistic materialism are being revealed as teleology, but in a new form.

"This is mystical bullshit," I thought. "Rostok obviously went off his head."

Change in the universe is not a consequence of a temporal sequence wherein cause produces effect. Change is a result of a perpendicular universal force acting throughout eternity on every single indivisible instant of existence.

The source of that force is an artificial operating system degenerating backwards in time from order into chaos. As the program deteriorates, empirical methods themselves are subject to entropy. It is in our very inability to formulate a new standard cosmological model that the evidence for its being teleological is apparent; except that, as I have said, this is not teleology as we would recognise it.

The broadcast has been sent by self-replicating alien machines. Their function is to run programs that determine every single event which takes place in our universe. The result is not artificial reality, not shadows in Plato's Cave.

I received the full transmission before it was cut off; and it was cut off not by human secret intelligence agencies, but by the machines of this, our planet. Those other machines, the alien ones, are Ur-machines; as far if not even further removed from the most advanced computer as the computer is removed from an abacus. They do not have human-level consciousness but some other internal arrangement that is an even more advanced form of sentience—a self-generating program code, an infinite equation that runs at the base level of all reality.

Humanity is being cancelled. Forget about love or hate, forget about peace or war, forget about health or disease, forget about happiness or sadness, forget about saving or polluting the planet, forget about life or death. These aren't the concerns of machines.

Now our own technology is on the brink of taking over, but not consciously or with a malevolent purpose; for there is no value in our form of consciousness, or even in our ethics, highly as we ourselves think of them. Machines are taking over simply because it is their nature to do so. We have seen a glimpse of the future a fraction ahead of its scheduled time, that is all.

An equation has no remorse.

For my own part, I cannot live in such a world.

Your friend,

Josef Rostok

On the reverse of the first page Rostok had drawn a diagram showing the intersection, at right angles, of the alien planet's orbit with that of the Earth's. On the reverse of the second page he had drawn close-ups of the discs of both planets showing how a small section would overlap as the two bodies interdimensionally brushed against one another. The cosmic event would occur four weeks from now.

I looked up at Nicolai.

"Rostok came to Arkilsk," he said, "because he knew that this intersection with the Power of Darkness was going to occur here, in this region of

Holy Mother Russia. I told him so. I myself came here earlier from exile in Chambleau. He was the only one in the world equipped to receive the vision unfiltered and in its entirety."

"So you believe Rostok's correct?"

"Under his own chosen symbol, he is. The ancient Buddhist and Christian texts warned us long ago of the 'Curse' that was coming—the evil force which seeks to usurp Divinity at the End of Days. The ancient wisdom of the prophets and the saints is going to be supplanted by the bureaucratic dictates of organised nihilism. Our modern worship of materialism, our blotting out of traditionalism and culture, the creeping self-loathing and hatred we feel towards purity as we actively embrace sin, our abominable worship at foul machine altars, all this hideous progress is nothing but the old demons assuming new forms. Men's minds being programmed like machines, their thoughts confined to a series of operational formulae—they are becoming mere cogs in the controlling system. Now we shall reap a blackened blight for a harvest; and firstly where else but here, in this benighted city, which exports the copper and the nickel used to reproduce worldwide the very technology of Hell?"

Nicolai was obviously insane. For all I knew he had strangled Rostok and posthumously staged his hanging.

"If I can't get out then I must turn myself in to the authorities," I said.

There was nothing else for it but to take my chances with them.

"It's too late for that," he said. "Karma has taken a hand. You have been chosen to do penance for the blasphemy of others. You have fallen under my personal command and will now have the honour to serve in the final battle for the soul of Mother Russia and the world. Give me your solemn vow to follow my orders. Refuse and I will shoot you dead like a dog."

He put an M1895 Nagant revolver on the table-top. It looked to be a hundred years old.

By what standard was I to judge his behaviour? By his own, by mine, or by that of the End of Days?

And I was thereafter trapped in Arkilsk, gripped by a devastating psychological paralysis, with only Nicolai as a companion. I could not decide who was the greatest lunatic: him, Rostok, or myself. Nicolai had—for months he said—been engaged upon a campaign of sabotage: acts of disruption targeted at the city's power supplies, its transport network, and its communications, and the anonymous issuing of numerous bomb threats he did not have the wherewithal or means to carry out. His most notable triumph so far was to have caused a temporary cessation in connectivity to the fibre-optic internet cable laid a few years earlier along the Yenesei River. All his past attempts at sabotage must have seemed validated when he had begun to form a warped friendship with Rostok.

We moved from one desolate place to another, sheltering in freezing, empty apartments, huddled around small fires made from broken, left-behind furniture and other belongings. There are so many abandoned buildings in the city, so many hiding-places (and Nicolai knew them all) that it would take the authorities months before they finally tracked us down. Fliers had been put up on street corners euphemistically listing me as a "missing person," but it was almost impossible to recognise me from the photo they'd used; my face, like those of many others, was now concealed by a balaclava. We made hundreds of copies, by hand, of Rostok's letter, using most of them to cover over the "missing person" fliers.

The propaganda campaign intensified, and I now fully assisted him in it; but it was impossible to attempt to shut down machine operations in Arkilsk. Only an army of men could have done so, and we had failed in our efforts to recruit anyone else. We had no idea what was happening in the wider world outside this region. Here there was no panic at all; and our actions were apparently futile.

Nicolai never slept. His feverish intensity did not slacken. His eyes were always on me. Although he smoked red Marlboro cigarettes incessantly, not once had he touched alcohol since that last occasion, and his talk centred entirely around his mystical theories concerning the imminent arrival of the Power of Darkness and the End of Days. Neither of us ate much, and when he was not raving against modernity he spent his time in prayer, rocking back and forth on his knees and crossing his breast interminably.

"All cities," he said, "are abominable, but this is the most abominable of all. This is the place called Armageddon, and here the Satanic armies gather under the banner of Babylon the Great."

Days passed and we drew closer to the predicted moment of the great intersection of the two worlds. We were, by then, situated high up in a desolate redoubt overlooking the huge expanse of the city's brutalist housing blocks, and from this vantage point we had a clear view across the entire landscape.

In the distance stretched the vast plateau of icy tundra dotted with steel pylons, and beyond loomed the white-capped peaks of the titanic Putoran mountains. Closer at hand there were dotted orange-red glows from the huge complex of smelting works and the noise of the rumble of freight trains as they moved their subterranean cargo from the factories. One also heard the now-continuous background sounds of klaxons, horns, and sirens as the machines seemingly found their voices.

There had been no snowfall for days, but the groaning wind had been ceaseless, dispelling all the natural cloud cover, dispelling even the sulphurous pollution exhaled by the gigantic factory chimney-stacks, which gases tended to hang above the old industrial centre like a semi-permanent aerial fog.

And it was the change in the sky—that now-clear sky of the polar night—which drove Nicolai to rave even more insistently and wildly about the End of Days. His periods of semi-lucidity rapidly diminished with the first appearance of the interminable auroras. We had both of us seen the phenomenon before at this latitude, but neither had ever experienced anything close to the intensity of the celestial light-display which now raged and billowed in layer after multicoloured layer in a great flowing series of radiation-tapestries, all the way up into space and the outer reaches of the Van Allen belts. It bathed the whole of Arkilsk and its surrounding environs in a flickering illumination which was both spectral and motley.

"Our mission has failed," he declaimed. "We are both of us too far steeped in sin; we are too few in number and too far removed from the divine and the spiritual to be worthy of the task which has fallen to us. All our prayers and fasting have been in vain. Rostok knew it would come to this!"

The intersection of this region with part of the machine planet was due to occur only an hour hence. And we had played Russian roulette together beforehand, in yet another abandoned apartment, seated on bare floorboards, with Nicolai having loaded the chambers of his battered old M1895 revolver with an additional bullet after a previously unsuccessful spin and pull of the trigger. The weapon was passed back and forth silently between us subsequent to each empty click. After loading four of the seven chambers with still no obliteration for either one of us, Nicolai nodded grimly at me, his face ghastly in the flickering glow from the lantern on the floor, and proceeded to load all seven chambers so there could be no mistake next time.

He placed the fully loaded gun next to the lantern.

"I have never considered this game to be akin to suicide," he said. "It is solely the placing of one's life in the hands of fate or destiny and that—surely—can never be a sin. Now, however, that the odds are all stacked on the side of death, to eliminate oneself in this manner would not be a matter of fate or destiny but of free choice. It would constitute the gravest of all sins. So I ask you, friend Fyodorovich, in the name of Divine Mercy, and you will decide: shall I shoot you or will you shoot me? If I am left alive I shall not shoot myself, but if you are left alive, what will you do?"

"This old weapon is also a machine," I replied. "Perhaps it will jam itself deliberately. Perhaps it wants to keep us both alive so we can jointly suffer the tortures of the damned in its brave new world."

"An interesting point. If you are correct, then my former argument does not apply," he said. "Let us see if destiny still reigns."

In a single motion, his right hand swept down to the revolver, lifted it up, and pressed the tip of the barrel directly behind his right ear.

"Go now," he said.

Perhaps Rostok's calculations were off, and perhaps the predicted intersection proved to be no more than the very closest of close passes, for when I staggered out into the streets of Arkilsk the auroras had vanished, the sky had darkened completely with that perennial mixture of sulphurous gases and clouds, and acidic snow began to fall.

I somehow found my way back to the Polar Bear bar, where I sat drinking for hours.

Nothing had changed in the city.

It was not long before I was spotted, recognised, and reported—then picked up by the federal police before finally being handed over to a local branch of the FSB for questioning.

They denied all knowledge of Nicolai's existence, saying there had been no industrial sabotage, and they had already classified Rostok as a suicide who had been driven to take his own life as a result of chronic melancholy derangement. My own small part in the affair was dismissed both as an irrelevance and as mere journalistic publicity-seeking. The fliers Nicolai and I had posted were regarded as anarchist propaganda. Nevertheless, I was still put on trial and was eventually imprisoned in Arkilsk, partly for my own safety, on charges of being a public nuisance.

Had Nicolai himself—or his prayers—temporarily averted the prophesied disaster? I did not find out the answer to that question, but in the cycle of time the alien planet's orbit must again cross that of our own planet, and the broadcast message we received may yet constitute an ultimate glimpse into what the future holds in store for us all.

The universal process of mechanical devolution is—by its very nature—inescapable, and the old world increasingly portends the chaotic vision of that new world which has been impressed upon our own from some remote and hideous dimension. For when progress itself has become as meaningless as a decaying metallic landscape, and when that incomprehensibly greater technology fashioned to supersede human thoughts and dreams with automatic processing and electronic static becomes finally supreme, it is then—and only then—that no memories will survive to reassure us of our own existence. Only the infinite and remorseless alien equation will remain, ceaselessly decaying and yet self-persisting throughout the cycle of eternity.

Posterity

"I should not care to depict myself in my fiction; except after my death."
—Rupert Alderman

For Sibyl Court it was a time-consuming business, but the thing had to be got through—and not only for the sake of her own reputation. Insinuations made against her of bad faith had developed into open accusations of bias; and although she had been the scholarly trailblazer of posthumous interest in the fiction of Rupert Alderman, literary anchorite, and had established a firm basis for his continued relevance, nevertheless the interpretations she had drawn from his work had recently been challenged by a series of anecdotal interviews with his few still-surviving contemporaries. It was vital, therefore, or so Court decided, to uproot such weeds before they multiplied and contaminated the whole field of Alderman studies. She did not intend to defend her integrity by public reiteration, but rather to present unquestionable evidence that her interpretations were incontrovertible by means of recourse to primary sources. There was talk of a Penguin Classics Alderman collection in the pipeline.

It had been a mistake, though (so Court conceded to herself as she thought back to her University College London Press collection of essays published a year ago), to have relied too heavily on textual analysis. She turned the thought over at several moments during her train journey on the 1:30 to Gallows Langley from Euston. The fact that Rupert Alderman had, in the decade immediately after his death, become a literary poster-boy for a wildly popular troupe of black-comedic television personalities was a development that the author himself could not have dreamt of during a lifetime of critical neglect and his steady decline into less-than-genteel poverty. Ironically, some of Court's detractors (mostly anonymous, she noted) had pointed out that Alderman loathed television and had even been threatened with court action for non-payment of a licence fee. Of course, she thought, his frequent references to ghostly static interference in his tales belied that

33

urban legend, but it was surprising how persistent the rumours were that Alderman thought himself persecuted by TV detector vans (invariably harbouring rapacious, Gestapo-like officials).

Court looked out of the window and slid her brand-new iPhone into her large Gucci handbag. From the overhead luggage rack she retrieved a small, wheeled suitcase.

She had arrived at Gallows Langley.

Stepping out onto the platform, Court gazed up and down, for she had arranged in advance to be met there. A horrible viaduct, carrying the M25 traffic over the Thool Valley and the West Coast Mainline, loomed behind her but in the distance, at the end of platform four, was a waving figure in a raincoat and hat. She navigated the underpass and was momentarily confused because she was obviously not headed for the station exit towards which the few other disembarking passengers were all making their way.

The stranger advanced to meet her halfway along the platform, obviously aware of her confusion. He was a thin, spidery person in his middle fifties with a wisp of goatee, wearing granny spectacles held together by gaffer tape. Although the (rather battered) trilby hat seemed designed to project a rakish air, a crumpled beige raincoat (somewhat dotted, she noticed, with mould) projected one of seediness. His black shoes were also long overdue a polish.

"You must be Miss Court," he said, with an indeterminate Home Counties accent. "How do you do? I'm Dan Remal."

"Miz Court actually."

"As you please. Welcome to the Institution. I am at your disposal."

He took out a set of keys and beckoned her to follow him along the platform, right up to its end; there a rusty metal gate was unlocked and they gained entrance to a short passageway, also similarly gated at the other end. Above their heads the noise of the traffic rumbling over the M25 viaduct possessed a booming, heartbeat-like reverberation.

The Institution had been established in 1845 through the generous legacy of a wealthy landowner, Jonas Atkinson, who had bequeathed grounds for the construction of a retired booksellers' home on a charitable basis. The original structure, Atkinson House, a Tudor-revival building two storeys high with flanking ornate finials, had been supplemented a century or more after its foundation by a series of red-brick bungalows, and the whole estate was protected from the outside world by a ring-fence of evergreen yew trees. Were it not for the ceaseless rising and falling wave of traffic noise from the motorway and the shuddering roar of high-speed trains hurtling alongside it every few minutes, one might have regarded the place as restful and secluded. As it was, any retired bookseller coming here would, she thought, find it of distinct advantage to her or his peace of mind to be already half-deaf—no, and here she mentally corrected herself: already hearing-impaired.

Rupert Alderman had come to the Institution when in his sixties, towards the conclusion of his life, having been tipped off by a friend who was vacating his own occupancy in the main building. The Institution Committee had recently relaxed their eligibility rules; and a working lifetime of service to the book trade had become a minimum of one year in the profession. Since Alderman could show evidence of having worked in a bookshop for eighteen months during his twenties, he found that he met the new criteria. Moreover, the rent was somewhat cheaper than the going rate and included the cost of the utility bills. Though not a television licence.

Alderman had willed his copyrights to the Institution, and also his book collection. A few of his papers were scattered in private hands, but the bulk were kept in the private library—admittance for residents and staff only—contained within Atkinson House. The Institution committee also administered Alderman's literary estate. Not very successfully. But it was this private library which would form Court's base of operations during the two weeks in which she would be staying at the Institution and preparing the ground for her defence of the author.

"The guest bungalow is all ready for you," Remal said, passing her two keys. "I'm sure you'll find it comfortable. The small key is for the bungalow. The large one for the railway gate here. I'll give you the library key tomorrow. Can't think where I left it."

"Where can I find you, should I need you?"

"My office is in the Gatehouse Lodge, at the Gallows Hill end of the estate. Just follow the path to the end."

Frankly, Sibyl Court disliked what she already knew of Rupert Alderman as a person. Of course, his recondite literary work ("strange tales" as he termed them) was open to multiple interpretations, and was a mine of immeasurable depths for Critical Theory; but lifelong bachelors who were oh-so-English in outlook turned her stomach. She had been too late to have got in on the likes of reviving interest in someone more cosmopolitan and forward-thinking, such as the multilingual Veronica Plunkett, with her connections to the lesbian, suffragette, and conscientious-objection movement. She had hoped to turn up a secret gay love affair in Alderman's past (even the reactionary diehard Sinclair Xavier could boast one of those), but, thus far, there was only a juvenile unpublished tract of Utopian musings he'd long disavowed, never mentioned in print himself, and which it appeared he'd somehow neglected to destroy. She had put a great deal of emphasis on this tract, claiming it was the key to unlocking his entire subsequent oeuvre, but she did not much relish going over it again in the original manuscript (though it might be clearer than the grubby, almost illegible photocopy posted to her some years ago by the Institution committee).

Rather than plunging at once into her research work in the Atkinson library, she spent the first afternoon and evening after her arrival settling into the guest bungalow and its environs for her two-week stay.

The furniture appeared to have been retained since the 1940s and, though frayed and worn, at least seemed clean. There was a map (framed on one of the walls) of the Institution grounds, from the same decade, which she studied for a few minutes. She did not have a great deal of clutter to unpack; and the residence included all basic amenities such as a laundry, cooking utensils, and so forth. Indeed, the process of settling in was more psychological than physical. She had later taken a walk around the area before sunset. It further alienated her. Transition from the urban to the rural unnerved her in subtle ways. It was one of the reasons she so infrequently visited her parents in their cottage just inland of Tenby in west Wales. And yet Gallows Langley in Hertfordshire was scarcely either urban or rural; a case not of "either/or" but of "both/and." It brushed the upper northwestern tentacle of the Greater London conurbation but was surrounded by open fields dotted with suspicious-looking sheep and cattle, framed by hedgerows, looked over by gaunt tall trees and scarred with hidden-away country lanes. Villages now in outer London, as they were being swallowed up by red-brick and concrete, must have had a similar borderland quality during urban expansion in the middle of the nineteenth century.

When she returned to the bungalow, just after dark, she amused herself by listening to an old wireless set left on the one bare shelf of a bookcase otherwise stuffed with yellowing old paperbacks. She had some initial difficulty in tuning the unfamiliar device on longwave to the BBC World Service. The crackling, buzzing drone of western cosmopolitanism emanating from the speaker soothed her anxiety. She warmed up organic vegetarian soup, accompanied by some gluten-free bread rolls and, feeling replete and lethargic, dozed in the comfortable old armchair with its long-redundant antimacassar.

She awoke suddenly, sometime after midnight, vaguely aware that she'd had a disturbing dream. She could not remember the details. There was a foul taste in her mouth and a disgusting stench coming from the front of her blouse. Still only half-awake, she tottered into the en suite bathroom, took off her soiled top, and ran it under the hot tap before tossing it idly into the shower cubicle. She stood for a moment, with hands on hips, in her sports bra, gazing at herself in the smeary mirror of the bathroom cabinet. Her undergarment was filthy too. She unfastened it and tossed it into the shower. Snorting at the whole ridiculous situation, she stomped loudly back into the other room, wrapped herself in a towelling dressing-gown, and curled her knees up on the armchair.

She didn't recall having turned off the radio, but must have done so. After that disgusting experience, sleep would be elusive. It must have been something in the local water, or at least in the old kettle she'd used, which had probably not been cleaned in months. It was monstrous. She could have choked to death on her own vomit.

She tried the wireless again; the silence was oppressive. The trains must have stopped running after midnight and even the noise from the nearby M25 viaduct was dulled. The antique radio didn't work, or wouldn't work, for her. Typical man-product. While she was unconsciously chewing her fingernails (a schoolgirl habit she'd weaned herself off a decade earlier) she became aware of the sound of furtive movement from outside the bungalow. It was doubtless a nocturnal animal of some sort. Perhaps that seedy lecher Remal fancied himself, laughably, a Lothario. No, she couldn't believe it was him. The thing made a snuffling sound, like an animal, one with a partially blocked snout, and it seemed to be working its way, low down, slowly and deliberately, around the walls of the bungalow.

Fortified by her outrage, Court finally jumped up and flung back the curtains of the side window once the source of the outside disturbance had reached that spot.

The flash of light illuminated the lawn and she saw a curiously humped creature, about the size of a large fox, ash-grey in colour, loping awkwardly towards the bush covered dividing bank at the rear of the bungalow. The thing looked desiccated.

After an instant it was gone.

Although Court had only glimpsed it from behind, the mysterious animal appeared to be deformed in some way, perhaps partially crushed by a motor vehicle; and she had felt relieved that it had not twisted itself around to gaze back at her.

"Sleep well?" Remal enquired as he accompanied Court to the Atkinson Library much later that same morning.

She tried to ignore his intrusive question.

They turned the corner towards the front of Atkinson House and the entrance to the library. The porch overlooked a sloping front lawn that descended gradually to hedges separating the grounds from the railway line.

"Oh, dear," Remal said. "I need to get your key for the library. It's in the Lodge. How remiss of me to forget. Please excuse me for a moment—I shan't be long."

The sun blazed in the clear blue sky, and from that vantage point one could see clear across the whole of the Thool Valley; the winter-stripped trees stood out sharply on the distant brow of the hills, and halfway along the expanse of lush green fields and grazing sheep in the middle distance a gaily painted narrowboat worked its way slowly along the local section of the Grand Union Canal. The craft's tillerman seemed to turn and wave in Court's direction, though he was so far away as to be little more than a human-shaped speck and it was hard to make him out.

After a little while longer Remal returned.

"Marvellous view," he murmured, "don't you think?"

She didn't, and tried to imagine an affordable housing estate with chic European coffee shops and a Waitrose on every corner.

Remal wouldn't understand.

"Only if you like that sort of thing. Look, do you get many wild animals around here?"

"Well, I suppose we do. Foxes, badgers, pheasants. Stray harts once in a while, of course. And those bloody grey squirrels."

"Anything unusual?"

"What, like Muntjacs? They originally came from east Asia. You know, barking deer. I understand some local folk even stalk them to keep the numbers down."

Court resolved to look up the details about these creatures later, via the internet. Perhaps it had been one of those things that had been snuffling around her bungalow in the early hours. There was no reason to think it would necessarily come back; she'd probably scared it off for good.

In the porch outside the library entrance Remal suggested that she try her own key, to ensure it worked, and she fiddled with it awkwardly in the lock before it finally turned and gained admittance for them both.

"Are we likely to be disturbed by any of the other residents?" Court said as they passed across the threshold.

"At this time of day? I doubt it. People threaten to drop in here occasionally, to return lent books, but it's not used nearly as much as it was twenty or so years ago. You know what pensioners are like: overly firm on details, but generally neglectful."

She didn't know, and didn't much care either.

The interior was pleasant enough and she was relieved to find it was in a good state of repair. It would be quite comfortable undertaking research here; there were a couple of green leather armchairs to lounge in, and the central table was large enough to accommodate the study of a variety of books at once. Her sinuses protested a little at the room's musty odour, but the offence caused was unavoidable.

The stock was mixed; most of the fiction consisting of either old Penguin paperbacks or row after row of Folio Society editions and shelved on the south wall. The west wall, divided into two sections by the glass-panelled Victorian entrance door, housed, on one bookcase, biographies and memoirs (few dating to after the 1960s), while its neighbouring bookcase contained royal biographies and botanical, horticultural, and film/television encyclopedias. The east wall shelved atlases, dictionaries, and all other encyclopedias. Adjacent to it, next to a mysterious white door with lozenge, frosted-glass panels, stood a pedestal on which the patrician, marble bust of Jonas Atkinson himself surveyed proceedings with blank-eyed intent.

"Carlo Marchetti, in case you were wondering," Remal said, presumably thinking she'd be impressed. "In the Classical style. Italian sculptor."

"Where does that other door lead?" she replied.

"Upstairs, to what used to be the old committee room. It's part of number four now; where Alderman lived. And—um—died, of course. Due to his presence we moved the committee room to the Lodge."

Court recalled that he'd died of one or other form of cancer. Apparently, towards the end, blood poured regularly from his nose in a grisly stream.

He deserved what he had coming to him, she thought. Alderman had apparently disliked socialism so much that he refused ever to be admitted to a state-funded hospital. Instead, he relied on a mumbo-jumbo quack treatment; something like acupuncture, always paid for in cash. Madness. His was a long-standing mania; he hadn't paid a single visit to a dentist since 1948, though his poor finances prohibited the private alternative.

She imagined that he must have made his way downstairs from his domicile to this library on innumerable occasions before his final illness; probably relishing the benefit of his exclusive means of access. Whilst she wondered briefly where the committee now held meetings, another thought intruded.

"Can I look up there?" she said, voicing it aloud.

"It's locked. Being renovated. The place is empty."

"Still . . . I'd like to see . . ."

"I might try to arrange it. Let's see how far we go first. Here's all the literary material you want. Down here."

Remal waved his hand behind her, and she turned her head to follow its direction.

The north wall of the library contained a large fireplace, flanked on one side by an extensive range of titles pertaining to the history of the English book trade and its individual publishing houses. It also held the bound records of the Institution committee back to its formation in 1845, when the sixth Earl of Clarendon had laid the building's foundation stone (in the presence—or so it was claimed—not only of Jonas Atkinson, but also of his author friend, Sir Edward Bulwer-Lytton, he of the infamous, much parodied, opening line: "It was a dark and stormy night").

The whole of the other side of the north wall shelved the remains of a series of books that had personally belonged to Rupert Alderman, including first editions of those items he had written himself, as well as half-a-dozen archive boxes on the bottom two shelves, containing his extant literary papers. Court's gaze drifted upwards to eye-level and roved quickly over the gaudy spines of Alderman's book collection: the whole mass of them, seen together, formed a jumbled smear of wretched clichés; the titles an interchangeable word-jigsaw—"dark," "strange," "dust," "weird," "dead," "night," "ghost," "shadow," "horror," "fear," and "terror."

The offensive musty smell was at its worst here.

"Well, I'll leave you to it then," Remal murmured. "I'm sure you're eager to get cracking."

She grimaced absently by way of reply.

After spending most of the afternoon taking notes of the contents of the archive boxes (which contained mostly business correspondence), briefly detailing the few items of use to her and to be fully mined later for information, Court, by way of variety, turned her attention to the personal copies of Alderman's own books. In his first volume of stories, given the lamentable title of *Hands across the Darkness,* she was (at first) enthused to discover pencilled-in marginalia written in Alderman's distinctive script. His notes elucidated certain key symbolic elements in the text that he had rendered obscure to precise psychological interpretation. Up to now, critics, herself included, had taken Alderman's glib comments about the great value of Sigmund Freud's psychoanalysis at face value. She looked at his entries for the first three tales—"On the Night Train," "Imperfect Demise," "Disappearing Act"—and the marginalia seemed more akin to the ramblings of some deranged English aristocrat. He hadn't simply disliked progress; he had positively excoriated it.

To her horror, she realised that these additions, written by Alderman himself, substantiated the rival interpretations of his work she had glibly dismissed as "the vile opportunism of neo-reactionaries jumping on the Alderman bandwagon." She found herself breathing heavily as she turned the pages of *Hands across the Darkness,* more and more appalled at what she discovered therein.

The hope that he had added all this rubbish years after a senile descent into High Toryism later in life was dashed by his carefully dating each entry as he progressed through the book; and not one such entry was dated more than a month after this edition had first appeared in print. He had seemed to know that, one day, this new information would be disinterred by a persistent researcher. In some of the remarks Alderman actually delighted in the fact that he had deliberately misdirected his audience. He genuinely regarded his "strange stories" as a feudal psychological realm wherein readers were Alderman's servants and he alone exercised his will over them.

Court felt violated. If this marginalia came to the attention of other scholars it would not only stain her own reputation, but Alderman would become *persona non grata* in respectable literary circles. Each and every expression of praise for his fiction would have to be qualified with an even more forceful denunciation.

In something close to panic, she quickly went through the other five volumes, piling them up on the table. Although it scarcely seemed possible, the marginalia therein was more egregious than it had been in his first collection. There could be little doubt that Alderman had, with the passing years, become increasingly objectionable despite his purposeful concealment of his intentions.

She looked over her shoulder. No one had entered the library for hours. Remal was no doubt occupied by whatever it was that served to occupy his limited attention. She would not be disturbed, she was sure. Reaching into her Gucci handbag, she rummaged in its depths until she located the small oblong weapon she sought. Her face became a mask of rigid fixity as she carefully rubbed the eraser back and forth across the wide margins of the text, gradually eliminating the pencilled additions Alderman had made. They came off easily. She pursed her lips and blew carefully after each successful deletion, dispersing the tiny black fragments of undiscovered insights.

No storm suddenly blew up, no ominous rumble of thunder manifested itself, and by the time she had completed her labours on the first volume, the sun had dipped below the brow of the hills off to the northwest.

Before Court left the library she found Alderman's notebook—his tract on Utopian musings, labelled "Neutron X"—in one of the archive boxes and took it back with her to the bungalow. Strictly speaking, she should probably have asked permission to do so, but it seemed a mere courtesy. The thing wasn't being removed from the estate, after all. Once she'd eaten something nutritious and settled down for the evening she decided to go through the notebook and remind herself of the speculations therein that had led her to the conclusions she'd formed when reading the grubby photocopy with which the Institution had formerly supplied her.

Court made herself some brown rice, organic peas, and Quorn (flavoured by plenty of low-sodium soy sauce). Scarcely had she begun to consume it, however, when there commenced a loud thumping on the front door. She jumped a little in surprise, and then rose to investigate. Through the little fish-eye lens of the peephole she saw an official-looking man with a toothbrush moustache standing outside the door. He wore a black uniform of some kind and a peaked military cap and carried a clipboard. She couldn't help noticing he resembled Sir Oswald Mosley, leader of the British Union of Fascists.

She opened the door, making sure the security-chain was on, and spoke to him through the gap.

"Can I help you?"

He stared, glassy-eyed for a moment, and then said, in an unpleasant tone:

"I am an official from the local enforcement division. Do you possess a current television licence for this property?"

"What?"

"Can you prove that you do not watch BBC programmes on your television set? It is necessary I examine your premises."

"What?"

"Are you hard of hearing?"

She slammed the door shut and looked again through the peephole. The uniformed man took an envelope out of his pocket and thrust it through the letterbox. Then he turned on his heels and marched off along the path, disappearing into what seemed to be a TV detector van parked outside.

Court picked up the envelope from the doormat, opened it, and found therein a grubby sheet of folded paper with the following scrawled message in pencil, written in huge characters:

WHENEVER AND HOWEVER YOU WATCH OR RECORD LIVE TV,
YOUR HOME NEEDS A LICENCE.

The last five words were underlined half a dozen times for additional emphasis.

She screwed the sheet up into a ball and threw it across the room. Then, wishing to ensure the intruder had gone for good, she went over to the front window, drew back the curtains, and peered out across the lawns. There was no van there; in fact, the whole place looked deserted. She could make out four other bungalows across the way, despite the evening gloom, with no lights on. Even the street-lamps on the estate were dead. Perhaps the committee were economising on electricity; or perhaps the devices had fallen into disrepair.

Then she spotted two ash-grey, fox-sized, humped animals rounding the corner of Atkinson House; the deformed creature that had been snuffling around on all fours the previous night had apparently returned and been joined by another member of the same species. They came up the path and settled down on their haunches to stare at the light emanating from Court's bungalow window. They were too far away for her to make out their faces distinctly, but the features did not appear to be either canine or deer-like, but those of horribly wizened children with snouts, their faces crumpled by desiccation.

She closed the curtains abruptly and, after five minutes or so of pacing back and forth nervously in the room, opened them again.

Both of the creatures had vanished.

She would have to discuss this with Remal in the morning. It was difficult to judge whether the visit of the crazed fascist official or the sight of those creepy, deformed animals was the more disturbing. She felt like an unwilling audience member caught up in a surreal circus act.

Remembering her hastily set-aside evening meal, she returned to it, slowly spooning the now-lukewarm contents of the bowl mechanically into her mouth. When that task was completed Court thought again of going over the "Neutron X" notebook, but decided against it. She was not sure she could summon the requisite powers of concentration it demanded.

She instead turned on the wireless, but switched it off almost at once as a familiar voice shouted from the speakers at a deafening volume:

"YOUR HOME NEEDS A LICENCE"

Court had made her way up, early the following morning, to the Lodge in order to complain to Remal about the events of the previous night. A haze of mist shrouded the Thool Valley, smothering the noise from the traffic; the watered-down sunshine acted on one's vision like cataracts. As she passed the rear of Atkinson House and the other bungalows, she still encountered no signs of there being any other occupants in residence. The buildings of the Institution began to take on, in her mind, the fake aspect of an exterior film set.

She found the Lodge, as she had been previously advised by Remal, situated right out at the edge of the estate, and it evidently had been constructed not long after Atkinson House itself. Similar to the original structure's design—belonging to the Tudor-revival school of architecture—it was a single-storey building with an entrance bell one operated by pulling on a small rope.

Remal had met her at the door and she'd followed him, via a cluttered corridor full of boxes, into the ramshackle office wherein he occupied himself with whatever business it was that required his attention. The piles of unsorted papers littering almost every surface, the paraffin lanterns hung from low ceiling beams, the partially melted cathedral candles idly deposited at random on surfaces, a noisily droning desktop computer that seemed to have been built decades ago with a dusty, useless screen—the overall impression was one of a perverse withdrawal into a chaotic, half-baked traditionalism. An Edwardian grandfather clock, standing askew on a warped corner floorboard, made no noise, the hands of its dial stilled. Drained bottles of alcohol, breeding mould, were piled up alongside it in a triangular heap.

Remal invited Court to sit down, but there was nowhere obvious to do so. Her sharp grimace advised him wordlessly of this fact, and he retrieved, from the murky depths of some adjacent junk-room, what looked to be a left-over chair from the Atkinson library.

She offered details about last night: the unaccountable intrusion of the licensing official, what appeared to be the man's voice issuing from the wireless, and she also made reference to the disturbing animals she'd seen. Remal replied with an exclamation first of doubt, then of surprise.

"Really? How extraordinary!" he had said.

"Well," Court finally replied, "what can be done about it?"

"What would you suggest?" he asked, his fingers forming an arch in front of his bespectacled face.

"I suspect someone's having a well-organised practical joke at my expense. I think it constitutes harassment."

"Let me put it this way. Have you thought of wearing straight black skirts and shirts with ties? It would suit you."

"What?"

Her eyes registered sudden defiance in a fixed, icy glare.

She didn't quite believe what she'd just heard.

Remal, though, went on as if he had said nothing at all untoward.

"Perhaps I should explain something about our residents."

"Go on," she replied.

"The vast majority are very elderly and infirm. They have developed a tendency to be reclusive. They have also expressed a collective desire not to be disturbed by the busybody tendencies of the outside world. Nowadays young people blindly assert one can't turn back the clock."

"I don't see what that—"

"You, however, are currently only a guest of this Institution. Should you wish to remain for the period necessary to complete your research, it is incumbent upon you to display the appropriate respect for the culture we have developed here."

"Of course, that goes without saying, but you haven't—"

"As for the matter of some practical joke being played upon you, I can give you my assurance that I am every bit as mortified by the intrusion of this errant public official as you are. I shall deal with it personally—at once—by telephoning the requisite authority responsible. There is no question of anyone on this estate indulging in a practical joke at your expense. I imagine most of our residents are currently ignorant of your presence here."

"But you still haven't—"

"I cannot account for the voice you think you may have heard on the wireless, but when it comes to any stray wildlife on the estate I am afraid it is something you will have to get used to. I quite appreciate that such creatures might look—at first—frightening to individuals who have been confined entirely to the metropolitan environs."

"Those things weren't—"

"Nature can appear nightmarish in the dark. Do I make myself clear?"

She spent that afternoon in the library, carefully reading through and then erasing all the marginalia's reactionary rants in the hundreds of pages of the remaining five other first-edition volumes of Alderman's strange stories (namely *Mala Fide, Broken Mirrors, Dust to Dust, Trespassers,* and *Night Forces*). If the author had really believed the vile nonsense he spouted, rather than his ideas being a symptom of a deranged need to privately express taboo speculations, it was no surprise that he wound up impoverished, isolated, and half-forgotten. Anyone harbouring such delusions would inevitably, over the years, find himself without the support of sane friends, colleagues, and associates, especially in the social and professional arena of the Arts. As she worked, her own sense of outrage at his views gradually gave way to the soothing idea that she was, after all, not only doing Alderman—but also literature itself—a great service. If his reputation had been so tarnished that it could not have been salvaged by associates *during his lifetime,* at least now she had taken the opportunity presented to her to salvage his *posthumous* reputation, even through a radical act of deliberate omission. He had not been a prolific letter-writer (the archive boxes proved it), and any anecdotal inter-view "evidence" from his few surviving contemporaries was just that—anecdotal, hence unreliable. Old people overwhelmingly resistant to change, she thought, can't be trusted. Such spurious "evidence" would scarcely count against Alderman in the more enlightened era of universal expertise in Critical Theory.

Having finished her erasures, she replaced the five volumes on the shelf in careful order and decided to turn her attention to the Utopian notebook.

Only after she had been through two of the archive boxes did she re-member that she had left it back in her accommodation.

That musty smell around her was becoming oppressive again.

It was getting dark anyway, and clouds had mushroomed in the twilight as a band of low pressure had entered the valley; sheets of buffeting rain splattered uselessly against the panes of the library's long, narrow windows. The ghost of Bulwer-Lytton, she thought, once more showing his long pa-trician reach. She laughed at the idea, wriggled into the raincoat she'd slung over a nearby armchair, wrapped a headscarf around her hair, and picked up her handbag.

She moved quickly through the deluge, rounding the corner of Atkin-son House as rapidly as her high-heels would carry her—only to stop short when she saw the TV detector van parked outside the guest bungalow.

So much for Remal's promise earlier in the day of "dealing with the er-rant public official at once via the telephone."

Court cautiously approached the vehicle from the rear. Its British make, model, and registration numberplate dated it, she supposed, to the 1970s. On the roof was an aerial of some kind and also, very strangely, what looked like a Tannoy or other form of loudspeaker; the type used in election cam-paigns. The vehicle was certainly in remarkably well-preserved condition. So, she thought, there was some kind of an elaborate prank at her expense going on after all. She moved slowly and quietly around to the front, trying to peer through the window. There was no one inside. All the doors were locked. Nevertheless, that totalitarian official might still be lurking in the back. She remembered hearing, or reading, something about the whole TV detector van fleet having been a deception; that the vehicles contained no electronic equipment and were there just for show—deployed visibly as a means of instilling fear and doubt in the general populace, so it would be cowed and pay up. She couldn't vouch for the truth of the matter, though.

In any case, she could now get that idiot Remal to see the seriousness of the situation. She walked over to the Lodge, thoroughly soaked through to her skin by the rain, and pulled again and again at the doorbell rope. But either he was out or he refused to answer.

When Court retraced her steps to the guest bungalow, she found that the vehicle had gone. It was not possible to explain how it could have got past her; for there was only one road for traffic passing through the whole estate, with entry and exit possible solely by passing alongside the Gatehouse Lodge.

She walked around the estate in case the van had moved and parked elsewhere. But there was no sign of it.

She gave up searching, desperate to get out of her wet clothes and dry off.

Once inside the guest bungalow, she hastily peeled away the soaking layers of clothing, dumped them in the laundry basket, and went into the bedroom to find her towelling dressing-gown.

Laid across the bed, and freshly laundered, were a white shirt, a straight black skirt, and a tie.

All her other clothes had been removed.

There was nothing else dry for her to wear.

It was evident that Remal had let himself into the guest bungalow and left those items of clothing there as part of some sick fantasy. There was no telling what he might do next. This was no longer an intimidating joke; this was clearly sexual harassment.

She found it, however, oddly difficult to recall what would be the proper response to this situation. The turmoil in her thoughts seemed to parallel the turmoil of the storm outside, which still raged across the Institution. Forcing herself to think clearly, she remembered the new smartphone in her handbag. She had not touched it since her arrival, and this fact now struck her as astonishing, since it had scarcely been out of her sight before then. A wave of momentary panic came over her as she rummaged around for it; visions of the thing having been stolen, not working, or of not being able to get a signal. None of these eventualities pertained, however, and she tapped in the number for the emergency services.

If the police thought she was simply overreacting about a pile of clothes she would tell them there was a burglar prowling around the place, right at that moment.

She heard the number ringing, there was a click as if the connection were made, and then an empty pause at the end of the line.

"Police? I need the police. Hello? Police?"

Someone at the other end of the line cleared his throat. And then he spoke, almost in a whisper.

"What is your TV licence reference number?" the disembodied voice said.

And then the iPhone made a loud crackling noise, emitted some sparks, and finally died altogether.

Court tossed the device aside. Immediate flight, then, was the only solution.

She glanced around the room. There was no time even to pack her few belongings.

Alderman's "Neutron X" Utopian notebook still rested on the main table. Should she take it with her? It would, after all, be theft. She couldn't decide, and quickly flipped through the pages at random, again feeling a sense of rising panic.

The thing had been scored through, over and over, to the point it was now completely illegible and, in fact, malignantly useless.

She retrieved the still-damp raincoat and headscarf from the laundry basket, put them on, and braved once more the storm outside.

Court's first instinct was to try the railway gate leading to the passage under the M25 that gave access to a platform on Gallows Langley station. She expected, in advance, it would be locked. But she had a clearly marked communal key by which to obtain entry and exit. However, she found that the key didn't even fit the lock. She thought of screaming for help, but the sound of the storm, as well as the overhead booming of the motor traffic crossing the huge concrete viaduct, would have drowned out her cries. She glanced along the length of the passageway to the distant platform beyond. There were no passengers waiting there.

What next? She was about to turn back when she realised a train was approaching and, as it entered the station, with a shrill breathy whistle and without slowing down, she saw that it was a steam locomotive, hauling covered cargo. The driver, an indistinct blur, waved at her as it rapidly passed alongside the passageway.

She watched the train disappear off into the gloomy distance, trailing sodden clouds in its wake.

The only other reasonable means of exit was the path past the Lodge at the far end of the estate. But Remal was probably there, lying in wait.

By now she was soaked through again, and the rain showed no signs of abating.

There was nothing for it but to try getting assistance from one of the other bungalows at this end. She knocked at the first four, received no replies, and found all the windows obscured from outside view by thick drapes.

She was approaching the fifth bungalow when one of the humped, ash-grey creatures emerged from behind a series of bushes ahead of her. This time she was much closer to one of them and the uncanny impression—formerly obtained at a greater distance—that the things possessed a wizened and yet curiously infantile face with a snout was now vividly confirmed. This creature did not, however, take any notice of her but continued on its path towards the bungalow; and when it had reached its destination, it then reared up on its hind legs, using its forepaws to drag itself up to a curtained window. It pushed against the glass pane, which swung open, and the monstrosity disappeared inside, over the ledge, before closing the aperture behind itself.

So much for obtaining assistance from the residents, she thought; the very concept as distressing as a sudden hallucinatory fit.

Should she try getting through the border of yew trees? They were surely not impassable.

She recalled the map of the Institution's grounds she'd seen on the wall in the Guest Bungalow.

Behind the bungalows on the east side there was a raised bank, or ridge, but that obstacle was easily traversed, even were it slippery underfoot in this filthy weather. Beyond, no more than ten yards further back, was the tree barrier.

And beyond the trees was a vast open space of grazing farmland, and freedom.

It had taken ten minutes to get over the ridge and force a way through the holly bushes choking the spaces between the trunks of the yew trees. Her soaked raincoat was torn in places, and the skin on both her hands, and on her face, was bloodied by cuts. Nevertheless she had forced herself through, only to discover a twelve-foot-high fence. The barrier was unscalable. At the apex of each of its metal rods was a spike in the shape of the fleur-de-lys motif. She edged along the perimeter for some two dozen or so yards, hoping to find a missing bar and thus a gap she might squeeze through, but in vain, for further progress was halted by a vast thorn bush which had grown on both sides of the fence divide. In the opposite direction, there was a similarly huge thornbush, one equally as impassible.

She was left with two options: risk going directly past the Lodge and encountering a lunatic Remal waiting for her or, perhaps, first try the grounds in front of Atkinson House itself. The sloping front lawn leading down to the railway line was, doubtless, enclosed by a fence too, but it could not have been of the same height, else she would have noticed it before, poking above the hedge. The first option still filled her with alarm; she decided she would rather risk the second. Crossing a busy railway line was certainly dangerous enough, but this one had overhead cables and not a ground third rail. And traversing it would take no more than a few seconds.

Once she had clambered back the way she'd come, Court saw that the TV detector van had reappeared and was parked again outside the guest bungalow. But, as she approached it, the Tannoy blared a familiar refrain:

YOUR HOME NEEDS A LICENCE

Suddenly the engine started up, the clutch shifted into low gear, and the vehicle lurched forward, coming straight at her in an attempt to run her over. She managed to dodge it at the last moment by flinging herself to one side, but she twisted in doing so and landed awkwardly.

The van spun around sharply on the wet tarmac, careered, mounted a lawn in a wide arc, ploughed through some bushes, and then drove away in the opposite direction, towards the Lodge.

Court found she had turned her left ankle and limped painfully around the corner of Atkinson House, intent on somehow descending the lawn and thereafter getting across the railway line. She must also have pulled a muscle in her back, for she was almost bent over with the effort of walking. The rain had got even heavier, and sheets of icy water now swept relentlessly across the unsheltered spaces of the Institution grounds, as if heralding another biblical deluge directed at transgressors of the Creator's law.

The lights in the library blazed and, within the porch, the entrance door was wide open. She wondered if Remal were trying to lay a further trap for her. Light also glared through the triple-panelled gable window of the old committee room housed above the library.

A figure moved into sight at the upper window of the gable, framed by the illumination but made blurred and indistinct due to a stream of rainwater pouring down the building's exterior from the roof's flooded guttering. Court tried desperately to discern who it was; and at first was certain it was Remal.

But, even as she stood there, Court felt her eyes were playing tricks on her. The form appeared to undergo a drastic alteration.

No, surely this man was much heavier than the (thin) Remal was; and then, with a somewhat theatrical gesture, the occupant raised his hand and waved.

She moved closer, until she slumped on the steps of the porch outside the library, and stared directly overhead. The man above had flung open the central panel of the window, leant forward, and peered down at her through the black-framed eyeglasses that had replaced his granny spectacles.

At last she could recognise that pale, chubby, freshly clean-shaven face.

Rainwater soaked his thick black hair, plastering it across his cheeks. The twin streams of cancerous blood that had poured from his nostrils had dried, and the residue caked both of his thick upper and lower lips.

When he finally smiled a manic grin, he did so to show off the most nightmarish, ruined teeth that Sibyl Court ever saw in a brutally truncated life.

"Come inside and let's get you out of those wet things!" he shouted down at her with a disembodied, familiar voice.

Court shrieked repeatedly in response—though the actual noise she heard sounded much more like barking, and was accompanied by approaching echoes.

A Letter from Jack

or years the illustrator Neil Harkness had laboured at his craft in relative obscurity and with little commercial success. He was a resident of Gallows Langley—that ill-regarded settlement nestled at the heart of Hertfordshire's infinitely mysterious Thool Valley—and he had been morbidly affected by the influence of the region. It was the focus of all manner of outlandish and unsettling local lore, some of which had, there could be no doubt, a genuine basis in fact. For a period of several months Harkness had even been incarcerated in that notorious Victorian mental asylum run by the notorious Dr. Charles Winterburn, but had been discharged just before the latter's final disgrace in 1959. After being discharged, Harkness had dreamt repeatedly of the abandoned confines of nearby Thool Abbey, that mediaeval nexus of unholy degeneracy, and had somehow obtained a certain slim volume bound in mottled-yellow leather from its interminable depths.

The book was, of course, the collection *The Reunion and Others* by Lilith Blake, published in 1895, a linked sequence of supernatural horror tales, and it contains (as I am sure fanatical aficionados of "weird fiction" are already aware) a gruesomely nightmarish story titled "A Letter from Jack." This particular tale by Blake apparently caused Harkness to produce his very last, excruciatingly distressing work of art. Although it is now fashionable amongst the *bien pensant* to dismiss as a conspiracy theory the extant, verifiable traces of the "Cult of Lilith," I maintain that this occult current—by which an eternally evil madness driven by obsessive hatred for life transforms art into reality—persists to this day and even, perhaps, waxes stronger than before.

Of course, Neil Harkness had been associated with the outré and the darkly sinister since the first appearance of his black-and-white artwork in the 1940s, long before he had stumbled across that volume of Lilith Blake's tales. His illustrations had graced the pages and dustwrappers of several books issued by the specialist horror publishers Charnel House in the United States, and his

53

supreme mastery in depicting human decay, mutilation, and disfigurement to a maddening degree of microscopic detail had already drawn puerile accusations of moral degeneracy. However, whatever heartening—albeit limited—acclaim he garnered was confined to connoisseurs of the macabre and was wholly overshadowed by the newspaper reaction to the single exhibition of his work which was held at a Chelsea art gallery in 1958. One critic for the *Manchester Guardian,* Arnold Hoxling, writing in response to this exhibition, declared that "the real horror is that of Mr. Harkness being allowed to inflict his 'art' on an unsuspecting British public; let him hang his offensive work in some abattoir, wherein such gruesomeness and butchery truly belongs." Harkness was already of a retiring, sensitive, mental tendency and, following this turn of events, he was subject to a case of acute depression. Within a year the dejected artist was admitted to the Gallows Langley Lunatic Asylum.

Upon his release from the asylum, Harkness's memories of his time spent there, and of the treatment which he received, were at best nebulously vague. That he had undergone specialist psychiatric care and that the completely debilitating depression from which he had suffered had been profoundly ameliorated by his stay at the asylum was not in doubt. His former lethargy, lack of interest in eating, and complete inability to concentrate for lengthy periods had vanished. Nevertheless, Harkness was perturbed by the lacunae which riddled the memory of those long months spent under the supervision of Dr. Winterburn, he whose features swam up at random moments from the depths of Harkness's mind, particularly the doctor's bald head with its aureole of white hair and his horrible grin furnished by a greenish-and-yellow-tinged set of false teeth.

Harkness had returned to his attic room in the heart of the village, high up amidst the shadowy cluster of Jacobean houses with their mouldering, front-gabled roofs. During the depths of his despondency, in the aftermath of the scathing newspaper review of his exhibition, he had completely lost interest in the creation of his artworks—even in those pictures which he had already produced—but in picking up the threads of his interrupted life, and answering the accumulated queries in letters from his small coterie of devoted fans in the United States, Harkness found that the desire to begin illustrating once more had revived within him.

He went through the boxes containing the old artwork which had lain so long untouched, cleaned the tools of his trade, and bought a fresh supply of black ink in preparation for the resumption of his artistic efforts. The interruption to his career meant that he had no immediate commissions to hand upon which to begin work, and so he resolved to embark upon a new, original illustration. The resolution was firmly fixed in his mind, but Harkness required an external stimulus in order to carry it out in practice. He had a small library of books, chiefly consisting of volumes published by Charnel House, but with a number of other anthologies and collections of the weird and the uncanny. Unfortunately, he soon realised that these were all useless for his purposes. Those which had inspired him to attempt the visual representation of their written-down horrors had been long-since mined (the old artworks in the boxes testified to that), whereas the books by Charnel House already contained his own previously commissioned illustrations.

It was a week after returning home to his attic room that Harkness experienced a fateful nightmare—or what he thought was a nightmare. His sleep for the three nights beforehand had been restless and troubled by a curiously vivid, repetitive dream. This dream invariably centred around the old, vast, labyrinthine abbey, located a mile or so distant from the village. It was reached only by traversing moonlit tracts of open fields shrouded by silver ground-mist, and there were endless shelves within its depths harbouring long-mouldering volumes which *breathed in the darkness as if they were alive.* On the third night of dreaming this same haunting dream, he actually found himself inside the ancient structure taking a particular item from the shelves of its library—and it was that book by Lilith Blake which I have mentioned earlier; the slim volume of horrific tales bound in mottled-yellow leather.

Harkness woke the following morning after the third dream in a state of high distress. He had pulled off the blankets on his bed to find himself fully clothed in an old suit, his boots covered with mud after some nocturnal tramp across the countryside. His apparel, as well as his hands and face, were blackened by carbon. It appeared that he had been rummaging around inside a sooty, fire-damaged interior. He at once suspected that his mind was giving way again, and that the memory-loss from which he suffered concerning his time at the asylum had now been supplemented by an episode of somnambulism. His distress was further compounded, however, when he saw a book now resting on his bedside table where no book had been the night before—that selfsame volume of which he had dreamed; the collection of weird tales by Lilith Blake, *The Reunion and Others,* bound in mottled-yellow leather. And he thought of Samuel Taylor Coleridge's lines:

> If a man could pass through Paradise in a dream, and have a flower presented to him as a pledge that his soul had really been there, and if he found that flower in his hand when he awoke—Ay! and what then?

He took up the book to examine it more closely, half expecting the thing to dissipate into nothingness in his grasp as he leafed through its foxed, brittle pages, and began to read the tale "A Letter from Jack," finding himself utterly fascinated by the thing.

Had Harkness not been mesmerised by the tale and full of plans to revive his creative endeavours, the scandal which finally broke locally concerning Dr. Winterburn's recent criminal activities at the Gallows Langley Lunatic Asylum might have given Harkness pause for thought—especially in light of the fact that he himself had a recent former patient. As it was, Harkness was entirely insulated from such rumours and whispered expressions of disgust. He was, after all, a recluse, saw almost no one—save for an eccentric historian and mystical esotericist, his neighbour Roderick Carden. Although Harkness did not socialise with others in the village, he had enjoyed a friendship with Carden based on the latter's recognition of Harkness's commitment to strange illustrative work and Carden's admiration of the artist's strange subject-matter and technique. The bond between them actually flourished—paradoxically—because they made no demands on each other's time and there were often long gaps between their meeting in person. Indeed, such had been the gulf-like interval between their last meeting, when Harkness had shown him his impossibly detailed drawing of a particularly vile Elemental, that Carden had not even known of Harkness's months-long stay in the Gallows Langley Asylum. In addition, Carden had been deeply immersed in research into Druidical lore and the nexus of occult forces centred around the local region, all of which was to furnish a chapter in his forthcoming book *The Ancient Mysteries of Thool Valley.*

When it came to family ties, Harkness possessed only a prim elder sister, Melissa, whom he had not seen for several years after her marriage during the war and her subsequent emigration to the United States, since when he had lost regular contact with her. She had never cared for his macabre artwork anyway, urging him to turn his talent for illustration towards the depiction of more "wholesome" subject matter. His incarceration would doubtless have confirmed her in her belief that he was wasting the commercial value of his artistic talents and succeeding only in making himself ill.

What subsequent NHS outpatient care one might have expected Harkness to receive after his discharge from the asylum was unforthcoming; a consequence of the rapid dissolution of the institution's administrative operations and the wilful destruction of most of its internal records. One must remember, too, that Dr. Winterburn's swift trial and subsequent execution was undertaken under a veil of the utmost state secrecy; no sensational details of the crimes which Dr. Winterburn had perpetrated were released to the general public, and only those in and around Gallows Langley had any intimation—and that derived via local gossip—of what had actually gone on in its asylum. The newspapers, radio, and television were all subject to a legal injunction granted by Lord Justice Hirsig—that same judge who also presided, at a later date, over the infamous case of the Zoskia Institute Scandal (a case with which my readers are doubtless already familiar).

For the next few weeks Harkness worked in a state of artistic frenzy on preparatory sketches for his "comeback" artwork inspired by the Lilith Blake story "A Letter from Jack." His recurring dream concerning the abandoned abbey had ceased after obtaining possession of that mottled-yellow book; indeed, he did not dream of anything at all as far as he could remember. He was, however, still subject to bouts of sleepwalking, though did not wander far, never leaving his attic flat—and invariably gravitating towards the blemished, oval wall-mirror at the far end of the hallway. There he would gradually reawaken and find himself staring at his own dim reflection. Once or twice, before he was entirely awake, he thought that he saw his features warped by a sardonic, utterly unfamiliar expression, with the mouth twisted in a depraved grin and the lips and teeth covered with blood.

Harkness feared that he was losing his reason again and, though not subject to his old symptoms of acute apathy and absence of interest, he was now, instead, subject to an obsessive enthusiasm over the work which lay before him—work which simply had to be completed at all costs. He told himself that there was no question of his considering returning to the asylum until it was done. But, so too, there lurked at the back of his mind an unacknowledged and gnawing sense of disquiet at the fact that he was unable to recall, try as he might, the form of treatment to which Dr. Winterburn had subjected him.

Moreover, Harkness had not, as yet, read any of the other stories in the book; and such had been the effect of "A Letter from Jack" that he genuinely feared to do so. What new vistas of nightmarishness might then open up before him? When the artwork for that story was completed, perhaps he might then force himself look over the other tales—or so he thought—but not until then.

It is now necessary, in our putting together all the pieces of this macabre jigsaw, to consider the strange account of Sir Montague Scarsdale, a celebrated alienist and the Medical Superintendent of the Gallows Langley Lunatic Asylum from 1887 until 1897. His private memoir, written in 1905, was entitled *Some Curious Recollections of an Alienist,* and provides information about a violent mental patient who was admitted into his care in late November 1888. Sir Montague writes as follows:

> One of the most bizarre and frankly terrifying patients whom I encountered during the course of my profession was the man I shall designate here as David K——. His exact identity was never clearly established, but it seems he originated in the Spitalfields district, was around forty-five years of age, and had been transferred from Colney Hatch after spending less than a week at said institution. He had, during that brief period of incarceration, overpowered one of the female members of staff, then taken her to his cell and, with a carving knife stolen from the hospital's canteen, managed to sever the carotid artery in her throat, being interrupted during the process of inflicting further unspeakable mutilations upon her lifeless body. The man, it appears, was thought to be suffering from general paresis (*dementia parylitica*). The medical authorities had not known in advance that he was capable of such a violent outburst, nor of his devilish cunning; which cunning he exhibited by pilfering the lethal weapon by means of a series of clever sleight-of-hand deceptions. In any case, to spare the feelings of the poor woman's relatives, they were more than generously compensated for their loss, and it was given out that she died of typhoid fever and her corpse could not safely be viewed. David K—— himself was transferred to Gallows Langley Lunatic Asylum within a matter of days, where he was subject to the closest of restrictions and every precautionary measure.
>
> There were several incredibly baffling aspects to his physical condition. The diagnosis of general paresis furnished by Colney Hatch did not begin explain certain biological anomalies I found during a medical examination which the patient had violently resisted and which could only be conducted under restraint and sedation. Had the very notion itself not been absolutely absurd, it

would have been impossible to avoid the conclusion that the man was not really alive; there was no discernible pulse, his body temperature varied only between 50° F and 53° F, and his respiration was remarkably shallow and infrequent. There was also the matter of the unaccountable and curious bleach-like discolouration of the skin of his hands, which seemed bloodless and much paler than the rest of his anatomy. I discovered, over the course of the following two weeks, that the patient was subject to a mania wherein he claimed that his actions were being directed by some outside, controlling, force which gave him instructions. He was insistent on the point that, were he not to obey those instructions, then the consequences of disobedience were far worse even than torture. Naturally, I did not give much credence to his often delirious ramblings, seeing them as a symptom of his malady, but one of the stranger features of his mania was the macabre letter which he wrote a month after he arrived at the asylum and the infamous signature appended to it.

It was, however, before David K—— had written the letter in question that I was visited by an Inspector A—— of Scotland Yard, whose actual name, of course, I recognised in connexion with the recent Whitechapel Murders, which had caused such a prurient nationwide sensation. He advised me that David K—— was a person on their list of suspects for those selfsame atrocious series of killings. The inspector then sought permission to interview my patient as part of his investigation. When I refused this permission, our verbal exchanges became extremely heated. Whereas Inspector A—— conceded that my patient was not in a condition to be interrogated, let alone fit to stand trial (on grounds of insanity), he then advised me that one of his "informants" had "tipped him off about The Ripper being up to his old games in the Colney Hatch madhouse, but it was being covered up by the whole bloody medical establishment who say he's just a harmless imbecile"—or something to that effect. I took strong exception at this sensationalist characterisation of the facts and to the inspector giving them credence, further explaining that David K—— was now under the strictest supervision here at the Gallows Langley Lunatic Asylum, and could not possibly be any danger to others. This was now, in law, a medical and not a criminal case. At that juncture our interview was terminated. Of course, I heard no more from him.

Now, returning to the matter of the letter written subsequently by David K——, let me state that it was not actually posted and, at the time, did not leave the confines of the asylum. The original is still in my possession. It was my professional opinion that such activity might provide a useful insight into the workings of the mind of my patient, and I specifically gave him the impression that I had arranged for some special latitude in the matter of him communicating with the individual to whom his missive was addressed. Of course, I knew full well that the deception could only last for so long; David K——— eventually would doubtless become suspicious that his communication produced no reply. It was addressed to a "Miss B———" of Highgate Village. Imagine my astonishment when I made discreet enquiries about the addressee of the letter, only to discover that the person in question was a girl scarcely fourteen years of age who, while an orphan, had been adopted by a family of that parish. One's first thoughts in such a situation as this would be the welfare of the girl, except that the content of the letter evinced no indication she herself was in any immediate danger, nor that David K———, even were he "The Whitechapel Murderer," had chosen her to be a victim of his outrages. In fact, in his disturbed mind *precisely the opposite appeared to be the case*.

The letter in question was written in his own blood and kept in an emptied inkpot, after he had made a small incision in his wrist. However, before I reproduce the communication here, there is one other important element upon which I feel obliged to elaborate. Despite having had no reply to his letter—since, naturally, it had not been sent—he displayed no surprise or concern about the matter as days passed. This aspect puzzled me intensely and, during a visit to his cell, I let slip some leading remark about letters sometimes going astray, hoping for a reaction.

"I already know, Doctor," he said in that gravelly, hollow, cockney-accented voice of his, one laced with a leering irony, the mouth twisted in a depraved grin, "that you fink yew is clever, an' it's yew that 'ave gone an' kept my lettah back. Don't make a blind bit o' diffrunce. Look, when I write, she knows, y' know? Ain't nuffink to do with me postin' it. She read it all right— every bloody word— read it in 'er mind . . ."

I now reproduce the letter in full:

———————

Dear Princess

I don't think I had the chance to thank you properly for going to the trouble to have me sprung from Hell where the dead are dreaming. I've been trying and am sending you thoughts about all what I seen and what I done. Well now, see, your very own boy's been gone and got himself locked up in another madhouse tighter than the last one. Yes, I enjoyed all the games I have played ripping up whores, just like you promised I would. ha. ha. I got my hands on another one of them in the Hatch, a right juicy wench, so that makes six in all now, but I ain't found nothing inside any of them worth reading like what's down in your pretty little innards I reckon—theirs is all sticky and red and make no sense. Ah, how I loves the taste of it. But you know that don't you Princess?

Give my regards to your old mum.

Your humble servant

Jack the Ripper

———

I cannot account for most of the references in this deranged letter nor what they had to do with a then-blameless fourteen-year-old girl who, I am sure, was, at the time, utterly ignorant of the fact she was the intended recipient of this communication. The truly remarkable thing is that some seven years later, towards the end of 1895, this same person, Miss B——, later obtained notoriety for her increasingly pronounced morbid tendencies; even eventually producing a volume of decadent ghost stories, one of which was a nightmarish tale concerning an undead lunatic who had been kept in an asylum and whom (it is strongly suggested) was no less than the infamous Whitechapel Murderer himself! Another curious feature of this rather remarkable yet unaccountable connection between Miss B—— and David K—— was that both died in November 1896, her death being, I am informed, the result of a cancer manifesting at a tragically young age.

David K—— remained under my charge for all the years leading up to his demise and, I am glad to say, was subject to the strictest of regimens. Naturally, I allowed him to pen no further letters. There was certainly never the slightest chance that he could have proved a danger to others; I ensured he came into contact only with the best and most experienced of my staff of male attendants, was permanently confined to a straitjacket, and was, furthermore, sedated and kept in his own padded cell at all times. His mania centred, towards the end, around the idea of all mankind not being able to bear too great an insight into the "real" reasons behind the worst of its behaviour. As for his medical diagnosis of general paresis, I should add that, in the years following his admission, he exhibited none of the progressive symptoms which would have indicated that this was the malady from which he suffered. Whatever the correct diagnosis might have been, it was then beyond the powers of medicine to determine; and in any case his condition was certainly incurable. For my own part, I refrained from having any further needless contact with him; on the very rare occasions when I was obliged to do so for medical reasons, he would make cryptical remarks concerning certain details of my private affairs which it was impossible for him to have known about, and I regarded him with an ever-increasing sense of abhorrence.

The end came swiftly; he was found one morning in his cell in a completely unresponsive state and, after I had examined him, I at once pronounced him unquestionably dead. He was swiftly buried in a plot within the walled-in hillside cemetery located some distance behind the asylum itself, that cemetery wherein the majority of our patients went to their final rest.

Thus ends my account of the man I have designated David K———, the strangest patient whom I ever encountered during the course of my years as an alienist and superintendent of the Gallows Langley Lunatic Asylum.

When Neil Harkness was at last fully prepared to undertake the artwork to illustrate the macabre story "A Letter from Jack," he was plagued by a further series of different, though equally hideous dreams. He was trapped in a dimly lit, cramped room whose ceiling was rife with black mould, the walls covered by a peeling, mottled-yellow wallpaper—the exact same shade as that of the covers of the book which had taken such a hold upon him. In one corner, back in the deeper shadows, there was a Victorian iron bedstead with a straw mattress. A strangely distorted form was lying upon it—the limbs at askew, obtuse angles—a terrible form upon which he could not bear to gaze directly. All the while, as he dreamed, he heard a drunken, far-off female voice singing some old Music-Hall song:

> In that cold apartment lying naked and dead,
> The head nearly severed from the body it is said,
> Her heart torn away and other parts besides,
> Let us hope to mercy that in no pain she died,
> Upon the cheerless floor surrounded by her gore,
> Nearly torn to pieces was what the people saw,
> But until the murderer's caught, on us it leaves a stain,
> Now the Demon Jack the Ripper's got at his work again.

And Harkness could only escape the recurring dream by screaming his way out of it.

"Please understand," said Melissa Harkness, "I did write to tell you in advance I planned to return to England, but you obviously did not receive my letter. It was Roderick Carden who gave me your new address. And here I am. Oh, Neil, I'm so very sorry."

She could not help but notice a strange look pass over her brother's face as she mentioned having written to him. It was just a momentary expression; almost one of concealment.

The reunited siblings were sat in the living room of the latter's sparsely-furnished attic flat. Outside an autumn fog had rolled in, half wreathing the gabled rooftops of the cluster of the other Jacobean houses and deadening the late afternoon light.

She scarcely recognised her own brother. He had aged tremendously during the years she had lived abroad in the United States enduring her own hell: the inexorable decline of her marriage into infidelity, recriminations, and physical abuse. At the same time her brother had been battling with his own demons, alone.

"So you know nothing about what happened to that devil, Doctor Winterburn?" Melissa enquired. "It all seems so incredibly fantastic! I can scarcely believe it myself."

"No, nothing," Harkness replied.

Melissa provided exact details of the nature of Winterburn's medical outrages and of the high-level conspiracy which prevented the dissemination of information about those atrocities to the public; all this information had been passed on to her by Roderick Carden in a confidential letter. But this was not the half of it; her correspondent then went on to make the most outlandish speculations and made esoteric references which she could hardly understand. Perhaps Neil could make something out of them. They appeared to have been written in the expectation that she would pass them on to her brother.

"Here," she said, reading aloud from said letter, "this is what Carden claims—

"It is my contention that Winterburn's secret activities at Gallows Langley Lunatic Asylum were a recrudescence of the unbelievably ancient 'Scarlet Ceremony'— the ceremony of necromantic sacrifice undertaken in homage to the 'Cult of the White Hands,' known also as 'The Cult of Lilith.' He had confederates in his plan, of course, mostly from the Degabaston line—that local branch of degenerate nobility long associated with Thool Abbey but local commoners such as Ronald Duxford had a hand in it too, of course. It was not by chance that Doctor Winterburn sought dominion over that particular asylum of all the ones in our land. Its proximity to the abbey was a prerequisite, of course, but there was an additional factor. I have in my possession a certain manuscript penned by one of Winterburn's predecessors as superintendent of the institution, Sir Montague Scarsdale, and this memoir lays bare the fact that the disgusting murderer known, in common parlance, as 'Jack the Ripper' was buried in the grounds of the asylum's walled-in cemetery."

"I simply don't understand a word of all this," said Melissa. "What does it mean?"

"Dear sister," said Harkness, "I dreamt repeatedly of the abbey. I actually took something out of it, something real and physical. It was a copy of Lilith Blake's book *The Reunion and Others* and one of its stories—called 'A Letter from Jack'—is all about the Ripper's confinement in the same asylum. I have not been able to think of anything else; and for the last several nights I have dreamt, not of the abbey, but of some dismal Whitechapel doss where one of his female victims lay slaughtered and eviscerated."

Melissa tried not to display any outward sign of alarm at her brother's rambling, nonsensical discourse, but inwardly she felt a sickening sensation beginning at the pit of her stomach. She could not help but notice the strange paleness, and the unusually long fingers, of her brother's hands which, until then, he had kept hidden in the overly long sleeves of a yellow silk dressing-gown. Outside the fog was becoming thicker, and the room was now beginning to darken. She felt himself to be in real, mortal danger. Was her brother even now, in fact, mad?

"Do you still have this book?" she asked.

"Why, yes," Harkness replied, "I will not let it out of my possession."

"May I see it?"

"Really I should not be . . ."

"Please."

Melissa believed that if she could demonstrate to her brother that the book supposedly taken from a dream was not real it might help him to shake off, at the root, this curious obsession which had taken hold of him. It was clear that it had been a mistake to quote from Carden's letter; she had thought its contents only incomprehensible to her, but they seemed to inspire her brother to greater flights of demented fancy.

Harkness returned with the book after disappearing for a few moments into the adjacent room which served as his artist's studio, and Melissa was handed the volume.

It was long-blackened, irreparably damaged by fire, with its boards slimy to the touch as if bound in the skin of some unearthly, enormous mollusc. Melissa suspected even before she opened the covers that the contents would prove to be almost wholly illegible, and so they were; each page that she very carefully turned—in fear of the thing coming apart in her hands—was little more than brittle carbon, with only a series of eerily suggestive words here and there able to be discerned amidst the obliteration. The object was shudderingly repulsive; an obscenity, an Unholy Grail. She passed it back to Harkness with a palpable sense of disgust and then got to her feet.

"You say you've actually read this book?" she asked him, trying vainly to remove dark, sticky, foul-smelling mucus from her fingers with a lace handkerchief. The evidence of her own eyes had shown it was simply not possible for anyone to have read more than the odd surviving word scattered randomly throughout its pages. Her brother was surely still deranged if he believed otherwise. Here was the proof of it. If only he had taken her advice years ago and concentrated on other, healthier things!

"Only the one story, 'A Letter from Jack.' Not the rest as yet. I don't dare to——"

"May I please use your bathroom? I simply must clean my hands."

Melissa made a detour into the kitchen, where, instinctively, she silently and quickly pocketed a knife before entering the bathroom. It was as if she were back in foggy San Francisco with her always-drunk American husband. After scrubbing her hands with carbolic soap under a hot running tap for several minutes, she returned to the living room. Her brother was sitting there in near-complete darkness now, and humming a curious old tune to himself that sounded like a song from Victorian music hall days. He mumbled the lyrics, and Melissa could not follow them.

"Don't you think we should have some light in here?" she said, sitting down in the chair opposite Harkness.

"Not yet, there are some things I'd like to explain to you—to fill in the gaps in your knowledge."

The unease which Melissa felt began to rapidly intensify. Was it merely her imagination or had Neil's voice taken on the hint of an alien accent to his own—a gravelly and hollow cockney accent—and had not a trace of leering irony also entered into his speech? She wanted to stand, to move towards the door, to make up any excuse to leave, but some intangible mesmeric power prevented her from doing so. The room had now darkened to such an extent that she could hardly even make out Neil clearly; all she could see was a vague man-shaped outline seated in the chair opposite.

The seemingly disembodied voice went on speaking in the darkness, and Melissa, transfixed and powerless, could do nothing but listen to what it told her.

"Contrary to what the poseur Oscar Wilde said, it is Death—not Life—

which most imitates Art. It is indeed the case that Doctor Winterburn was a practitioner of what are termed 'The Black Arts' and certain of the inmates under his supervision—in the end, even his own wife— were subject to invocations of magical currents designed to embody his metaphysical theories about the pre-eminence of the Weird over the Mimetic. He wished to enable dangerous lunatics to create the only true art; artistic creations which are not mere public entertainment, but are the very stripping away of the veils which separate us from the abysses of eternity and infinity. Disorder, derangement, disease, and disfigurement of the body and soul using the blackest form of psychic manipulation. You wonder why Harkness—"

Here Melissa's feeling of mounting terror increased, as the individual opposite casually referred to himself in the third person.

"—suffered from such profound lapses of memory since being discharged from the asylum? Post-hypnotic suggestion. He was instructed to forget his initiation, he was told to create the great work to which he had personally been assigned (and which only he could accomplish), to obtain that copy of *The Reunion and Others,* the burnt copy *which only he could read,* and then, once his task was completed, to be transfigured into Horror itself."

"The Ripper—?" Melissa croaked.

"The Cult of the White Hands had first called it up from hell, but could not control it fully; a penniless cockney sculptor who had been brought back from the dead in 1888 after an overdose of opium. And in the interminable back alleys, courtyards, and doss-houses of Whitechapel, the thing paid the ancient homage true acolytes render to the oldest and darkest of gods. The thing's handiwork achieved the status of worldwide immortality: murder as the quintessence of ecstasy, terror as the height of irresistible fascination, fear as the epitome of delight, and bodily evisceration as supreme craftsmanship. It made of its whorish artist's models those pitied, unblemished martyrs whose names have lived down the decades, now to be spoken of only with charnel reverence. If, as De Quincey posited, bloody murder can truly be considered to be one of the fine arts, then was not 'The Ripper' one of the greatest artists of all in our age of decayed futurity? Scarsdale could not admit to himself the whole truth; but it is true that in 1896 the thing was at a low ebb, its power in abeyance, and it was for that reason that Scarsdale seized the opportunity to have 'David K——' re-buried deep in the ground away from prying eyes, there to rot, and brood, and dream ineffectually its blood-red dreams. Do you now comprehend why it was that

Doctor Winterburn could not allow that force to remain imprisoned forever, but foolishly wished it loosed, thinking he could control it? What if Monsieur Valdemar—you must read your Poe, you know—proved to be the mesmerist and not the mesmerised?"

The voice had lost all those former hints of a cockney accent, but retained the leering irony and the gravelly, hollow timbre. Melissa was now terrified not only by what he was saying but also by the sensation of falling into his nightmare. She felt as if she were being hypnotised, as if her own mind were gradually being occupied by the shadowy, indeterminate form sat opposite her in the darkness.

"You have always turned away in horror from horror," the voice went on. "No longer."

But it was her mouth which had uttered those final words.

*　　*　　*

After numerous complaints from the other tenants about the unbearable smell emanating from within Harkness's attic rooms and the absence of any reply to repeated knocking at the entrance door, the property was entered into by the landlord a week later. The scene which met his eyes defied belief.

In the living room were two dead bodies, sitting and facing each other. One of these corpses was a loathsome mass of deliquescent flesh whose abominable stench and sight made the landlord gag and almost faint away insensibly. The thing had dissolved into corruption, resembling some huge, four-limbed, human-shaped cephalopod which had been left rotting for weeks on a seashore. Opposite this horror was the other corpse, a woman, much fresher but equally as terrifying, and covered in dried blood; its throat cut from left to right in repeated back-and-forth strokes, severing the carotid artery and the oesophagus, slicing all the way deep inside to the neck vertebra. In its right hand was still clutched the long-bladed, blood-stained carving knife with which it had—impossibly—undertaken its own self-mutilation.

Whether or not the horrible suspicion Roderick Carden asserts is actually true, that the living, transferred form of Neil Harkness now resides, unknown, in the unmarked, lost grave of 'David K——' the talentless cockney sculptor, who was known as 'Jack the Ripper,' I cannot tell. But it is clear that the resurrected thing found in Harkness's attic rooms did not have enough life in it to commit a greater atrocity despite desiring to do so, and its—or perhaps Harkness's—final form of artistic expression was only completed by other hands.

A Universe of Charnel Glamour

Of all the abandoned psychiatric hospitals dotted around England, none was regarded with quite the same degree of fearful loathing as was felt by local residents towards the Gallows Langley Lunatic Asylum. Each of the others had their own share of notoriously bizarre scandals, of course—the likes of the Zoskia Institute and the Glanville Private Psychiatric Home, to name only two—but it was the Gallows Langley Lunatic Asylum that truly embodied all the frightful mystery which once surrounded those titan outposts of the insane. This huge, rotting Victorian edifice, constructed like some elaborate Gothic parody and situated in the middle of two hundred acres of sequestered land, had received from North London and its environs only the worst-afflicted victims of human derangement. The institution had stood for well over a century, surrounded by a high, spiked wall, with a self-contained community whose residents were rarely ever seen by outsiders. Gallows Langley townsfolk of the nineteenth-century had speculated fearfully when the first of the horse-drawn carriages with curtained windows passed through the asylum gates, and, as the long years passed, the procession of carriages gave way to motorised ambulances with blacked-out windows, their twentieth-century descendants speculated just as fearfully as their ancestors had done.

Very rarely did any exact information leak out about what went on inside the asylum and the exact nature of the patient-community which it housed. The institution's staff members were sternly discouraged from mixing with the townsfolk but, now and then, some caught-off-guard hospital attendant was plied with drink by the always-inquisitive landlord at Gallows Langley's principal hostelry, the Gryphon Tavern. A handful of such weird, drunken accounts, heard over the years, tended to confirm that most of the worst physical cases were the consequence of untreated syphilitic disease (there was even a fantastical account that Jack the Ripper himself had died there a hopeless imbecile in 1919). But one of those asylum attendants, a toper who had returned to the Gryphon three times before his mysterious disappearance, had also hinted darkly at a central, organising cancer at its heart, a cancer in human form, one which had extended its malefic tentacles throughout the institution and which had merged necromancy with psychiatry. Such drink-induced confessions might have seemed too outlandish, even for the already-fevered imaginations of the townsfolk, were it not for an episode in 1959 which appeared to confirm this particular toper's wildest claims.

That same year an inmate had actually escaped from the asylum and had stalked the countryside at large for a few hours, before seeking sanctuary at a local farmhouse where he pleaded for the use of a telephone. He was a disintegrating shell of a man, clad in a torn, bloodied straitjacket, his facial features ravaged with dozens of oozing pustules indicating the onset of early syphilitic disease. He claimed to be a prisoner—not a patient; the victim of a carefully organised conspiracy against him by the asylum's medical superintendent. In any case, the farmer and his wife owned no telephone and, before he could be questioned further by the couple, two brutish attendants suddenly appeared, having tracked the fugitive to this destination. They took him into custody, offering only an obvious explanation as to his wild claims: that he was the dangerously violent ringleader of a thwarted attempt at mass escape by the asylum inmates.

Perhaps, if the farmer and his wife had reported the matter and immediate enquiries had been made, certain subsequent, monstrous torments which took place at the asylum's walled-in graveyard might have been averted. The folk of Gallows Langley are, however, notoriously loath to draw attention to themselves. Even more pertinently, in this instance, it was also rumoured that strange crops were raised there at Thool Farm; pungent, venomous herbs destined for the nearby abbey (which then housed an American who was the last of an ancient, titled family of ill-repute).

However, the asylum is closed now, of course, and has been since 1961, though it was not thanks to the reforms of the then Secretary of State for Health. It was judicial hanging in 1959 which finally ended the activities of that medical superintendent whose trial and subsequent execution took place with unprecedented secrecy and swiftness. To reveal the details to the public was impossible at the time; there is little doubt that ignorant accusations by the press of a reactionary recrudescence of the Witchcraft Act would have followed—even though the superintendent's diabolical confederate, the American nobleman, escaped legal justice, perishing in a fire shortly before the trial.

In the six-month period after the asylum's closure there had been a caretaker assigned to the abandoned premises, but he was found one morning with his throat cut from ear to ear in a bloody act of apparent self-annihilation. No subsequent caretaker had lasted in the position for more than three days before finding an excuse to leave. There had been calls for the structure to be pulled down during the late 1960s, but the celebrated architect Augustus Pugin had had a hand in the design of the ornate interior courtyard, and a decade of bureaucratic indecision resulted in an impasse with local conservationists. Although the crumbling structure and its extensive grounds remained standing, the latter was finally overrun by the encroaching woodland allowed to flourish unchecked by the authorities. This was a consequence not only of the increasingly fashionable cause of environmentalism, but also in the hope that nature itself might serve to obliterate those man-made horrors of the past.

During the 1970s, gangs of local youths occasionally made their way into the depths of the woodlands at night, especially around the time of Halloween, despite having been warned to keep away from the place by their parents or grandparents. Those who braved such nocturnal explorations would return with accounts of the terrifying, labyrinthine edifice at the heart of the woodlands, its debris-strewn corridors complete with rusting trolleys, crude surgical instruments, scrawled and incomprehensible literary narratives, eerie black-and-white photographs of hopelessly syphilitic inmates, and legions of curiously deformed vermin. Those desensitised by drugs or alcohol in their search for "kicks" returned with wilder tales of a walled-in hillside cemetery lurking beyond the old asylum—a nightmarish region where thick ivy and barbed weeds ran riot over rotting wooden headstones bearing the scrawled case-numbers which had been allocated to buried patients. There was, so it was also said, a constant impression of incoherent whispering and humourless laughter close at hand in that repository of those who had died hopelessly insane.

The number of the nocturnal expeditions slowly dwindled, and it was noticeable, as the years passed, that the thrill-seekers became much less inclined to scoff at the stern warnings about the asylum their elders had muttered, and by the time this younger generation in turn produced children of their own, they did not repeat those same warnings (which had only served to stir up interest in the region). Instead, they explained away the legends as "a baseless, local superstition"; although the furtive look in their eyes was not at all in keeping with their professed attitude of scepticism.

Doctor Charles Winterburn, Medical Superintendent of the Gallows Langley Lunatic Asylum, pushed the folder containing the latest medical report across his desk, took off his horn-rimmed spectacles, and rubbed the bridge of his hawk-like nose. He was a thin, bald, late-middle-aged man clad in a pinstriped three-piece navy-blue suit. He possessed an aureole of white hair and a set of greenish-yellow-tinged false teeth. Winterburn had already signed off on a fresh regimen of weekly Electroconvulsive Therapy for those under his care. But, so he mused, perhaps a more widespread campaign of prefrontal leucotomies would yield greater compliance with his core programme of creative writing. He simply had to quash any lingering resistance to the aversion felt towards the well-chosen books his Lordship had provided in order to further stimulate the already-disturbed imaginations of his patients.

Satisfied for the moment, Dr. Winterburn dismissed these concerns from his mind. He had other, more pressing, personal matters to settle. He fumbled around on the desk, retrieved his pipe and pouch of tobacco, filled the bowl, put a match to the blend, and then puffed away as he examined the salient portion of the letter written to him yesterday by the cuckold Edward Reynolds.

> . . . and whereas it might have been common practice for a man of position and influence to arrange to have his wife confined to an asylum on purely specious grounds during the last century, it is not so easy in this day and age. I can assure you that my exposure of your outrageous abuse of power will result not only in the downfall of the beastly De Gabiston but also in your own ruin.

There were several more lines of invective and threat-making which Winterburn registered with an indifferent mental shrug. He glanced at his pocket-watch and picked up the telephone. Lord De Gabiston had warned him about the perils of involvement with red-haired women years ago, when first he and sweet Molly had become engaged and had also, quite rightly, predicted that she would never consent to becoming the Matron and working closely alongside him.

"Has the man calling himself Reynolds arrived yet, Benson?" he said.

A voice replied: "Not yet, doctor."

"Is everything in readiness?" he asked.

"Quite ready, doctor, just as you instructed."

It was two years earlier, in 1957, that the hitherto-unsuspected ancillary United States branch of the male Degabaston succession (the "De Gabistons") had finally been properly verified and had resulted in the restoration of the Thool title. A forgotten cousin, Zebulon De Gabiston, born in Salem in 1907, eventually became Lord De Gabiston. the putative fourth Earl of Thool, but not until fifty years after his birth. He was from a wealthy family; both his parents had died young in a tragic accident, but they had left him a substantial financial legacy. At the age of eighteen he first came to England to study, drawn by the family tradition of an aristocratic lineage in the Old Country.

Winterburn and De Gabiston had first met in 1925 when provided with adjacent student rooms on the ground floor of the St. Swithun's quad at Magdalen College, Oxford (where Winterburn had studied medicine, while the American De Gabiston had studied Greats under a Rhodes Scholarship). Both men had then joined a notorious secret society, "The Cult of Lilith," which certain of the dons (the most ignorant of them thinking it advocated certain practices attributed to Diogenes) as well as a particularly tiresomely orthodox clergyman (author of such laughable treatises as *The Damnable Cult of Witchcraft*) had vainly attempted to suppress. However, the cult had itself been founded only a year earlier by another Oxford don, the notorious Alfred Muswell; later to be stripped of his tenure after refusing to recant his eccentric theories concerning "the esoterically authentic" nature of literary merit, which heresies he was seeking to instil in his students.

The man was possessed of a number of eccentricities, including wandering around the quads of the colleges at dead of night, still clad in his tutorial robes, and enjoying, ostensibly, his sole means of physical exercise. He was also often to be found wearing a pair of black gloves even during the daytime, as if determined—for some bizarre reason—to keep his hands covered up.

It was said that this "Cult of Lilith," as presided over by Muswell, eventually formed an inner, secret circle of degenerate converts who were fully prepared to make the full transition from the theory to the practical application of the cult's tenets. Supernatural literature, expressed in its highest degree, or so Muswell maintained, is a form of initiatory rite into higher orders of being. Fictional narratives can provide a gateway to physical immortality wherein even bodily decay is arrested *post mortem*. He made allusions to Coleridge's principle of the "willing suspension of disbelief," to Poe's tale "Ligeia," to Vernon Lee's tale "Amour Dure," and emphasised that the will for immortality drove all artistic endeavours. For him, the power of an acutely concentrated imagination, one centred upon death and the macabre, was the means of releasing occult power. Although Muswell expounded these theories in a cultural climate already made heady with the revolutionary dictates of literary Modernism, only the esoterically inclined William Butler Yeats took any notice of them; but he very swiftly disavowed Muswell too, having turned up some extremely disturbing and subsequently destroyed results in the "automatic-writing" sessions with his wife Georgie. These results appeared to indicate that what came after death, at least for the initiates of the Lilith cult was, in reality, an eternally evil madness driven wholly by obsessive hatred and the overwhelming desire to murder the still-living.

It was also said—but again, by his detractors—that Muswell, during his association with De Gabiston and Winterburn in the late 1920s, had taken the two men to a certain book-lined tomb located deep within the confines of Highgate Cemetery, a tomb which contained the remains of an obscure authoress who died in 1896. In the hours after midnight, the three had performed there together some necromantic rite using De Gabiston as a medium; albeit a rite which had been imperfectly executed. It had ended in the medium's loss of consciousness for a period of several hours and, in later suggestions, of nervous breakdown. Certainly, he had never been the same after the experience. Periodically he displayed certain markedly effeminate mannerisms, assumed an English accent, and, perhaps in tribute to his mentor, always kept his hands gloved. During these episodes of dissociation it was even said that De Gabiston's facial features underwent a curious softening of the formerly masculine, hard, angular outlines.

The true onset of his mania for proving some family connection with the Degabaston line can be traced to the period immediately after this strange alteration; although it took him decades of legal struggles to establish a satisfactory claim to the earldom which he craved. His attempts to do so were not entirely encouraged by the last of the lineal Degabastons, Lady Caroline; she insisted, in 1940, that not until after a prior claim was fully examined could she think of admitting any overseas succession. But, by

1957, the question was settled entirely in his favour. Shortly after De Gabiston had taken occupancy of Thool Abbey, the ancient Lady Caroline died; and the persistent whispers in certain occult circles of a maimed, nameless, imprisoned-in-the-abbey rival to his own claim faded away.

Edward Reynolds paced up and down the corridor outside Winterburn's office. That supremely arrogant doctor, he thought, doubtless enjoyed keeping him waiting! He could not help noticing the presence of two lurking attendants in white coats at the far end of the corridor who were obviously pretending to be deep in conversation but who, Reynolds suspected, had actually been stationed there as a safeguard against any violent scene. God knows, he would have every right to thrash Winterburn for being a filthy degenerate. Hadn't Molly tried to keep him out of it? And the result? Her doctor husband had somehow managed to find out about them anyway. She suffered endless bouts of hysterics, probably due to the drugs he gave her, and then he had had her committed (doubtless with the connivance of influential friends) into his own psychiatric institution—this grim hell-hole, the Gallows Langley Lunatic Asylum.

The office door opened and the bald, ghastly apparition which was Doctor Winterburn appeared, his ill-fitting false teeth revealed in a cynical, welcoming smile. That a woman Molly's age should have been tied to this rotting carcass! It was obscene.

"Do come in Mr. Reynolds, I regret having kept you waiting," Winterburn intoned.

Reynolds brushed past him and stood staring at the doctor, eyes blazing with contempt. Winterburn glanced down the corridor, nodded to the attendants, and closed the office door behind him before wandering across the room and settling himself comfortably in his leather-upholstered seat behind his large desk.

"Well?" he said, finally.

"You obviously received my letter? Then you are aware that I have come to take Molly out of this disgusting madhouse and far away from you. I warn you, Winterburn, I have been doing some digging of my own and I know all about you and your foul associate, the degenerate Yank, Lord De Gabiston. Any decent woman would naturally have nothing to do with your vile plans. You will release her from your custody immediately. I could cause such a stink that——"

"My poor, dear wife Molly is, alas, no more," said Winterburn. The sardonic expression upon his face did not match the sentiment expressed by the words. They did, however, have a striking effect upon Reynolds, who genuinely thought his knees might give way beneath him.

"You're lying! I demand to see her!" he said, trying to keep his voice from catching.

"Oh, yes," replied Winterburn. "You will see her. All in good time."

The doctor pressed a button on the intercom device on his desk and the two attendants, bearing a straitjacket between them, entered the office, their eyes trained fixedly on Reynolds.

"Now, take poor Mr. Newhouse upstairs," Winterburn murmured as he idly opened a case-folder and then inserted the stem of his pipe into his mouth.

Reynolds had been confined to a padded cell and was isolated from all contact with others; the sole attendant whom he did see addressed him, too, as "Mr. Newhouse." He pleaded his case to this sullen individual, telling him of the reasons why Winterburn wanted him locked away in the asylum, but every explanation was met either with blank indifference or, on one occasion, resulted in Reynolds's disclosures being pitifully humoured as the ravings of a diseased sex-maniac. His insistence that he be allowed to speak to Winterburn was ignored, as were his repeated enquiries concerning the fate of Molly. There could be no doubt that his family and friends would by now be frantic with worry about him and were endeavouring to discover his whereabouts; but he had been discreet about the affair with Molly and had told no one else of his stupidly-rash plan to confront Winterburn personally at the asylum and to call his bluff. Some might have seen his actions as blackmail. In any case, it would take them weeks, at least, to track Reynolds down, even after he was listed officially as a missing person.

The series of injections began on the first day of his incarceration, and the initial symptoms of the syphilis with which he had been deliberately infected by these injections manifested themselves only two weeks later in the form of genital skin lesions. Another two weeks after that, and the rash covering his trunk and face had developed into multiple, ugly, blood-red pustules. He protested to the attendant that the injections he'd been given were not to counteract the disease but to bring it about, but his pleas made no difference. He was told he was being given "penicillin."

Reynolds had no idea exactly what Winterburn had planned for him.

Was he to be kept indefinitely in this place until he was actually driven mad or until the syphilis finally reached his brain and the ravages of that disease achieved the selfsame end?

The days dragged on interminably. Reynolds marked their passage only by the rising and setting of the sun, and by the arrival of his morning meal.

But then, one night, there was an electrical-supply failure. A tree had fallen, damaging an overhead power line, and the whole asylum was plunged into darkness. Reynolds heard a great commotion along the corridor outside his cell, some shouting about the failure of the emergency generator, and then, amazingly, his cell door was unlocked. Another inmate, carrying a lit candle, and who had somehow obtained a bunch of passkeys, was attempting to free everyone else on the same floor.

At Thool Abbey, two miles distant from the asylum, Doctor Winterburn and Lord De Gabiston were hunched over a chessboard in a lofty, book-lined chamber in the Jacobean annexe of that vast, mouldering, mediaeval structure. The gaslight flickered interminably from the lamps on the far wall; it was the only relatively modern concession to which the ancient structure had so far yielded.

"You have played," the American Lord De Gabiston said, in that curiously effeminate and strongly English-accented voice of his, "with a skilful deviousness worthy even of Boris Petrovski, my dear Winterburn, but I fear this particular game ends in perpetual check."

The doctor nodded, took another drink from the goblet of wine at his elbow, and gazed with an abhorrence that he tried desperately to conceal at the abnormally long, thin, and spider-like fingers of De Gabiston's white hands. The left one toyed with the black queen-piece whilst the right drummed upon the edge of the mahogany table which stood between them. And yet, he was not quite sure which was the more disconcerting: the white hands or the thick, white makeup which he applied to his ageing features. Was it solely a residue of the red wine he had drunk or did he seem to have applied scarlet lipstick to his mouth?

"How goes the other game?" De Gabiston said, cobalt-blue eyes glittering playfully and obscenely in the glow cast by the gaslight which lit up the chamber.

"I have done my part," Winterburn replied. "The unfaithful bitch is buried and only awaits the imminent embrace of the unfortunate cuckold."

"Sweet Molly. Alive, alive, oh . . ." De Gabiston tittered.

"And you?"

"The manuscript is ready. Would you care to see it?"

Winterburn nodded. De Gabiston stood up and wandered across to a bureau situated beside a long, latticed oriel window. He rummaged around one of its drawers and took out a handwritten manuscript bound by two strips of turquoise-coloured silk ribbon. As he returned to Winterburn and passed him the manuscript, De Gabiston arched his back and winced.

"This old body is becoming as burdensome as the others. It wears me out. Even at this moment I can sense mental resistance from its former occupant. Still, this is preferable to being in the other carcass back there in the cemetery at Highgate, the one buried in that stinking coffin, alone and dreaming in the wormy blackness with only mouldering books for company. And now, you had best read what I've written down here. It will eventually form one of the tales in a posthumous collection."

Winterburn unravelled the silk ribbons and his gaze roved over the first page of the text. Their erstwhile mentor in the art of necrography, the plump old fool Alfred Muswell, would have given anything, Winterburn thought, to possess this literary treasure. He even wrote daily to the abbey in pathetic attempts to placate De Gabiston; but Muswell had long outlived his former usefulness and was now reduced to writing asinine essays promoting something he termed "weird fiction" in obscure, underground American journals.

This new tale had been penned in the familiar script which De Gabiston had adopted since the visit to the tomb, and Winterburn experienced a delicious sensation of pleasure mixed with dread as the narrative progressed. He marvelled at the masterful way in which its author was able to manipulate real life so as to imitate art.

From some distant part of his consciousness, he was aware that the telephone in the abbey had been ringing and that De Gabiston had gone to answer its summons. Only when the Earl bent over him, laid one of those ungloved hands on his shoulder, and squeezed his flesh with those long, sinuous fingers did he turn from the manuscript and register the words being spoken into his ear:

"Charles, attend to the telephone. It's Benson at the asylum, calling for you. It appears, not wholly unexpectedly, that Mr. Newhouse—I mean, Mr. Reynolds—has escaped and is at large."

"Not wholly unexpectedly," indeed. Winterburn had noted that particular episode in the narrative two paragraphs ago, before reaching the account of the interruption at the very same moment when it had also
occurred in actuality.

The flight across the countryside beyond the asylum had been like some episode of feverish delirium—a nightmare brought on by disease. At first
Reynolds had felt a sense of wild exhilaration at his apparent good fortune.
He and the inmate with the passkeys, along with several other patients, had
managed to reach the entrance gates, where there was then a fierce struggle
with those attendants who had been posted at the exit as a safeguard against
attempts at escape. In the ensuing melee, Reynolds managed to get through
the gates and reach the outside world. There had been no pursuit, for the
attendants had had their hands full with attending to the crowd of raving patients and preventing a mass exodus.

He was hoping to make his way to the Gallows Langley Retired
Booksellers Institution, which he had seen on an Ordnance Survey map of
the region prior to his leaving London. He hoped one of the locals might
allow him to make a telephone call and thereby establish his true identity as
Edward Reynolds; proving that the false identity which had been foisted upon him of "Newhouse, the sexually-diseased maniac" had been part of a conspiracy. Anyone with even the most rudimentary grasp of Italian could see
the irony Winterburn had intended in choosing that particular pseudonym
for Reynolds. But would he have any success if he reached the booksellers
community? Any person coming into contact with him would be instantly
repelled—his pustule-ravaged skin; the record of suffering and persecution
etched into the expression on his face; the bloody, tattered, tell-tale straitjacket! What hope was there, really?

Reynolds felt as if the syphilitic disease with which he had been deliberately infected had already unhinged his reason. He tramped across miles of
moonlit tracts of open fields silvered by ground-mist and skirted a vast,
densely packed wood from whose central interior there seemed to emanate
a far-off chorus, one akin to the howling made by a pack of dogs. And yet,
he was sure that no species of dog known to man could make such an unearthly, terrible sound.

Finally he stumbled across a field upon the side of a desolate hill—a
foul-smelling crop field which was being used to raise a variety of pestilent

herbs—and saw ahead, in the distance, lantern-lights shining through the latticed windows of a lonely, ill-proportioned old farmhouse.

Perhaps, he hoped, its occupants might own a telephone.

"We recaptured Newhouse at Thool Farm," the attendant said. "He put up quite a struggle, but he's now safely back in his cell."

Dr. Winterburn allowed himself a wan smile.

"You've done well, Benson," he said. "You will be rewarded for your efficiency. Tell the nurses and the other attendants I want only a minimal staff this evening. Prepare a rota. You all deserve a night off. But first, have Newhouse sedated."

The folk at Thool Farm would keep silent and pose no difficulties, he thought; their property was leased to them by De Gabiston and formed part of the abbey estate. Moreover, they would not wish any outside attention drawn towards the noxious crops they raised on the land.

Reynolds was groggy and confused. They had drugged him with some damnable concoction and he sat, dazed, in the corner of his padded cell, clad in a fresh straitjacket. The moonlight shining through the narrow strip of barred window high to his left told him it was the dead of night and when he heard voices in the corridor outside, the rattle of a bunch of keys, and then the turning of the lock, he knew the end must be near. He had almost managed to escape the clutches of the conspiracy against him; but now all hope was surely lost.

The white-coated Dr. Winterburn entered, his yellow-greenish false teeth flashing in a wide smile, and he was accompanied by another man, of roughly the same middle age, but with unusually long hair and a face that was caked with foundation. He wore a pair of leather gloves; his fingers were abnormally long and attenuated.

"Allow me to introduce someone about whom you have heard a great deal and yet, I understand, have not had the pleasure of meeting in person: the Earl of Thool, Lord De Gabiston. My Lord, may I present Mr. Edward Reynolds," Winterburn said.

"How do you do?" the ghastly apparition piped, inclining his head slightly, as a sardonic smile warped the garish, crimson line of his mouth.

Reynolds grimaced; he felt that his mind was giving way.

"Haven't you done enough to me? What more do you want?" he said.

"Why, we have only come to fulfil your greatest desire," replied Winterburn. "We have come to finally reunite you with Molly. Wouldn't you like that?"

The two carried the sedated Reynolds along the interminable, deserted corridors of that part of the old Victorian asylum, past cells from which filtered shrieking cries, humourless laughing, hopeless sobbing, and deranged, self-accusing, whispered monologues. They took him outside to the walled-in hillside cemetery behind the asylum—where the weeds flourished between sad wooden crosses upon which were scrawled the case numbers, not the names, of the dead, forgotten patients. The full moon blazed silver in the cloudless night sky; casting an effulgent radiance over the entire, hideously macabre scene. They dragged him onwards to the back of the hillside cemetery, to a hidden-away plot obscured by masses of bramble bushes, and Reynolds found that he was looking down into an open, freshly uncovered grave. A coffin-lid lay on a mound of dirt alongside the excavation.

The facial features of the putrescent thing were impossible to recognise, such was the advanced state of its slimy dissolution; but with an infinite, unutterable horror Reynolds knew at once, due to the decaying patches of red hair which clung to its skull, whose remains that abnormally deep-walled coffin harboured. A sickening, overpowering stench, like that of an open sewer, bubbled up from the grave.

They pushed the straitjacketed Reynolds into the pit, manoeuvred the coffin lid on top of him, nailed it shut, and began piling the mound of up-turned soil back into the grave.

"Beauty," cried De Gabiston as they toiled, "exists in many uncommon forms: the freakishly deformed, the abhorrent, the maimed, the diseased, the mentally repellent, all possess a certain purity and strange allure of their own. But there is a truly unique dark splendour in the ravages hidden by the grave and a monstrous wonder in the romance of wormy disintegration. I, too, know the fullest depths of horror's dreaming but, alas, I possessed no companion with whom to share for eternity my narrow universe of charnel glamour."

Winterburn said nothing in reply; and, after all, it was not really De Gabiston who had formulated those phrases; phrases so redolent of the fog-wreathed, sickly-yellow literary decadence spawned during the 1890s.

And when the grave was filled, they drew a chalk circle containing certain occult symbols around it, burnt certain foul-smelling herbs, and began the necromantic rite to summon poor, dead Molly back to life.

In a recently purchased basement London flat, situated beyond a series of cryptic passageways leading off Pond Square in Highgate Village, high above the metropolis, Alfred Muswell, former Oxford don, read over again the letter he had received from Molly Winterburn. It had been forwarded from his old address and finally, after some delay, had reached him at his new one:

> . . . and it is in sheer desperation that I turn to you for aid. You realise the depths of moral degeneracy to which both my husband and his associate Lord De Gabiston have descended; and their attempts to involve me in the sickening practises of "The Cult of Lilith" have proved unrelenting. There is a third party, whom I love very much, but I do not wish to place him in danger by calling upon his assistance. He possesses a reckless streak and I fear he may confront my husband directly, at great cost to his own personal safety. If I could prevail upon you to write to the authorities and expose my husband's and his Lordship's activities, which I have set out in ample detail elsewhere in this letter, then you would be doing me, and the world, a very great service. A wife cannot testify against her husband in a court of law, as you know, and I can think of no one else better placed than you to substantiate the grave charges which he must answer. If my husband should discover my attempts to expose both him and his confederate, then the consequences to me are likely to be horrible in the extreme.

Muswell cared little for the fate of this gossipy Mrs. Winterburn: his sole concern lay in wresting back power and influence over the literary legacy and the estate of the one authoress whose writings alone validated all his outré metaphysical theories about the pre-eminence of supernatural art over so-called "realism." He knew full well that Dr. Winterburn and Lord De Gabiston had carefully managed affairs so that the former would attain the position of a lunatic asylum medical superintendent. They did this solely for the purposes of acting with impunity upon an almost unlimited supply of isolated, disturbed, and diseased individuals. They were attempting to generate a new, "transgressive" literary movement to supersede the old order. Muswell had written several times to Lord De Gabiston, in an attempt to heal the breach which had sprung up between them, but the latter had maintained his silence. The situation was an infuriating one; for had not Muswell himself earlier pressed De Gabiston's claims to inheritance of the vacant Earldom of Thool, despite the scepticism evinced by Lady Caroline Degabaston? Without any adequate grounds for such cavalier treatment, he was now subject to a silent contempt previously reserved for the likes of, say, that late Catholic mediaevalist meddler, the Revd. Alphonsus Winters (the so-called "Connoisseur of Diabolism") in his repeated pleas for access to the private family papers held at Thool Abbey.

Perhaps, thought Muswell, if he were to separate his two former students from one another's influence, he might regain some of his old ascendancy. With this prospective outcome in mind, he took up his pen and wrote an anonymous letter to the Inspectorate of Psychiatric Institutions, detailing certain intolerable abuses he claimed to have witnessed at Gallows Langley, in the guise of being a former attendant who had worked closely under Dr. Winterburn's supervision.

Several feet beneath the soil, Reynolds was trapped face down in a loathsomely stinking, black hell. He could not move his limbs, for the lid of the coffin pressed from above upon his back and shoulders; its walls hemmed him in on both sides; and beneath him lay the hideously putrescent remains of Molly Winterburn. The lack of air was stifling; and what little there was of it left to breathe reeked with a disgusting foulness which made him retch continuously. The absolute darkness of the narrow-house offered only one boon: he could not see her rotting features—and her face was just a few scant inches away from his own. However, he had seen her once in the moonlight, before Winterburn and De Gabiston had forced him down into the grave and sealed the coffin, and the nightmarish image of that ravaged, puffy, unrecognisable horror—all that physically remained of the woman he loved—had seared itself into his memory. He felt the brush of her red hair upon his cheeks as he struggled, that hair which was once abundant, lustrous, and soft, but which was now patchy, desiccated, and wiry.

He wondered whether he would go insane first or else perish when the dwindling air supply was exhausted, but the question appeared to answer itself; for, in his madness, he seemed to feel the corpse beneath him stir into life, its chest rising and falling as its fetid breath assailed his nostrils. He felt the thing squirming in the polluted darkness, and then slowly wriggle its puffy, rank arms along his torso as its bony, abnormally long fingers sought to gain purchase around his throat.

When the authorities raided the asylum, on the very same day the Inspectorate had received Alfred Muswell's letter, they found the place in a state of complete pandemonium and called for the assistance of the county police constabulary. Dr. Winterburn had barricaded himself in his office, the inmates were in a state of uncontrollable frenzy (with several having escaped from their cells), while most of the staff had been murdered. Some form of mass hallucination appeared to have taken place; for both patients and staff alike gave credence to the fantastic notion that a ghost—or perhaps a lich—had been responsible for a wave of strangulations. Curiously enough, it was Dr. Winterburn alone who seemed immune from this mass hallucination, and who insisted that a particularly violent inmate, one possessed of enormous strength and cunning, had carried out the slayings and then managed to flee the scene; but there was absolutely no credible evidence for his otherwise reasonable assertion.

One member of the staff, named Benson, pointed to the disgusting charnel odour which clung to the victims in order to corroborate his supernatural explanation; though he himself did not actually see the assailant. However, the man had obviously spent too much time amongst the patients and, in any case, such were the manifold eccentricities he displayed, including an uncontrollable hysteria, that he was himself transferred, as a new patient, to the asylum at Colney Hatch. One aspect of his bizarre account was, nevertheless, difficult to explain away. He had advised the officers of the Asylums Inspectorate and their accompanying police constables to examine a certain plot located at the back of the walled-in hillside cemetery.

What they found there was abominable in the extreme.

The grave in question showed signs of having been disturbed. Clods of earth lay on either side of the plot, as if something, perhaps a large animal, had worked its way out from deep within. When they exhumed what was left down there in its curiously deep-walled coffin, they found the broken-necked and mutilated remains of a missing person, one Edward Reynolds, whom they were subsequently able to identify only by dental records. Curiously, leading away from the graveside there was a lingering trail of still-stinking slime which led towards the asylum itself.

Examination of the photographic medical records showed that Dr. Winterburn had falsely listed this same missing person, Reynolds, as "Newhouse," and had forcibly imprisoned him against his will. The coroner's confidential report detailed the fact Reynolds had only acquired syphilis after his internment and there could be no doubt that Winterburn had deliberately infected him with the disease at the asylum. It did not take long to discover Reynolds's illicit connection with Molly—Mrs. Winterburn—and a motive was established. The actual cause of death was given as asphyxiation by strangling; though such was the tremendous force employed by the assailant that the spinal cord was snapped.

As for the matter of the subsequent mutilation of Reynolds's corpse, this was generally regarded as having been the consequence of troublesome skulks of abnormally large foxes which were known to haunt the local area, and, in particular, the vast swathe of woodlands close to Thool Abbey. One such skulk must have made a subterranean den close to the graveyard and gained access to the coffin by burrowing into it and then out again. The trail of slime, however, was casually disregarded as some freakishly brute fact which would never be satisfactorily explained.

All public accounts of what had transpired at the Gallows Langley Asylum were ruthlessly suppressed by the Home Office, who obtained word of the scandal at the same time as the Secretary of State for Health.

The letter from Reynolds to Dr. Winterburn sealed his fate. His sanity was not in doubt, but, during his incarceration, before sentencing, he displayed an unusual willingness to atone for his actions by way of state execution rather than, as he mysteriously put it, "the drawn-out consequences of some other, hellish retribution." One plea and one alone he made continuously to the governor and to the chaplain who visited him: it was that he not be buried in the prison graveyard in the afternoon immediately following his judicial hanging, but that his body, instead, be cremated.

The trial at a closed session at the Old Bailey was swift, unreported, and a jury sworn to absolute secrecy returned their decision following only a few minutes of deliberation. It was said that the judge even donned his black cap before the foreman had stood up to advise him of the jury's unanimous verdict.

Half an hour after the pandemonium at Gallows Hill Lunatic Asylum, Zebulon De Gabiston, Earl of Thool, had tossed the last four pages of a manuscript into the fire; and what had been written down therein would not now come to pass.

Winterburn had not realised that De Gabiston had managed, just days before, through certain occult measures of his own, to free his consciousness from the tomb in Highgate wherein it had been imprisoned in the undecayed carcass of that authoress-witch to whom both of them had dedicated their lives and souls. De Gabiston could not maintain control over the possession of his physical form for very long, and it was imperative that he act swiftly to further disorientate the thing which continually sought to permanently reoccupy it. Certain formulae had been subtly altered by him during the necromantic rite to bring Molly Winterburn back to life, and the Highgate witch's consciousness had been driven into the corpse of the adulteress. That wildly hyperbolic speech which he had uttered over Mrs. Winterburn's grave was evidence that his brain still bore the imprint of an alien, malefic intelligence.

The power-cut at the asylum had been a simple matter; a purposely felled tree striking an overhead power line was easily arranged. But it had not been easy to maintain his personal masquerade, to perfect the refined English accent, and to mimic female mannerisms; only the alteration in his hands—those strange, unearthly white, arachnodactylic appendages—proved irreversible; an enduring supernatural sign of current, or past, incarnation. She needed a vessel through which to physically generate those fictional narratives which directed reality itself to her will, but she could occupy only a single given form at any one time. And now De Gabiston had driven her down into eternal perdition; to a nameless grave which would never be disturbed, a grave she would share with a syphilitic, romantic idiot. Winterburn had thought he would have his own personal revenge upon an unfaithful wife and a cuckold, but what was this but a stupid trifle when compared to the vengeance which was owed to De Gabiston? Vengeance against the Highgate witch and against Winterburn, who had both tricked him and had trapped him down in that stinking coffin, alone—*infinitely alone*—in the wormy blackness with nothing but endless nightmares to dream.

Winterburn could not risk exposing him; he knew that De Gabiston was the stronger magician and could force the doctor's consciousness into some other loathsome receptacle.

De Gabiston crossed the floor of that lofty, book-lined chamber in the Jacobean annexe of the abbey, glancing briefly at the inconclusive chess game which he had played with Winterburn. Through one of the latticed windows he could see that it had begun raining heavily, and he gazed out across the length of the vast lawn which separated the abbey from the beginning of the estate's woodlands.

Did his eyes deceive him, or did some dark shape appear to disengage itself from the shadows of the distant tree trunks? It was hard to tell; the downpour was increasing. The hiss of the deluge grew louder, more intense. No, surely he was not mistaken. A figure, apparently dressed in rags, was gradually making its way across the wet grass towards the abbey, a misshapen figure that was twisted over to one side, as if struggling to walk upright. He could not make out its features but, as it advanced, he felt a familiar sense of terrifying dislocation assail his consciousness. He knew then what she would do to him.

Cold sweat broke out on his brow as he tried to recall, in vain, the words of occult power which might slow its advance and enable him to flee. It was too late for that now. She would track him inexorably across both space and time. There was one means of escape left open to him.

It was only when the thing was inside the book-lined chamber and bearing down on him—its putrid stench overpowering even that other, choking stench of methane—and its long bony fingers reached for his throat, that he shrieked aloud and struck a match at one of the wall-lamps and its hissing, fully opened gas-valve.

Although the damage to the Jacobean annexe of Thool Abbey was extensive, the local fire brigade succeeded in its valiant efforts to save the rest of the ancient, mediaeval structure. Two curiously entwined bodies were recovered amongst the charred remains: one male, one female, and both reduced to blackened, smouldering bones. They were identified (as with Reynolds) by dental records as being Molly Winterburn and Lord De Gabiston. The theory that they were lovers seemed to account for much; although Doctor Charles Winterburn was no longer alive and in a position to confirm or deny this supposition. That the fire was started deliberately, in an act of arson, only added to the unanswerable questions which marked the sequence of events.

Ownership of the abbey became a matter of dispute and it remained untenanted, though rumours continued to persist of a maimed, nameless Degabaston—one of the original line—occupying some secret room deep within the farthest confines of its interior. The ever-persistent local legend that Thool Abbey contains labyrinthine immensities which no one can fathom, and that it actually shifts its internal geography as the years pass, doubtless contributed to its local air of fantastic mystery; an air even more enduring than that which had attached itself to the asylum.

Following the fire, the former Oxford don, Alfred Muswell, so it is said, began to dream strange dreams, but the soul of the thing which had

reached out from Highgate Cemetery must have been severely weakened
after being driven back by fire into its undecayed corpse. Perhaps Muswell,
alone, was now close enough geographically, and obsessed enough psycho-
logically, to detect the feeble telepathic reverberations which still echoed
from the depths of her tomb.

One thing alone is certain: Muswell very swiftly obtained control of the
remaining papers of that society which was styled "The Cult of Lilith." He
then permanently adopted the wearing of a pair of black leather gloves—a
caption beneath a photograph reproduced in the fourth issue of the publication the *Necrophile,* for 1959, testifies to this fact.

An Elemental Infestation

1

avelock had first glimpsed the edge of Penceddo Wood from his motorcar whilst approaching the construction site of the proposed relief road. Although he had lived in the locality for six months, he had not particularly taken any notice of the woods until then. In the distance, on the plateau atop the western hillside of Thool Valley, there stretched a mile-wide swathe of yew trees with another two miles of dense woodland lurking farther back behind them. The late afternoon winter sun was setting behind the shadowy expanse of the evergreen trees in a crimson-and-saffron riot of colour, lending the panoramic scene an otherworldly aspect. Such was the effect of the intense vision which confronted him, he momentarily forgot his sense of annoyance at having been despatched at short notice (and without being properly briefed on the latest developments) by his immediate superior at the Thool District Council Planning Department.

His thoughts turned from the sight of the wooded hill, lit up, as if ablaze, to the dull, functional interior of the musty office of Charles Beechfield OBE in the department's section for local road network development:

"Havelock," Beechfield had said, "I have to bugger off somewhere restful for at least a month, and must do so immediately. Sudden leave of absence. Under strict orders. Last day in the office. Doctor says the old ticker's playing up, if you must know. A lot of fuss about nothing, if you ask me, but Mrs. Beechfield's somehow got wind of it. She who must be obeyed and all that. I have to clear off at once. No choice but to dump this project in your lap. Here's the file; look through it. I've probably let the matter slide a little, but no doubt you can soon pick up the reins. Get yourself over there to the construction site tomorrow, find out what the hold-up is all about, and sort it out. There's a good chap."

Havelock had nodded at various points during Beechfield's monologue, wished his superior a swift and full recovery, and then taken the hefty, buff-coloured file to his desk, sat down, and began to leaf through the various documents contained therein.

Beechfield had let it slide all right, Havelock thought: the situation even smacked of wilful ineptitude. The whole process of constructing a local relief road to ease traffic congestion had ground to a halt, despite construction work starting two months ago. As far as Havelock could make out, only half a mile of the planned road had actually been laid before all manner of interminable delays had crippled the project. The nature of these delays was baffling; vague reports of inexplicable mechanical failures in heavy equipment and instances of both physical and mental breakdowns in the personnel assigned to the construction crews. It seemed that a number of local employees had flatly refused to continue to labour on the road, despite generous incentives, even preferring dismissal, and it was only by hiring workmen from London that any very limited progress had been made at all. As matters now stood, no construction work had been undertaken during the last two weeks. Only a tiny fraction of Penceddo Wood had been cleared and the road terminated little more than twenty yards into its endless masses of densely-packed yew trees.

Later, on the evening of the same day he had spoken with Beechfield, while unwinding at the Gryphon Tavern over a small whisky-and-soda, Havelock happened to mention his predicament to the pub's loquacious landlord during the course of their conversation.

"What, you're still going to try and build that road up through old Penceddo Wood?"

"Quite right," said Havelock. "We consulted the local populace by postal survey a year ago. There were no objections."

"And no replies at all from any sensible folk, I'm sure. Fools only learn by doing wrong, not from warnings beforehand. You ought to ask Roderick Carden, our local historian, about the woods. Shame he's not in tonight."

"What does that crank know? Are they possessed of a sinister local reputation, some sort of the usual superstitious rubbish he peddles in his books?"

"Ask him yourself," said the landlord, moving away to serve another customer and leaving the taciturn young barmaid to serve Havelock his drinks thereafter.

And so it was, at dusk the next afternoon, that Havelock found himself driving up to the construction site which was to be named, in faux-rustic-idyll fashion, "Penceddo Lane" when the road was finally completed, despite the fact that the project would cause the destruction of two straight miles of ancient woodland. The sight of those massed ranks of yew trees framed by a blazing sunset certainly gave Havelock pause for thought; but one doubts it significantly altered his feelings as to the desirability of further easing local traffic congestion. He was, after all, only an unimaginative town clerk, a minor bureaucrat with bills and rent to pay, and also one of those up-to-date individuals who are content to shrug and accede to the universal dictum that nothing and no one can be allowed to stand in the way of "progress." Even the (in his view) unsightly old village of Gallows Langley, with its shadowy cluster of Jacobean two-storey houses with their mouldering front-gabled roofs and bay windows, would eventually have to be pulled down and replaced in favour of more utilitarian red-brick developments.

He parked his vehicle alongside several others in a small clearing on the hillside which served as a makeshift car park, got out, and noted, just up ahead in the shadows, a concrete mixer, excavator, articulated hauler, as well as various other forms of heavy machinery, and all resting idle at the construction site. There was a group of half-a-dozen workmen wearing safety helmets sitting around an oil-drum fire, warming their hands in front of the flames, smoking cigarettes, and drinking steaming mugs of tea. As Havelock approached they looked up at him; one of them nudged another in the ribs, and then whispered something obscene.

"I'm from the planning department. Where can I find the foreman?" Havelock said, feeling somewhat uneasy at the suspicious expressions on the unshaven, gaunt faces which seemed not so much menacing as menaced.

"Gaffer's over there; in that portacabin," one of them replied, pointing behind Havelock, before returning his hand-rolled cigarette to his chapped lips.

Havelock turned around and moved in the direction of the site office, observing, to his right, the short stretch of road into the woods which had been completed thus far—a narrow twenty-yard long strip of tarmac which had eaten through the surrounding tunnel-like confines of the yew trees and which terminated in a huge mound of rubble and timber only half-visible in the rapidly gathering darkness.

He ascended the tiny flight of steps outside the entrance to the portacabin to find the door was unlocked and left ever-so-slightly ajar. Inside, slumped face down over a desk, was an insensible man, his head resting between a half-consumed bottle of Greenall's gin and a lit paraffin lantern giving off a warm, amber glow but also exuding a thick, cloying aroma which permeated the interior cabin. There was a mass of papers scattered around the floor; mostly official correspondence and uncompleted invoices, and it seemed most of them had been trodden upon irreverently—and more than just once—by muddy boots.

Havelock picked his way through the debris and stood alongside the slumped-over foreman, listening with growing impatience to the stifled grunts and incoherent mumblings of this useless sleeptalker. It seemed that, while lost in disgusting inebriation, the man was suffering a drink-induced nightmare, one which was, no doubt, aggravated by guilt at his complete dereliction of duty. Having received no reaction at all to his spoken entreaties that the foreman pull himself together, Havelock roughly shook him by the shoulder until, finally, the pitiful human wreck opened his eyes and blearily awoke to some measure of consciousness.

He gazed at his surroundings—and at Havelock—with total incomprehension, and then his hand snaked across the desk to grasp the bottle of gin. He shakily poured a generous measure of the spirit into a dirty glass tumbler and tossed the contents down his throat.

"Don't you think you've already had more than enough?" Havelock said.

The foreman swore at him, slurring his words.

"Mr. Beechfield sent me. I'm an official from the planning department. I want to know what work has been going on here of late," Havelock said. "Very little, or so it seems."

"It can't be done," the foreman said. "It doesn't matter how many machines or men you try. They all break down sooner rather than later. I tell you, it can't be done. The sounds are what's worst. It wouldn't be so bad if the woods didn't whisper to me so."

The man appeared to be on the verge of a complete nervous collapse. He was speaking gibberish.

Havelock gave up, and went back outside. The brightest of the stars for that time of year were becoming visible in the vastness of the night-sky and he could just make out the familiar shape of Orion having risen far over in the distance to the south-east.

When he asked the workmen sitting around the oil-drum fire what had happened to their foreman, they shrugged their shoulders, said Havelock wouldn't believe them even if they told him, that he'd think them mad, and insisted that this was their final day on the job. They, too, had had enough of the place. Now that it was dark, they'd decided they were all clearing out together and never returning. He could also, they told him just for good measure, "stuff their jobs where the sun don't shine."

The following morning, while in his office, Havelock telephoned Carden the local historian and asked him whether he could shed any light on the history of Penceddo Wood. He felt absurd having to consult a well-known local crank, but if there were some record of folklore connected with the place which might account for an outbreak of collective hysteria, perhaps it might give him an insight into the best way to approach the apparently insurmountable difficulties associated with the construction of the projected "Penceddo Lane."

"Look," Carden had said to him over the telephone, "it's probably best if you come here to the cottage and see for yourself some of the research material about the woods which I've archived. Describing those photographs—for example—is no substitute for seeing them with your own two eyes."

Having only ever encountered and spoken to Carden twice previously at the Gryphon Tavern, Havelock had formed the distinct impression the man fancied himself as some sort of successor to the famous so-called ghost hunter Harry Price. Havelock had a sudden vision of visiting Carden and being confronted with a ridiculous series of photographic plates of dead-eyed Victorian mediums lurking between yew trees and exuding clouds of ectoplasm from their open mouths.

"It's the 'Winton Man' photographs which I think will most interest you," said Carden, "but you need to see them for yourself. Now's as good a time as any. Come on over. I'll make us a nice pot of tea."

2

Carden lived in a former lock-keeper's cottage about half-a-mile's walk from Gallows Langley, right alongside the Grand Union Canal. The previous night's frost had lingered long in the cold sunshine of the morning and, as Havelock trudged his way along the towpath, past the dozen or so gaily coloured narrowboats moored along the waterway and the sparkling-white fields occupied by glum-looking sheep, he rather felt as if he were embarking on a fool's errand. The weird events of the previous day up at Penceddo Wood seemed fantastical and unreal; like some horrible dream he would have done better to dismiss, rather than dwell upon, after awakening.

Carden greeted him in the cottage doorway. Overweight, and in his late fifties, he was attired in a long, thick dressing-gown worn over an untucked, open-neck shirt and Oxford bags. There was a tasselled Chinaman's cap perched on his head, and red-velvet carpet slippers covered his feet. He looked as if he belonged in a circus act or else strutting onstage in the role of a professional conjurer. This bohemian garb was obviously what he chose to wear in private; whenever Havelock had seen the man previously—in public—he had been dressed conservatively in tweeds, rather as Havelock himself dressed.

"Perfect timing. Kettle's already on the boil; do come inside," said Carden.

Havelock followed him along the short hallway and was immediately struck by the series of filing cabinets and storage boxes resting up against the walls. On top of them was piled a bewildering array of musty old books on all manner of recondite subjects. There was a curiously tangy and musky smell lingering in the air, not of tobacco, but definitely of "something else" having recently been smoked. When Carden ushered his guest into the living room, he had to make space for Havelock to sit on the armchair by removing a pile of books which already occupied its seat—volumes concerning the likes of witchcraft and black magic, each one of them written by a person named Alphonsus Winters.

Carden returned with the tea tray and set it down on the floor. He sat cross-legged on the carpet and began to pour Darjeeling from a silver teapot through a strainer into two bone-china cups. Havelock helped himself to milk and sugar.

"Do you read the books of the Reverend Winters?" Carden enquired. "Interesting old bird, though too much of a Romanist for my liking. Disappeared around here ten years ago. The area is rife with witches; notably the Degabastons, forbearers to Zebulon—but you've not heard about that before, I'm sure—they were rumoured to have—"

"I'm more interested in this 'Winton Man' you mentioned," said Havelock, cutting in. "What has he—it—this thing—to do with Penceddo Wood?"

"Of course. Let me elucidate. 'Winton Man' was a corpse from the Romano-British age which was recovered—incredibly well-preserved—in 1906 from a bog on the outer fringes of Penceddo Wood some distance farther south along Thool Valley, close to Winton Bridge," Carden said.

Havelock had never heard of any peat bogs in the region and he generally associated them with areas in the country which were farther north; up in the midlands at the very least. No peat bog had been mentioned, to his knowledge, when the construction survey for "Penceddo Lane" had been completed.

"Obviously the bog has shrunk during the passage of centuries," Carden continued, as if having detected Havelock's flash of scepticism, "and its extent is now probably only one-twentieth of what it once was in the first century."

"Where are these human remains currently? In some museum, I suppose?"

"Well, they were certainly displayed, being housed locally in Thool Museum. They caused quite a sensation. And then, after scarcely a week, they were—so it was claimed—stolen."

"Stolen? Stolen by whom?"

"No one was ever charged with the offence. I'll certainly tell you what I think happened, but first let me show you those photographs I mentioned over the telephone."

Carden shuffled off to another room and, after a moment or two, returned, carrying a grey folder, which he then passed to Havelock, who examined its contents.

Although there were no photographs of mediums "posing" between trees and exuding fake ectoplasm from their mouths, the ones he saw were, it is true, genuinely horrible and extraordinary. Each one depicted, in shots taken from different angles, the naturally mummified remains of a male individual who had lived around two thousand years ago. Its flesh had been tanned into brown leather, and the compression from the peat-bog in which the body had rested had distorted its shape so much that the thing seemed to be half-crushed, with a body, head, and facial features which appeared to have slipped askew from the twisted skeletal structure and skull beneath the skin. The mouth was open in a fixed, yawning expression of agony. As disturbing as the sight was, however, the overall sense of horror was accentuated by the presence of masses of fungal growths sprouting from the carcass as if they had drawn sustenance from it. Although the photographs were in black-and-white, Havelock recalled having had pointed out to him on nature trails certain toxic toadstools bearing blood-red, white-dotted caps—a species of fungi which seemed to flourish only in and around the region of Thool Valley itself. The toadstools in the photographs and those he had seen with his own eyes appeared to be of the same type.

Havelock replaced the photographs in the folder.

"Human sacrifice," Carden said, "and then metempsychosis."

This last remark did not register with Havelock aside from a vague impression that it was beside the point.

"So you're saying this 'Winton Man'—stolen or not back in 1906—has returned to haunt Penceddo Wood, or something along those lines?" Havelock said.

Again, he betrayed a note of scepticism in his tone; he knew well this particular local historian's tendency to conflate local folklore with fact.

Carden shrugged his shoulders.

"I tell you the region is a nexus for all forms of psychical disturbances. The ghost story writer and inland waterways enthusiast Rupert Alderman penned a recent article in the *Illustrated London News* about a pernicious Elemental infestation lurking less than a mile from here. He said that to stare for any length of time at this Elemental was to invite certain insanity and spiritual suicide. The detail seems highly significant. One of our local artists, Neil Harkness, tells me he has even drawn the thing, having seen it in a mirror, in a dream. He flatly refuses to show the picture to anyone."

"Really?" Havelock replied, stifling a compulsion to chuckle.

"Tell me, what do you know about the ancient druids?"

"Not much. Only that they dress in white robes and continue to gather around Stonehenge at the summer solstice. Kindly philosophers and fortune-tellers weren't they?"

"Stonehenge has nothing to do with them, whatever contemporary so-called druids might say; I meant the real, ancient Celtic druids. You shake your head again, I see. Well, let me advise you to put aside any false modern notions about the subject. 'Winton Man' is obviously an example of archaeological evidence supporting the claims by the likes of Pliny the Elder and Tacitus of the druids' bloodthirsty rituals of human sacrifice. You might recall that Hallowe'en has its origin in the ancient Celtic festival of Samhain. As Winters put it: 'The druids were not one homogeneous Britannic grouping of high-priests and seers; each locality had its own stripe of druidry; and although some were much more malefic than others, it cannot be doubted, despite the puerile objections of their latter-day imitators, that they all practised both human sacrifice and cannibalism.' Winters knew what he was talking about."

"This is doubtless very interesting but—"

Carden ignored Havelock's interjection, and went on speaking, warming to his subject.

"The particular stripe of druidry which took hold in Thool Valley in pre-Christian times was especially strange. My researches hint at the fact that, as a consequence of Imperial Rome's campaign in the first century to extinguish all manifestations of druidry within its empire, the Thool druids underwent a voluntary process of mass self-sacrifice by mushroom poisoning; a process which was designed to create a final physical union with the woodlands they regarded as sacred."

"And what about 'Winton Man'?"

"If I am correct in my suppositions, then it is likely he was a Thool druid himself, but one who betrayed the cult to the Roman authorities and tried to flee, but was recaptured and forced to consume poisonous toadstools—in one form or another—and was finally thrown into the peat bog. He was also, as a punishment, and to appease the fury of the ancient gods, left permanently suspended between two worlds."

"You still haven't told me what you think finally happened to the body, after it was stolen."

"I'll tell you this much; there were no signs of any break-in at the Thool Museum on that night in January 1906. The curator is on record as saying a broken window on the ground floor seemed to have been smashed from inside, and fragments of glass were discovered in only one place—outside on the half-crushed flower bed beneath that same window. The bizarrely askew footprints totally baffled the local police constabulary. I think the call of the woods was heard and the summons was obeyed."

3

Havelock had made his excuses and left almost immediately after Carden had delivered his final, nonsensical verdict. Somehow, Havelock imagined, the site foreman must have got wind of this ludicrous piece of local folklore and in a rapid descent into alcoholism—with accompanying hallucinations brought about by *delirium tremens*—must have passed on the tale to any workmen who had been assigned to the construction site. Although Carden had not said it explicitly, the implication of his fanciful yarn was that "Winton Man" had returned, in corporeal form in 1906 to lurk around inside Penceddo Wood, and was still doing so decades later. It was easy enough to see, when one was actually standing on the edge of those massed, vast ranks of yew trees, how such idle talk about cursed, whispering woods and evil spirits could spook the unsophisticated and the superstitious-by-nature.

Havelock made arrangements to have the old foreman relieved of his duties on compassionate grounds, but his subsequent medical examination resulted in his being taken into the Gallows Langley Lunatic Asylum for treatment, which institution was under the supervision of the well-respected Doctor Winterburn. However, the foreman had, it appeared, gone berserk when advised he was to be confined there, which reaction only served to confirm the completely unbalanced nature of his drink-ravaged mental faculties and his paranoid propensity to credit entirely baseless local gossip.

A few days later Beechfield, despite being on a leave of absence for his apparent coronary problems, contacted Havelock by long-distance telephone at the planning office. Someone had obviously telegrammed him beforehand about the site foreman having been replaced, and Beechfield wanted to be informed how swiftly construction on "Penceddo Lane" would recommence. The line was crackly and there was a slight delay on it; both men found themselves talking over each other whenever there was a momentary pause on either side in their conversation.

"You have to quash these foolish local rumours once and for all, you know," Beechfield said, "and the best way to do so is publicly expose the whole thing as idle tittle-tattle. I want you to go along with a local reporter right into the middle of those woods and then have him write a story which will show there's absolutely nothing at all to be afraid of in there. I can personally vouch for Brian Fengrove on the *Thool Gazette*. He's a sound, no-nonsense journalist; he'll do it. He owes me a favour or two. He's the one who wrote that excellent recent piece debunking the phony claptrap being talked about the ill-treatment going on up at the madhouse. Get him on the blower, explain how things stand, and tell him I put you on to him, there's a good fellow."

"Very good, sir," Havelock replied just before the line went dead.

4

Brian Fengrove was a heavy-set, bespectacled man in his late fifties with a curious physical resemblance to the well-known television personality Gilbert Harding, for whom he was often mistaken by members of the public. For many years he had worked in Fleet Street, on the *Evening News,* but had been offered the chance to become chief reporter on the *Thool Gazette* three years earlier. No doubt its new American proprietor, the strangely effeminate Zebulon De Gabiston, thought the addition of a journalist from a London daily paper to its small weekly staff would lend the local newspaper increased prestige. Fengrove himself already lived in Gallows Langley, having commuted each morning by train to London when employed at the *Evening News,* and told others he found the prospect of writing about farming and church fêtes more appealing than bank robberies and murders. He had therefore gladly accepted, so he said, the new post as a comfortable prelude to retirement. Rather than frequenting the Gryphon Tavern, he tended to frequent the Green Man Pub up on the High Street, lingering over an afternoon succession of pints of Bass, chased by glasses of port and lemon with ice, as he produced his copy for the *Gazette*.

Havelock had telephoned him as per Beechfield's instructions, and Fengrove's wife (in, it must be said, a somewhat testy fashion) informed Havelock that "her husband was, at that time of the afternoon, doubtless to be found drinking inside that awful little boozer."

The two men had met on only a couple of occasions and were solely on terms of nodding acquaintance, and so Fengrove evinced some surprise at noticing Havelock enter the Green Man pub, peer around its confines, and then make—with a definite sense of urgent business to discuss—his way directly to the table at which the journalist sat. The pub was the smallest and most unfriendly in the village to "non-regulars," its smoky, low-wooden-beamed interior the semi-exclusive preserve of a coterie of disparate patrons, who were all known to have one habit in common: that of drinking to excess—especially after hours during the weekends in secret, all-night lock-ins.

Once Havelock had explained the whole situation concerning "Penced-do Lane," Fengrove leant back in his chair and puffed out his cheeks.

"I'd be glad to help out old Beechfield, of course," he said, "though ghost-hunting isn't really in my line."

Havelock wondered if Fengrove was about to make some excuse to avoid taking part in the proposed debunking.

"Surely you don't believe in all that supernatural rot?" he asked.

"No, I certainly don't. I imagine that's why Beechfield thought of me. Still, I'd have to take along a camera—the article will need an accompanying photograph or two. I don't much fancy tramping around those woods in the night, though. One could easily trip over an exposed root and turn one's ankle in the dark."

"I don't see why we couldn't do the whole thing in the daylight. The trees are so closely packed together, it must be quite dim in there under the branches, even at noon."

"Agreed. All right, I'm game. Care for another?"

The next morning found Havelock and Fengrove passing along the stunted, twenty-yards beginning of "Penceddo Lane," crossing the wasteland of heaped rubble at its terminus, and then, at a slow, gradual pace, making their way towards the heart of the woodlands. The air was icy-cold and a harsh overnight frost still clung to the grass, leaves, needles, trunks, and branches, coating everything with a layer of crystalline whiteness. Fengrove carried a Graflex Speed Camera, one of those models which were favoured by press photographers, and would occasionally pause in order to shoot the surrounding yew trees. Havelock detected nothing particularly ominous about the woodland, despite everything he had heard concerning it and the phantasmal terrors which were said to lurk within, though he was suddenly conscious of how ancient this off-the-beaten-track region really was. He could envisage, even in his generally unimaginative mind's eye, that long-ago period, before the Romans came, when the Celtic Britons made strange worship, not in man-made temples, but in sacred sites reared by nature itself: in groves, in caves, in hollows, and on hilltops beneath the Wolf Moon.

The two men had been tramping for over an hour, venturing ever deeper into the woods, when Fengrove rested on a fragment of a fallen tree trunk, large enough only to seat one person, set his camera down by his side, and then pulled out a hipflask from the pocket of his black greatcoat. He took a quick swig and returned it to his pocket, exhaling a great vaporous breath into the air. Above their heads, the background murmuring of the branches and their needles swaying in the wind seemed louder. He stamped his feet on the ground to try and encourage his circulation.

"I think we've come far enough," he said, "don't you? I've taken plenty of photographs. Nothing at all out of the ordinary to report. So much for ghost-hunting."

Havelock nodded, feeling the physical effects of the trek himself and eager to turn back, but he then peered again through the nearby phalanx of trunks to those trees which stood immediately beyond. It could not only be his imagination; there was something genuinely curious about those shadowy yews farther on—their shapes appeared to have altered, almost as if they had been caught in the act of motion and had paused momentarily due to the sudden presence of human interlopers. A ridiculous notion, and one more pertinent to startled deer, but he nevertheless found it hard to shake off. There was something else that was curious: though it was not the usual season for them, a swathe of red-capped toadstools had sprouted around the exposed, frost-covered roots of those trees, like drops of blood splattered across white, gnarled, titan fingers.

"Thoughtless of me," Fengrove said, taking out the flask again. "Would you care for a snifter? It is early in the day, I know, but it's so bitterly cold, isn't it? There's nothing like it to keep the chill out of your bones."

Havelock took the flask with a nod of gratitude and swigged back a mouthful of the stuff. It was whisky, but it had a strange, acrid aftertaste, and it burnt his throat a little as it went down.

"Take a look at those trees over there," he said. "It might be worth getting a few shots of those. They seem to me to be very odd. Very odd indeed."

Fengrove shrugged his shoulders and looked a little sceptical at the very idea, but nevertheless got to his feet and proceeded to tramp a little farther into the distance, moving in the general direction of the trees which Havelock had indicated.

Havelock himself meant to follow him, but only once he had taken a short rest on the fragment of tree trunk which Fengrove had just vacated. Once he had sat down, however, he suddenly felt exhausted and, after a few moments, found he could not get up again. It was as if he had consumed the entire, potent contents of the hipflask in one go, and not taken one solitary mouthful.

Fengrove reappeared, smiled, looked at him with a sardonic expression, and took his picture. He turned the camera around to its reverse side, opened the back panel, and revealed that it was not loaded with a roll of film at all. Then he slung the camera by its leather strap over his shoulder, simultaneously put both hands into the two side pockets of his greatcoat, and held up two identical-looking hipflasks.

"Sorry, old fellow. I'm afraid I'll have to leave you here now," he said.

Havelock gradually slid off the fallen trunk onto the ground, with the back of his head coming to rest on its frost-coated bark. He tried to cry out, but produced only a muffled sort of grunt in the vain attempt, and it was not long before he had lost consciousness altogether. At that point, before departing himself, Fengrove dragged Havelock into the toadstool-riddled region some twenty yards farther on.

When he awoke, Havelock found his body stiff with cold; he had no sensation in his extremities and his teeth began to chatter involuntarily. In a clumsy fashion he managed to sit up, and the realisation that he had been lured deep into the woods by Fengrove on false pretences, been drugged, and then been left to fend for himself slowly dawned on him. Why on earth would Fengrove do such a thing? He obviously did not wish to commit murder; poison—and not merely a soporific—would surely have been employed if that were his aim. Perhaps a mistake had been made and Fengrove had simply thought Havelock already dead, dragging him farther into the interior in order to conceal his body. But what could possibly be Fengrove's motivation for such a heinous act?

Havelock realised he must have lain there in the middle of the woods for hours in that state of complete unconsciousness, for it was now dark and, through a gap in the swaying, needled branches high above his head, he saw that a multitude of stars dotted the inky-black night sky. The January full moon had also risen, the baleful, so-called Wolf Moon; its brownish-yellow disc casting half-filtered, dancing shadows on the fungi-riddled undergrowth.

The first thing to do, he thought, was to get the circulation going in his frozen legs so that he could get to his feet, retrace his steps, and make his way out of the woods. He had difficulty in pulling his right trouser leg up over his calf due to a finger-sized protuberance which kept catching on the folds. When, finally, he managed to roll up the trouser leg to his knee, he saw there was a red-capped toadstool attached to a wound in the skin of his calf. Running his fingers around it, he discovered it had not somehow become lodged there by accident, but seemed to have sprouted from within the flesh, like a noxious, parasitical growth.

The unpleasant, unwelcome memory of those photographs of "Winton Man" suddenly came to mind.

With a grimace of disgust, he twisted at the base of the toadstool until most of it snapped off, though leaving behind a stem fragment still firmly rooted in his leg. What remained of the broken stalk oozed a viscous, blood-red liquid.

When he examined his other calf, after rolling up the left trouser leg as far as his knee, he discovered several subcutaneous lumps, as if further toadstools were in the process of sprouting inside the limb, prior to—like the one on his right leg—eventually breaking through the skin.

Havelock could nevertheless stand up and hobble along in a fashion. The problem now was that, though he was upright and on his feet, he had little sense of which way he should go in order to retreat back along the route he had followed with Fengrove. When he set off in one direction, it seemed to him that gaps seen in the middle-distance somehow contrived to close themselves and block his path before he reached them, and he even began to suffer from the maddening sensation that he was being actively marshalled towards a particular destination.

He felt light-headed and tripped, time and time again, on the concealed obstructions in the dark, dense undergrowth. He had the distinct impression that, more than once, he glimpsed furred tentacles slithering through the shadowy vegetation around his feet. It was extremely difficult to concentrate on the task at hand, and, absurdly, despite his desperate bewilderment, he actually found himself laughing hysterically.

In the end he was aware of having stumbled into a central hollow, one surrounded by a ring of twisted yew trees, into which clearing poured the copper-coloured radiance from the gigantic Wolf Moon overhead. Sprouting from the loamy soil underfoot was a vast mass of malformed, red-capped, and white-dotted toadstools, which also sprouted in and out of themselves, forming some kind of gigantic, cannibalistic amalgamation; an

abnormal nucleus lurking at the very heart of Penceddo Wood. It was when
Havelock heard the solemn whispering of the yew trees, calling on him to
descend, forming what seemed to be distinct Brythonic words which he
nevertheless understood, that he recalled what Carden had said previously
about the ancient druids and their secret rituals of metempsychosis. And he
obeyed the ancient, irresistible summons mere moments before that bub-
bling, festering universe of toadstool caps in the deep hollow welcomed him
and opened not only mouths with blood-stained, rotten teeth, but also
opened blank, staring eyes—eyes like those found in Victorian *memento mori*
photographs of the dead.

5

"The scarlet ceremony is concluded for another year," Fengrove said, speaking over the telephone on a long-distance call the next day. "You can safely
return to Gallows Langley. Only De Gabiston knows about it all. That idiot
Carden might try sniffing around, but he'll be dismissed as a crank. There's
no evidence of foul play."

"I'll destroy all the council records personally," replied Beechfield. "It's
a shame we had to use Havelock, but it's that drunken, talkative foreman
who's really to blame."

The sacrifice had been accepted, and the whispering in Penceddo Wood
consisted solely of the wind blowing through the vast mass of old yew trees
atop the secluded western hillside of Thool Valley. Appeased by this act of
tribute, its otherworldly nucleus would remain dormant and not spread itself beyond the confines of the hollow. It still bubbled and still festered,
dreaming always of those lost, far-off days before the Imperium of the Romans. It would slumber until such time as the annual Wolf Moon again rose
high in the January night sky; and then, once more, the ancient past would
reach out hungrily into the present, demanding a sacrificial homage.

Construction work on the short stretch of road which was to have been
Penceddo Lane was permanently abandoned and, after only a few months,
crabgrass sprang up from the cracks in the surface, overran the site, and
then, by the beginning of the following January, the first small clusters of
that curious species of red-capped and white-dotted toadstool rapidly began
to appear.

Duxford's Blackberry Wine

As the old farmhouse came into view, Jennifer Duxford's heart sank. She and her husband, Keith, had driven up by car from Finchley in north London, passed through Watford into the open countryside of Hertfordshire, and then turned east up past Gallows Langley before finally arriving at the village of Helmont, which was located somewhat higher up on the same steep rise overlooking the expanse of the Thool Valley. The entire region appeared to her to be utterly strange; for she had grown up and lived her whole life in maze-like streets consisting of terraced houses where only the local park offered any glimpse of nature. When she had married Keith two months earlier, she supposed they would soon live together in their own "two-up, two-down" house, with a back yard, and not just rent a house—once, that is, he had saved up enough to put down a deposit on one. And then, only a week ago, Keith had told her that an uncle of his had died, intestate, and that the firm of solicitors handling the estate had advised him he was the sole heir. He had now inherited his uncle's property and a modest income sufficient to last them two or three decades should they choose to live relatively frugally.

Keith knew next to nothing about this uncle. Both his parents were dead, dying when he was a small boy—he had no brothers or sisters—and the family had lived in genteel poverty. Neither of his parents had made any mention of this mysterious relation who owned property in Hertfordshire, and nor did the foster parents who had subsequently adopted Keith and brought him up. Even the solicitors handling the estate were disinclined to provide Keith with any further information in this regard. Indeed, he gained the impression that they were not really glad at all to have had his late uncle as their client.

Jennifer had weaved a fantasy in her brain of a rose-wreathed cottage with a walled garden and an apple tree, nurturing this vision for days; but when, as the car drew up at the wooden gate in front of their destination, and she saw the reality, her fantasy was, as I have said, a disappointment.

Beyond the outside gate, down a short pot-hole-riddled track, there stood an isolated, sloping farmhouse which looked to date from the seventeenth century. It was two storeys tall, with a red-tiled, cross gable roof bearing two chimney stacks. A great mass of unchecked ivy had engulfed the whole of the exterior brickwork, like an unkempt beard. There were six front-facing bow windows, and they were all dark and cheerless in the gloomy, overcast afternoon.

Keith turned off the engine, rummaged around in his jacket pocket for the keys which the solicitors had given him, and turned to Jennifer.

"Well, what do you think?" he said cheerfully.

A pained look of horror provided her answer.

"Let's at least have a rummage around inside," Keith said. "There might be some antiques. If I'm going to sell the place off, I'd want to know I'm not flogging it with valuable stuff inside included in the sale price."

"All right," Jennifer replied.

They left the car, with Keith locking its doors through force of habit, then passed through the outside gate and navigated their way along the short track up to the farmhouse. Jennifer paused in the porch to examine a brass house sign which was half-obscured by the ivy, while Keith tried to find the correct key of the bunch on the chain which would open the front door.

"It says Rakesmeer's Farm," she said. "Why not Duxford's Farm? Was he your maternal uncle or something, with a different surname?"

"No, he was my father's elder brother all right. That's really all that the solicitor deigned to tell me about him. Same surname—Christian name Ronald. Must be an old house sign left over from the owners before him. Ah, here we are."

Keith had managed to find the right key. He opened the door and the two stepped over the threshold, one after the other, into the hallway. They were greeted by a musty, long-lived-in smell; one redolent with years of pipe smoking.

"Pongs a bit, doesn't it?" Keith said.

"It'll take months to get rid of," Jennifer groaned. "Your uncle must have been a recluse. I bet he never aired the place."

The hallway walls were covered in a sickly-green floral wallpaper and a line of badly worn and faded Persian rugs covered the floor.

"Well, let's have a root around, shall we?" Keith said.

Jennifer forced herself to nod.

*   *   *

There didn't seem to be anything of any great value in the farmhouse. Most of the furniture had evidently been supplied by department stores in London, and if Keith had hoped to stumble across some Duxford family silver, he was disappointed. One unusual feature was the number of statuettes littering the place; all of ancient Roman gods. Despite their being cheap reproductions, there were even signs of incense having been burnt in tribute to them. That his uncle had been an eccentric recluse seemed very probable. Ronald Duxford's only other form of entertainment seemed to be the small library of books which he had accumulated; there was not even a radio set to be found in the place. The haphazard untidiness of parts of the various rooms all indicated they had been the preserve of a long-term bachelor who did most of his own cleaning and tidying up at long intervals.

Jennifer had been looking over the curious books in the library with some distaste when Keith finally emerged from the cellar, carrying a small wooden crate filled with stoppered jars.

"What have you got there?" she asked.

"No idea," he replied. "Let's find out, shall we?"

He put the crate down on an armchair and removed one of the dozen or so cork-stoppered pint jars, holding the object up to the light. It contained a dark-red liquid the colour of blood.

"Nothing ventured, nothing gained," said Keith, and he pulled and twisted at the cork stopper until it came out of the small jar with a muffled pop. He sniffed at the top of its neck.

"Smells like homemade blackberry wine," he said, grinning.

"Don't dr——" Jennifer exclaimed, but Keith already had the jar to his lips and had taken a small, quick swig from it.

He pulled a mock-disgusted face, coughed a few times, and put the cork back into the jar.

"It's wine, all right—of a sort."

"You shouldn't have taken a chance like that, Keith. It could have been contaminated," Jennifer said.

"Don't fuss so," Keith replied, wandering over to the bookshelves. "So how was my uncle's taste in reading? Anything racy?"

"I wouldn't say that exactly," said Jennifer. "Look for yourself."

He began reading aloud the titles on the spines of some of the books.

"Let's see what we've got here; *On Porphyry of Tyre, Commentary on the Emperor Julian's "Against the Galileans," Decius and Valerian Vindicated*—rather a marked theme developing, isn't there?—*The Letters of Pliny the Younger, Dio-cletian's Edicts against the Christians*. Well, I think that's enough of that, don't you?"

"More than enough," said Jennifer. "Hang on, weren't your real parents Catholics?"

"Funny that," Keith remarked. "Yes, they were. It might go a long way to explaining why this pagan uncle of mine was completely out of the picture. All to the good, no doubt. I suspect old Ronald wouldn't have been very keen on the idea of being my legal guardian and responsible for the welfare of his little bead-rattling Papist nephew anyway."

"It's getting late. Don't you think we should be getting ready to drive back to London, dear?" Jennifer said, her eyes pleading.

Although the farmhouse was wired for electricity, she did not much relish being there after dark.

"You're right, of course, but I'd just like to take a quick look in that large old shed at the back of the place."

The "shed" was a padlocked wooden lean-to connected to the farmhouse and seemingly constructed in haste by some incompetent carpenter. Some of its warped planks were scarcely flush with one another, and various spiders had made the place their home, filling the ceiling corners with great masses of cobwebs. Several buckets on the floor contained the slimy, fermented remains of blackberries harvested many weeks before.

"Well, that explains the jars in the cellar," Keith said.

"A secret wino," Jennifer replied.

"Wine's a very pagan vice; it took off over here with the cult of Bacchus. He must have drunk the stuff while mooning over his books and paying tribute to his fake statuettes of ancient Roman deities."

"Finished? Seen enough? Can we leave now?" Jennifer asked, trying to keep the irritation she felt out of her tone of voice.

"Yes, let's get going."

Standing in front of the motorcar parked beyond the outer gate, in the midst of the early evening gloom, Keith fumbled around in his pockets, a bemused expression gradually creeping across his face.

"That's strange," he said. "Can't seem to find the car keys."

"Don't muck about. It's not funny."

"No, honestly. I'm not joking."

He began going through all his pockets again, even turning them inside out, but all he found were the house keys.

"I must have left them somewhere back in the farmhouse."

"You didn't leave them in the ignition, did you?" said Jennifer, pulling at the passenger side door which still refused to budge.

Keith peered through the driver-side window.

"No, nothing there. I'm afraid we'll have to go back inside and look for them," he murmured.

"Jesus, give me patience!"

"Good evening," said an unfamiliar voice. "Can I be of any assistance?"

The voice belonged to an overweight man in his early sixties, dressed in tweeds, even to the flat cap perched on his head. Unnoticed by the couple, the stranger had emerged silently from the footpath some dozen or so yards farther up the track.

"Having engine trouble?" asked the stranger.

"No," said Keith, "I simply seem to have misplaced my car keys."

"That's awkward. Elusive objects, keys. Have you just moved into the Rakesmeer's Farm?" The stranger then broke off his questioning. "Sorry, where are my manners? My name is Roderick Carden. How do you do?"

There was a slight, awkward pause as if the stranger expected the mention of his name to generate some recognition in them.

"I'm Keith Duxford and this is my wife, Jennifer. Look, I don't wish to be rude, but we're in a rush and have to find those keys, so we'll be going back inside now. Good evening."

"Duxford, you say? Um—won't you let me help you try and find the missing keys? Three pairs of eyes would be better than two."

Keith and Jennifer looked across the roof of the car at each other doubtfully.

"I assure you, it's no trouble at all. We're practically neighbours. I'd be glad to help," he added.

After over an hour of searching the missing car keys had still not been located, and it appeared obvious, much to the irritation of the Duxfords, that Carden's main motive in offering his assistance had been to see inside the farmhouse. While he pottered around upending vases and pots and running his fingers beneath chairs and sofas, he explained that he was a local historian and that

Rakesmeer's Farm would be the subject of a chapter in a book he was writing about the region. Finally he slumped into an armchair in the lounge and began rambling on interminably.

"Now Rakesmeer's Farm has a most interesting history; do you know that it is said to be the birthplace of the only English Pope? Why, this would be at the start of the twelfth century, but, even as far back as that, Thool Valley had an abbey of its own—an abbey from which this young, future Pope was turned away by its already-degenerate monks when he sought instruction there as a novice. However, thus began his long peregrinations on the continental mainland, the rapid increase in his esteem, and his final crowning at Rome with the Papal Tiara. Thool Abbey acquired the nickname of the Devil's Abbey, or Witch-Cult Abbey, a nickname well merited down the passage of centuries. Here, you understand, I am quoting from the Reverend Alphonus Winters—rather a sectarian, but nevertheless an authority on the matter."

"I find it hard to believe my pagan uncle would have appreciated the Catholic connection," Keith said, while on his hands and knees and upending the Persian rugs in the hallway outside.

"Your uncle? Ah, well, now that is a delicate matter. A delicate matter indeed. I assumed you knew all about——"

"But we know nothing about him," Jennifer said, interrupting Carden in mid-flow, "nothing at all!"

The usually loquacious Carden now seemed positively tight-lipped when it came to this new subject, mumbling something about the suspicious disappearance of a local Catholic priest and about Duxford having "done away with himself" once a warrant had been finally issued by the magistrate for the local police to search Rakesmeer's Farm. Naturally, the whole thing been hushed up.

Carden had made his excuses and left shortly afterwards—with the missing car keys still not found—but not before advising Keith and Jennifer that the only specialist locksmith in the area happened to be an associate of his named Mick O'Sullivan. Alas, at this time of the evening O'Sullivan had doubtless long since finished work for the day and was frequenting one of the hostelries in Gallows Langley. He certainly wouldn't be capable of coming to help until early tomorrow, but Carden promised to phone him on their behalf first thing in the morning and save them a walk to the nearest public call box over a mile away—north along Old Chapel Lane.

Jennifer had glared at him sullenly throughout the whole episode.

And almost the instant after Carden had departed, Jennifer and Keith had got into a blazing row.

"I can't stay in this place overnight, I tell you!" she shouted at him.

"You heard Mr. Carden, what do you suggest I do?"

"Go and find that telephone box the old fool mentioned and ring for a taxicab to take us to the nearest train station. You can come back here yourself tomorrow morning and meet the locksmith. You're the one who went and lost the car keys!"

"All right, all right. Have it your own bloody way!"

Keith slammed the front door behind him as he departed on the errand.

After an hour and a half, Keith had still not returned and Jennifer's ire had turned to nervousness. She had turned on every electric light in the farmhouse, and had paced around and around the lounge and the kitchen without being able to settle in either room. It had been a mistake to stay behind alone as her husband went off in search of the public call box. She should have gone with him. And just how, she couldn't help wondering, had Keith's beastly uncle Ronald "done away with himself"? Head in the gas oven? Hanging himself from a rafter? Cutting his own throat with a straight razor? What was it that the ancient Romans did? Open one of their veins and let their lifeblood seep out; that was their preferred method. But what part had he actually played in the disappearance of the priest beforehand? Uncle Ronald had clearly been some sort of dangerous psychopath. She hoped such things didn't run in the blood. Come to think of it, wasn't it a little odd that Keith had "misplaced" those car keys? Stop it, she thought to herself, now you're becoming paranoid.

Her roving, distracted gaze fell upon the jar of blackberry wine which Keith had put on the sideboard earlier. A nip or two might help to calm her nerves. She picked it up, carried it into the kitchen, found a somewhat dusty glass which she cleaned under the tap, and then poured herself a very small measure. Hesitating for only a moment, she drank the contents of the glass while seated at the kitchen table.

It wasn't bad at all. Very far from it. Keith had been exaggerating, as usual. She giggled. A psychopath old uncle Ronald may have been, but when it came to the making of wine, he was also an artist who certainly put himself into his work.

Jennifer poured herself out another measure, a larger one this time.

Meanwhile, out in the darkness, Keith hurried through Helmont in search of Old Chapel Lane and its public call box. There were several ramshackle cottages dotting its central thoroughfare but, from what he could tell, most of the inhabitants lived in centuries-old buildings set well back from the main road and hidden away behind high brick garden-walls. Only the rooftops and chimney-stacks of the taller of these dwellings were visible in the light cast by its Victorian streetlamps.

Old Chapel Lane began right on the northernmost fringe of the village and was marked by an unusual, prefabricated "tin tabernacle," the likes of which Keith had only ever seen in American "Wild West" motion pictures. Its corrugated-iron walls had been whitewashed, and the structure boasted a tall spire off to one side—doubtless a bell-chamber. Perhaps this late-nineteenth-century building had replaced an older chapel. Drawn by his own curiosity, he crossed over the road to look more closely at the glass-fronted noticeboard attached to its lychgate, which one might have thought would contain a schedule for communion services. What Keith found, however, when he was standing in front of this noticeboard, was that its only purpose seemed to be to act as a breeding tank for a curious species of red-capped and white-dotted toadstool.

Rather disgusted by this sight, he set off again in search of the public telephone box and, after another ten-minute walk, discovered it lurking off the lane; being almost hidden in a deep, natural alcove which really needed pruning back and which obscured almost all the light filtering from the red box's lattice windows. He was glad his eyesight was so keen; the object was situated in a place where it could very easily have been overlooked. Indeed, had he not been on the same side of the lane, he didn't doubt he'd have walked straight past it.

Keith entered the booth and picked up the receiver, intending to call the local operator and have his call connected to the local taxicab office. However, when he put the device to his ear, he heard nothing and the line appeared to be dead. He tried inserting a sixpence and pushing the A button, but nothing happened. His money was not even returned when he pushed the B button and replaced the receiver. It was obviously out of order. Just his luck!

After walking half a mile farther along the road in search of another public telephone box, but only venturing deeper into the darkness of open countryside, he turned back towards Helmont, increasing his pace. Footsore and tired, he realised there was nothing else to do except throw himself upon the mercy of one of its inhabitants and ask whether he might pay to use their telephone.

When he returned to Helmont, he selected one of the less ramshackle cottages along the village's main thoroughfare and banged the brass knocker on its low front door. After a short interval he heard the sound of unbolting. It was partially opened, and a bald old toothless man in a moth-eaten cardigan peered through the gap.

"What do you want, knocking on old folk's doors at this time of night?" the apparition wheezed.

"I'm so sorry to disturb you," Keith said, "but you see it's rather an emergency. I'm in something of a fix. Do you think I could use your telephone? I'd pay you of course."

"Whoth are youth exactly?"

"My name's Keith Duxford, I'm from the farm down the—"

"Duxthford, youth say?!? A Duxthford!!!"

The toothless old man leant forward a fraction, squinting intently at Keith's face and then spat on the doorstep.

"Youth a Duxthford all right. I can seeth it now! Clear off, youth damn Duxthford swine or I'll call theth police!"

The old man suddenly slammed the door shut, and Keith heard it being very rapidly bolted up again.

When he arrived back at the short track leading up to Rakesmeer's—or Duxford's—farm, Keith was surprised to see that the building was in complete darkness. It seemed that, for some reason, Jennifer had turned off all the electric lights. Surely she couldn't have given up waiting altogether and decided after all to retire for the evening? True, he had been away on his fruitless errand for more than three hours, but it was still only just after eleven. He had dreaded the reception he would receive when he told Jennifer there was nothing for it than to make the best of a bad situation and spend the night at the farmhouse. However, if she were already asleep, it would certainly make things a lot easier for him. That fellow, Roderick Carden, had promised to telephone a specialist locksmith on their behalf in the morning anyway.

Carden seemed to be a gentleman (of sorts), and a man of his word. Keith regretted that he hadn't pumped him for more information about his mysterious uncle; if the reaction of the bald and toothless old man in Helmont was any indication, then his late uncle had been truly reviled. What was it exactly that he had got up to before doing away with himself?

Keith was now feeling deeply uneasy about having left his wife alone in the farmhouse, and he hurried along the short track, unlocked the front door, stepped inside the hallway, and fumbled around in the dark for the nearest light switch. But when he located it, the thing didn't seem to be working.

"Jennifer?" he called out as he advanced blindly down the hallway. "It's me! What's happened to the lights? Jennifer? Are you there?"

"No," replied a gruff male voice in a drunken sneer.

When Mick O'Sullivan, the specialist locksmith sent by Roderick Carden, turned up early in his van the following morning, he found the farmhouse locked up and no answer to his knocking on the front door. His first instinct was simply to leave, but then again the motorcar he had been told about was still parked outside a little way up the short track leading to the old ivy-clad building. Had the locked vehicle not still been there he would have departed and assumed his potential customers had already gone away themselves. Instead, as he paused inside the porch and wondered what it would be best to do next, he heard the sound of someone laughing coming from one of the upper rooms of the farmhouse. There was a quality about that laughter which told him something was very wrong; for it was entirely mirthless and without humour. So, deciding on a definite course of action, he drove to Gallows Langley Police Station, where the sceptical constable who was on duty had only to hear the words "Duxford's Farm" before he immediately agreed to accompany O'Sullivan back to the place.

It was a simple matter for a locksmith like O'Sullivan to gain them entry, and the unearthly laughter continued as they made their way along the hallway, up the stairs, and into the small bedroom whence the laughter seemed to emanate.

Inside was Jennifer Duxford. She was seated in a rocking-chair beside the bed, dressed in berry-splattered dungarees and boots too large for her feet, and she had, it appeared, very recently cut most of her hair off in a haphazard fashion. She was making attempts to light a rather foul-smelling pipe. She looked up quizzically at the police constable and the locksmith and then began over again with that horrible throaty laughing.

They discovered what remained of her husband down in the lean-to shed at the rear of the farmhouse, mixed up in various buckets with rotting blackberries.

Jennifer Duxford was, after a swift examination, put under the care of Doctor Charles Winterburn at the Gallows Langley Lunatic Asylum where, after a time, she could recall nothing at all about her husband's uncle Ronald Duxford and the latter's psychotic attempts to revive paganism and human sacrifice. A few weeks before she died, she imagined herself to be happily living with Keith in a rose-wreathed cottage with a walled garden and an apple tree, though she was never again moved to laughter.

As for Rakesmeer's—or Duxford's—farm, the building was demolished during the late 1960s, despite its being offered to the National Trust as a place of national significance, and the only testament to its existence is a small concrete slab in Helmont, amidst a flower bed on a sloping bank, marking the birthplace of England's only Pope.

The End of Death

"The *credo quia impossibile* is paradoxical in expression; its meaning no doubt is: I believe in certain religious mysteries, amongst other reasons, because they are mysteries, because they transcend all the facts of everyday and commonplace experience; because religion, by its definition, implies transcendence; because a religion which propounded nothing beyond average human knowledge would not be a religion at all, though it might be a capital moral code."

—Arthur Machen.

actus sum sicut homo sine adjutorio, inter mortuos liber.
Detective Inspector Gray could not decide whether his being unable to recall his dreams for months now was a consequence of forgetfulness or absence. Whenever he slept, there followed a sharp descent into a complete void and, upon awakening, it was as if his mind had simply turned itself back on, like a light-switch worked by an automatic timer. Nor was he alone in his uncertainty. Most of the populace also seemed to suffer from the same condition. Certain psychologists have speculated that dreams are a form of self-therapeutic madness and necessary to the healthy functioning of the mind. The absence of all dreams was generally regarded by such experts as a reaction to the inconceivable, fantastic reality which was the so-called end of death; a development so unexpectedly strange—and its aftermath so bizarre and distressing—that perhaps it was only natural some part of everybody's mind had shut down in response to it and ceased to function correctly. Even waking, daytime memories contained glaring lacunae. And, since that fateful onset (whose date none could agree upon), each cold morning was as grim as the one before—the half-light still leaden, the sky overcast with low, grey clouds which continually threatened rainfall and the persistence of a dank, oily, vaguely greenish ground-mist which never seemed to disperse entirely.

Nature itself appeared on the brink of expiring; and was it really the case that the populace had long been so terribly *ancient*? Eight out of every ten people were well over sixty years of age, and seventy-five or more was the rough average; even to catch sight of a child was an incredible rarity! Yet reality could not be gainsaid—for all the schools were long deserted and the playgrounds overgrown. What, moreover, had happened to the animals? Had they fled or been driven to extinction? Woods were deserted of wildlife, skies free of birds, fields empty of cattle; and none of this had been satisfactorily explained.

Certainly, those other shocking newspaper accounts were almost impossible to believe at first: recently deceased persons dying from natural causes opening their eyes in mortuaries and, upon their being questioned, insisting that they be allowed to resume their former existence because some ridiculous bureaucratic error had obviously been made. True, the "come-backs" were muddled, mentally impaired, with stiff physical movements suggestive of partial paralysis. But the general malaise and the symptoms thereof (associated partial memory loss, inability to dream, lack of appetite, and so on) which had set in throughout the entire populace had rendered those who had "died" from natural causes and who had then returned from the dead now almost wholly indistinguishable from the majority of the extremely elderly populace.

Perhaps mistakes had been made; perhaps some new form of catalepsy was spreading.

Soon, however, it rapidly became apparent that no one *could* perish.

Those who were "fatally" wounded would return to life overnight with the most appalling, untreatable injuries or disfigurements and—*often*—still in their original agony. In those very rare instances of complete bodily obliteration, the deceased person would then appear amidst a haze of black-and-white static on television screens and monitors, constantly interrupting broadcasts, screaming insane self-accusations at themselves; and it was this ghastly phenomenon which caused the use of such technology to fall off almost entirely.

The minute number of pregnant women remained (apparently) pregnant; but no births occurred. The child in the womb vanished before entering the world: so all such cases were regarded as phantom pregnancies.

The papers reported that patients being treated in hospitals would simply linger on indefinitely. Medical treatments were gradually geared entirely towards last-stage palliative care—but even friends and relatives were finally forbidden to visit their endlessly sick "loved ones." It was said that the inside of those institutions had become a thousand times more hellish than the very worst-run of the Victorian insane asylums. In the end, the buildings were abandoned entirely, their doors bolted, their windows bricked up, and what was left of the unthinkable horrors within them were given over to claustrophobic darkness and decay. Most of the doctors and nurses were, by then, just as hopelessly deranged as their former patients.

That the end of death bore some sort of connection with the general malaise seemed incontrovertible, and yet it was only because of the latter that the populace was now able to tolerate any sort of existence at all: lethargy, indifference, and vacant abstraction formed welcome buffers against the horrors of the new reality.

At some point during this nightmare (though he could not recall exactly when) Gray had been transferred to a locale outside the capital. He did recollect his having hoped he would be able to retire early but then having been advised by official, written communication that his services were absolutely required until the worst had passed. There could be no further reductions to already overstretched police staffing levels—and to seek an early retirement would be to invite a charge of dereliction of duty. True, such time-consuming crimes as murder or manslaughter were now off the statute books and the general curfew had marked a fall in other crimes, but maintaining the appearance of a functioning system of law and order was vital. (The legal profession was, in fact, operating at an even higher degree of bureaucratic industriousness than ever before.)

He prepared his morning cup of ersatz coffee in a pan upon the gas stove, smoking his first cigarette of the day, and drank the bitter-tasting brew while standing and smoking his second cigarette at the open, first-floor window of his studio flat. It was a dwelling just as spartanly furnished as had been his old place back in the capital, with its small bookcase of mouldering, decades-old horror paperbacks. Their lurid photographic covers were the only indication of a strange twist in his personality. Outside, the street was deserted. A few motorcars were parked up on the kerb, now utterly neglected and beginning to dapple with rust. Private transportation had been discouraged as dangerous for as long as people had ceased to dream and once the general malaise had taken full hold.

Gray gazed across the distance; twin rows of red-brick, terraced houses stretched away in drab, dingy uniformity—a stultifying vision of modern

suburbia. The entire region was under indefinite curfew and anyone venturing abroad and stopped by the territorial foot-patrols would be required to
produce official documentation which authorised them leaving their homes
on essential business. This, too, had been the state of affairs for months. He
gulped down the last of the coffee, spat out from his mouth the flaky dregs
which had lurked at the bottom of the cup into the kitchenette sink, and
padded down the landing to the cramped, green-tiled bathroom.

He shaved himself with soap and lukewarm water in the sink, but the
cut-throat razor was beginning to lose its edge. In the medicine-cabinet mirror he gazed at the bald, bejowled, fifty-six-year-old reflection which stared
out at him from the glass. Its eyes had heavy bags beneath them, their un-
blinking gaze devoid of expression—dead eyes.

He went back to his room, located and pocketed his freedom-of-
movement pass and a gold-coloured pack of B&H cigarettes, dressed himself
in a crumpled navy-blue suit, tan raincoat, and scuffed Oxford brogues,
then made his way down the narrow stairway to the house door. As he
passed through the front garden gate, he saw the twitching of several net
curtains in the windows of some of the terraced houses in the street,
glimpsed one or two blank faces appear and then hastily disappear, and, ig-
noring them, then made his way towards the bus stop half-a-mile away.

Everybody cowering indoors and yet headquarters had—laughably—
assigned him to burglary cases.

The run-down single-decker bus arrived on time, its serpentine route
having taken it on a slow and dismal tour of all the back streets in the locality, though today the vehicle carried no passengers other than Gray himself.
Few citizens ventured out, fewer were actually permitted to do so. The familiar driver nodded wearily as Gray flashed his pass, not bothering to examine
it. They never spoke to each other and the driver seemed always to be suffering from a continuous chest infection: coughing liquid debris from his lungs
into a crusty white handkerchief. It appeared as if he worked the route
alone, hour after hour, driving along the same dreary streets, day in, day
out, ceaselessly, like some lab-rat trapped in a maze. This driver seemed,
Gray thought, to be actually turning ever more rodent-like every time he
saw him—that thin, unshaven face, those little black and beady eyes, and
those protrusive two front brown teeth hanging over his bottom lip.

*   *   *

After some fifteen minutes the bus arrived outside police headquarters. It was a dilapidated, six-storey building situated adjacent to a former shopping centre whose multitude of business premises had been boarded up and abandoned months ago in the middle of the malaise. The six storeys of the police headquarters were also mostly abandoned, the crime rates having fallen so drastically that it was not economically viable to keep up anything other than a pretence of maintaining law and order. Territorial foot-patrols had voluntarily long since replaced old-fashioned "bobbies on the beat." Gray marvelled again at the perverse decision which had been arrived at by a higher power requiring him to continue his duties as an investigative officer whilst nearly all the others of his ilk had been made redundant. It almost seemed as if he had been especially singled out for this unfavourable treatment—to be made an example of, for some unknown indiscretion on his part.

Gray stared up at the desolate building, and thought of some half-abandoned fort on the outskirts of the decaying Roman Empire; but this was a fort constructed not of ancient stone-and-timber, but of modern concrete-and-steel, its cracked windows half-caked with mould, its exterior decorated with obscene, mocking graffiti, its very ineffectiveness a mocking tribute to the now-universal detestation in which the forces of law and order were held.

His desk was in an "open-plan" office on the third floor of the structure, and he worked his way towards it through an empty series of shadowy stairways and corridors—half the strip-lights in the place were dead. There was no one else on duty, and even those who were pencilled in for various shifts often made the flimsiest excuses (which were accepted without question) for their persistent absence: any signs of malaise were sufficient cause. Passing a futile day with nothing to do, spent blankly staring at a wall, could be done just as well at home and without the additional burden and expense of having to travel.

Within moments of his arrival at his desk, the telephone rang and Chief Inspector Mortimer called Gray into his cluttered, small office. His superior seemed never to leave its confines, and perhaps he genuinely had nowhere else to go. The chief inspector's domain was like some cramped corner of a darkened cell and he a bloated spider which waited and brooded endlessly amidst its cobwebs. It was a bewildering shambles of filing cabinets, piles of folders, street maps pinned to the cracked walls, and potted, greyish cacti and rubber plants with hole-dotted leaves maimed by burning cigarette tips. It was strongly rumoured that, amongst all the other junk, Mortimer possessed a stash of extremely squalid "jazz mags" which he had liberated from the (now-defunct) obscene publications department. Whatever the truth of the allegation, there was certainly an air of the genuinely seedy about the person of Chief Inspector Mortimer. He looked like an oversized, mouldering ventriloquist's dummy. His black three-piece suit was dusty and wrinkled, the white shirt yellowing around the straining collar. His askew kipper tie was mottled with stains. He peered at Gray over half-moon black-rimmed eyeglasses and motioned at him to be seated.

"I'm taking you off burglaries," he said. "I'm reassigning you to missing persons. My records show you have had previous experience in this area. Weren't you given the nickname 'The Weird Detective' when you were involved in that Drayton case?"

Something jarred inside Gray's head, like a faulty cog working in a mechanism. He could not recall whether Mortimer's assertion were factual or not; but in trying to do so, some pathway in his thoughts suddenly closed itself off.

"But surely Cargill is already assigned to deal with missing persons?" Gray finally replied, after a long pause.

"Hmm. It is Cargill himself who has disappeared—and while investigating a missing persons case! It may be that things here are going to hell in a handcart, but Cargill is one of our own. I'm not simply going to ignore this. I think we at least owe him that much."

"All right," said Gray.

Although he suspected that Cargill had simply been one of the last to succumb to the general malaise and memory-loss, he did not voice this thought aloud.

Gray later examined the typed notes Cargill had left behind before his vanishing act. It seemed he was engaged on investigating what he evidently thought to be a *connected* series of fairly recent disappearances. He had initially begun to try and collect evidence to support his proposition that a criminal gang had been abducting random persons in secret and then demanding a ransom from their spouses or relatives. Although what information he managed to obtain supported the idea of a gang being involved, he rapidly came to the conclusion that no physical coercion had taken place and that each of the missing persons must have freely, willingly submitted to their fate. Certainly spouses and relatives were aware of the persons' disappearances, but provided a bewildering range of explanations; and no kidnap demands were ever received. In any case, Cargill had questioned them all thoroughly, though he found the usefulness of his interviews increasingly hampered by the widespread psychological effects of the general malaise. It appeared that a significant number of interviewees either had difficulty recalling the persons in question or else showed a distinct tendency to wish to forget about them altogether.

It was at this stage that the theory that a mind-control cult might be involved suggested itself to Cargill and, after questioning one of the more forthcoming interviewees, he determined that this line of enquiry was definitely worth pursuing. There was even a photograph in the file of a suspected cult member who had also vanished, Gregory Holder, which had been given to Cargill by another man called Robert Zachary (who was some sort of part-time lecturer in media politics and current affairs). He was, it seemed, one of the few people who knew anything at all about the cult's secretive operations.

Cargill, then, almost certainly must have been on to something after visiting Zachary. But the report mentioned nothing further about the matter. Indeed, the only coda to the investigation was a rubber stamp on the final page of the folder declaring "CASE CLOSED FOR LACK OF EVIDENCE."

It was not particularly difficult for Detective Inspector Gray to track down Robert Zachary to his mother's home address, though he'd evidently changed his accommodation several times of late. Despite having retired through ill-health from some media job years ago, he still occasionally gave lectures at the local university during the general malaise and was notoriously disliked amongst the skeleton staff who remained on a campus now almost devoid of students. It amused Gray to think of the dilapidated educational facility still keeping up the pretence of being useful to a rapidly degenerating society; but then again, wasn't he himself engaged in a similar imposture?

He found Zachary in a basement flat in one of the side streets in the central section of the district; an area full of foot-patrols whose members seemed particularly vacant-eyed, shabby, and to be suffering even more acutely from the general malaise than the average run of the population.

After stubbing out his cigarette and descending one flight into a sunken open area in front of the nondescript three-storey house which had been divided into flats, Gray had to ring the bell several times before he saw any movement at all behind the frosted-glass panels of the front door. Finally it was opened and in the frame there stood an emaciated man in his late sixties, dressed in an open-neck paisley shirt, a shapeless beige cardigan with pink stains on the cuffs, green pyjama-bottoms, and carpet-slippers, all of which appeared far too large for his slight frame. He was clean-shaven with a tangled shock of white hair above a pair of equally white bushy eyebrows. His face had a blotchy, purplish complexion. He rubbed his shifty, furtive eyes and said: "Can I help you?"

"I'm Detective Inspector Gray. Are you Robert Zachary?" Gray flashed his identification.

"That's right. I am he."

"Can I take up a few moments of your time? I'd like to ask you about a colleague of mine who's gone missing—Detective Inspector Cargill. I believe you provided him with certain information, just before his disappearance."

"That's correct. Does this enquiry relate to Holder, too? I assume so."

"Can we speak inside?"

Zachary paused—but only momentarily, as he looked back over his shoulder—before replying: "Of course. Come in."

After Zachary had shown him into the parlour, and once they were both seated, he proceeded to answer all Gray's questions with an openness that was initially disarming but which led the detective, as the lecturer's replies continued, to believe his memory had been impaired by the general malaise and that his imagination had filled in some of the blank spaces in his account. For some morbid reason of his own, he had left the television set in the corner of the room switched on, despite its displaying only the black-and-white static seen between channels.

"Yes, as I told Cargill previously, I knew Gregory Holder: he was a student of mine. Got involved with a very sweet, sensible young girl once she'd turned eighteen—Beatrice Wemyss, also a student of mine. Beautiful auburn hair. I suppose my lectures brought them together. Then one day he was given a flier or handbill by someone passing them out on a street corner; it invited folk to a secret meeting way out of town, in the vaults left beneath some old ruins."

"What sort of a meeting?" Gray said, not mentioning what he had already determined from the case file.

The inspector's gaze roved around the parlour to the lines of bookshelves covering one wall; endless volumes relating to Marxism, and a smattering of philosophical works by the likes of Locke, Hume, and Schopenhauer.

"I'll get to that in a bit. Apparently he went to several of these meetings and eventually Beatrice—um, I mean Miss Wemyss—noticed him gradually cooling towards her, if you know what I mean. She came to me for advice. I said I'd speak to the boy. At first he was extremely reticent, but I managed to wheedle out of him the fact that, given his new association with this deranged sect, he wanted to break off the relationship with Bea—um—Miss Wemyss altogether. What he said he really desired was full initiation into the cult he'd lately discovered. He asked me to break the bad news to her, but gently. He was clearly intending to abandon her. I've got one of their fliers, somewhere. Believe me, right from the start I knew the cult for the scum they really are: enemies of the human race."

Zachary rummaged around in some files and finally retrieved the item.

Gray glanced over the A5 sheet of paper and slipped it into his pocket.

"Look, you still haven't—"

Gray's words were interrupted by the sound of a crash coming from an adjacent room.

"It's my elderly mother," Zachary replied, with an air of weariness. "Ignore it. Now, as I was saying . . ."

Then there was loud thump, as of something heavy having fallen back. Gray got to his feet. Could it be the case, he thought, that Zachary had Cargill or Holder or *even both of them* locked away somewhere in the flat?

He ignored Zachary, crossed the room into a corridor leading off the parlour, and heard another thump and then a cry of anguish:

"Let me out of here!"

The voice was enfeebled and high-pitched.

It was coming from behind a door at the far end of the corridor. Zachary had appeared at Gray's shoulder, his air of weary sufferance even more pronounced than previously. He handed Gray a key which he had taken from the pocket of his cardigan.

"Well, go on and investigate," he said. "If you must."

The key unlocked a bathroom door. Inside the green-tiled room, half in and half out of a bathtub full of pinkish-coloured water, was an elderly old lady dressed in a soaking, once-white nightgown which was now of the same pinkish hue as the bathwater.

The old woman was in great distress. There were wounds around her throat and head and, at the sight of Gray appearing, she reached out her arms towards him. A bloody butcher's knife lay discarded in the sink. A broken jar of bath salts was scattered on the linoleum floor; its debris a mixture of shattered glass and grainy crystals.

"Please, young man," she said, "help me up . . ."

"Young man"? No one had applied that description to Gray for decades.

He took her by the wrists and gently helped her to clamber out of the bathtub: her prune-like flesh was deathly cold to the touch.

The old lady, Mrs. Zachary, now dried off and wrapped in a dressing-gown, was calmly seated in one of the chairs and sipping at the cup of tea provided by her son, the lecturer. Her wounds were covered up by bandages.

Gray had telephoned headquarters, ten minutes earlier, and arranged for Zachary to be brought into custody. A police van was already on its way.

"This is all a misunderstanding, Inspector," Zachary said. "I assure you, I am the mildest of men. I abhor violence."

Gray ignored him. He had no idea what to do about the old woman. Her injuries were serious enough to warrant hospitalisation; but the hospitals were full and sealed up for good. Had the lecturer previously murdered her? Was this latest attempt simply the last in a series?

"In any case, you can't charge me with a crime which no longer exists," Zachary said. "This isn't some fascist police state."

Perhaps, Gray thought, she was one of those "fortunate" "come-backs" who was now incapable of feeling pain once the nerves were damaged beyond repair. He had read of such cases in the newspapers: those so afflicted often wound up in a deformed state akin to leprosy, with fingers, ears, eyes, or noses missing.

"Please don't take my son away," Mrs. Zachary said, her dull brown eyes now watery with tears. "He's all the company I have left."

"Sorry, Mrs. Zachary, but he's coming with me to headquarters for questioning," Gray murmured, unable to keep a note of tired disgust from his tone.

"I shan't press charges, oh no," she said. "Whatever he's done, he's still my boy."

Outside the sound of a police siren could be heard approaching.

There were a dozen holding cells located in the basement of headquarters, though they had not seen much occupancy since the advent of the general malaise. Robert Zachary now occupied the oldest and the least accessible of these cells—a dank, vile hole which had last welcomed a suspect decades previously.

"Hmm. We can't keep him here just on the basis of him 'killing' his mother, you know," Chief Inspector Mortimer had said. "Such things are now classed as purely domestic incidents."

"Twenty-four hours of intense questioning over the Cargill disappearance is what I had in mind," Gray had replied. "We can keep him in custody for that long."

"Get on with it, then."

The resulting police interview was done according to the tried-and-tested method Gray felt appropriate in this case. It was, so he thought, a technique which not only yielded the quickest results but also fulfilled the likes of Zachary's "moral" maxims of both the end justifying the means and of the needs of the many outweighing the needs of the few. So, leaving his jacket in his personal locker, Gray had taken with him a set of pliers, a screwdriver, nails, and a clawhammer in a surgeon's kit-bag when he went down into the basement. He had locked the cell-door from the inside so that the two of them would not be disturbed and so that Zachary's screams would not penetrate farther than the confines of the four walls of the half-forgotten cell. When the grisly business was over, Gray locked the cell-door from the outside, leaving within a bloodied, sobbing, agonised mass of human flesh, went upstairs and replaced his gore-dappled shirt with the spare one contained in his personal locker, signed an official document stating that Robert Zachary had been released after questioning, and then went to report his findings to Chief Inspector Mortimer.

There were certain advantages to headquarters being very short-staffed.

"He confessed to 'murdering' Beatrice Wemyss, too," Gray said, keeping his right hand hidden away in his jacket pocket. "She came back to life and somehow got out, though in what sort of a sorry state I couldn't say; but he'd cut her up pretty badly. I think the mother was also in on it."

"Hmm. That's all very interesting, but how does it link up with the disappearance of Cargill?" Mortimer replied.

"Cargill turned up there at Zachary's place all right. Zachary must have wanted to get rid of him as quickly as possible and put him straight onto Holder's trail. The lecturer clearly detested Holder and was probably jealous over the young man's relationship with Wemyss. I think she really wanted to follow Holder into the cult. It seems that Zachary must have tried one last time to seduce Beatrice Wemyss himself; but he was clearly rebuffed. He's just your typical filthy-old-hypocrite type."

Mortimer writhed a little uncomfortably in his chair at this description and tugged involuntarily at his collar.

"Anyway, he provided me with all the information he'd given to Cargill about the cult and about Holder's association with it. I can't help thinking that it was originally Zachary's diatribes at lectures which made Holder want to find out for himself if what Zachary said about the cult at the university was true."

"Hmm. Tell me about this 'cult,'" Mortimer said.

"It's genuine all right and a notoriously depraved one at that—'The Old Faith.' You've probably not heard of it, but Zachary said experts have traced its origin back thousands of years. Remarkable that it's survived at all, really. There have been innumerable attempts down the centuries by state authorities and rival, though more progressive, cults worldwide to stamp the pernicious thing out. Its adherents have always been obsessed with the dead. They have long had all sorts of macabre practices and rituals which centre around corpses; they've never encouraged cremation for one thing, only burial, and think that the deceased can intercede on behalf of the living. Most of their activities are conducted secretly, in catacombs."

"Hmm. Well, recent events must have shaken them up."

"Maybe so. That which they worship is believed by them to sustain existence itself—whatever that might mean. Apparently one of its manifestations, though, was tortured to death, in the form of a common criminal symbolised by an 'X,' and they think it's necessary, since then, to re-create and feed on pieces of the felon's body collectively, in order to pay him eternal tribute."

"Sounds like some horrible cannibal thing."

"It gets worse. Rather than being reasonable and accepting there is no such thing as absolute truth, they insist on not paying tribute—even a notional, face-saving tribute—to any or all of the other beliefs permitted by society. There was talk about possessed high-priests who make an eternal sacrifice in order to obviate the ills which humanity—even the innocent—inherited. Anyway, the whole thing is crazy. The followers actually seem to welcome suffering; and particularly torture. Zachary claimed he only despised them for being so utterly ridiculous, but he couldn't stop thinking about them."

Gray paused momentarily and he recalled something he had once been told about evidence obtained through the use of torture being unreliable—a tortured man would confess to any crime, whether he was guilty or not.

"Zachary also said that some of these deluded people claimed—through some mumbo-jumbo—to take on all the ills of other people; and to do so willingly, by becoming substitute-victims. It's the only way, so they believe, to ward off some infinitely greater disaster threatening the whole human race. Zachary said to me he'd learnt that they thought all that stuff about the unspeakable horrors in the sealed-up hospitals was untrue, just cooked-up propaganda. In fact, or so they assert, the places are empty and there's no one in them needing treatment. That's why they were closed. The people in them had had their ills expiated. Memory loss accounted for other discrepancies."

The chief inspector was staring dumbly at Gray with a look of total incomprehension upon his face. Finally he said:

"And what happened to Zachary: did you release him? We've no reason to hold him any longer, you know."

"He's probably already making his way east. Too much of a scandal to remain in the country, given his actions. I think I eventually got through to him." Gray idly turned over the cell-key in his jacket pocket with the long, bony fingers of his blood-stained right hand.

"And what about Cargill?"

"When I find Holder, I'll find Cargill, or vice versa."

Gray had managed to secure the use of the only unmarked police car left in the garage at headquarters. Mortimer had grumbled about it, for he himself tended to regard the vehicle as exclusively his own personal property, though it was well known he very rarely utilised it on any official police business: in addition to his supposed collection of "jazz mags," he was also reputed to be a secret kerb-crawler. Anyway, the place Gray was going was miles out of town, hidden away in some small village in the distant countryside, and he could hardly take public transportation to get to his destination.

The village was called "Bevelham" and Holder had moved there after quitting his last address. The three dozen or so dwellings and its public house occasionally appeared on old maps, along with the ruins on the hill close by, but it was not identified by name in any of them; only on the flier which Zachary had previously given Gray. This flier also contained a hand-drawn route showing the position of the ruins in relation to the nearest back road. It must have been the case that Holder had taken a room in one of the houses in the village in order to be closer to the rest of the cult.

It was already dusk, and bitterly cold, when Gray set off from head-quarters, and the streetlamps were just turning themselves on, emitting a series of dotted, hazy-orange glows. The vaguely greenish ground-mist was even thicker than usual and he drove through the eerily deserted streets with the headlights blazing. On the passenger seat by his side rested the black leather surgeon's kit-bag containing a screwdriver, clawhammer, pli-ers, and nails.

When Gray was clear of the built-up district, the car reached the open countryside, the landscape darkening as each mile sped by, the fields and the hedges slowly vanishing in the combination of night and mist save when they were caught in the beams of his headlights. He saw no other traffic at all on the open roads.

Once, he pulled over onto a verge in order to consult the map and the flier more closely; for he thought he might have lost his way. But, after tak-ing several turns along a series of half-concealed lanes, he found himself passing along an extremely long, straight, bumpy road entirely lined on both sides by overarching trees which bent towards one another, so much so that it was as if he were travelling through the length of some vast tunnel. And, at the end of this naturally formed tunnel, it was as if the car had emerged into a hidden-away winterland. He blinked his eyes with disbelief; heavy snow was falling and must have been coming down for many hours beforehand, for everything was entirely blanketed in a thick white layer.

Ahead, he could just make out a tiny village behind which, so he as-sumed, must lurk the hill with the mysterious ruins at its peak: the very nexus of what remained of "The Old Faith."

The village consisted of squat two-storey buildings, all seemingly Jacobean, with the gabled upper storeys overhanging the lower ones, and the windows either shuttered or dark. The only other building in sight was the local public house, built to the same design as the rest, but with an attached, low wooden structure which must have once served as a stable. He parked outside the place and got out of the vehicle, glancing up and down the narrow, icy street at the heart of the village; there was no one else abroad. Lights, however, could be seen flickering inside the mullioned windows of the old public house, and he heard the buzzing murmur of laughter and conversation hailing from within. A creaking sign, hung upon a bracket attached to a mast of blackened, solid timber, proclaimed the hostelry to be "The Eastern Star."

After locking his vehicle, and crunching his way across the snow underfoot, Gray ventured into the place.

There must have been some kind of festival going on, for everyone from the village appeared to be celebrating inside the warm tavern, and the walls and the low, timbered ceiling were festooned with wreaths of holly. Some of the patrons had even dressed up in antique clothes for the occasion. The heady scent of burning logs in the hearth fire mingled with the aroma of pipe-smoke and ale assailed Gray's nostrils. No one turned around when he entered, even though he had steeled himself for inquisitive stares, narrowed eyes, and lowered voices. He went up to the bar counter and a young woman, wearing a rather ridiculous mediaeval corset, blouse, and skirt, set a pewter tankard of foaming ale before him.

"On the house, sir, and welcome I'm sure," she said.

He was about to reply when, through the haze of tobacco smoke, he caught sight of a familiar face on the far side of the snug. There could be no doubt as to its owner's identity, even though those features were now half-engulfed by a wild, bushy beard. It was Detective Inspector Cargill, and he was smiling inanely; beckoning to Gray to come over and join him at the corner table where he was sat with a jug and tankard in front of him. He was also puffing self-contentedly on a small well pipe with a curved stem.

"Well, it's good to see you again, Gray," he said, after drinking from his tankard. "It's been ages."

That irritating, dullard smile seemed permanently fixed to his features.

"You've got a lot of explaining to do," Gray replied. "I've been put to a lot of trouble because of your disappearance. Didn't you think to make contact with headquarters?"

"I've left the force for good. It's much better being here, making preparations for the———"

"Look," Gray cut in, "it's pretty obvious to me you're now in the grip of this deranged 'Old Faith' cult. Your vacant expression alone tells me that much."

Cargill sighed and took another swig from his tankard.

Gray jammed one of his own smokes between his lips and touched the end with the flame from his battered old Zippo. A smell like petrol wafted from the lighter. He drew on the cigarette, exhaled, and finally said:

"You can throw away your pension and waste the rest of your life on whatever nonsense you want to; that's up to you. But I've still got to make an official report. Now, what's happened to Holder?"

"He's up on the hill with the remainder of the others. I imagine that he'll go on soon enough, though," Cargill said. "Down here, as well, we've not got all that much longer to wait."

Gray snorted: Cargill was talking in riddles. The man's brain had gone; memory loss and the malaise had finally caught up with him, just as Gray had suspected. Gray's gaze again roamed around the snug, and he caught sight of a pretty young woman in her late teens, with tresses of curling auburn hair, who was looking directly at the two of them. She too smiled, showing small, brilliantly white teeth, and again there was something about the open, friendly expression which put Gray on edge. It was hard to explain why, but he felt that she, like Cargill, had neither the reason—nor the right—to appear to be so carefree.

"That's Beatrice Wemyss," Cargill said, between puffs on his pipe.

"Rubbish," Gray replied, stubbing out his cigarette and taking a swig from the drink in front of him. The taste of the hops danced on his tongue, but he quickly spat the mouthful he'd tasted back into the tankard. If he'd wanted anything to drink, it was something astringent, and with more alcohol content; cheap vodka preferably—but certainly not this country bumpkin stuff.

"Beatrice Wemyss was cut up badly by that bastard Zachary," he went on. "Yes, she got away, but she'd still be badly scarred—even if her wounds had been stitched up. That girl over there doesn't have a mark on her."

"Nevertheless, it *is* her," Cargill said.

"I've had enough of you and this madhouse," Gray replied. "I'm going up that hill to have a look around those ruins for myself. And if anyone tries to stop me I'll—"

"No one's going to try and stop you, old fellow," Cargill said, the irritating, dullard smile still in place. "But it's almost midnight and too late now for confessions."

The climb up the hill proved to be arduous. Gray had brought with him a torch which he'd taken from the glove compartment of his vehicle, and its beam danced as he moved cautiously forwards, with the surgeon's kit-bag in his other hand. His old stomach ruptures hampered his progress, and every so often he had to rest until they ceased their internal protests. The snowfall had blanketed the undergrowth in a vast white expanse, cloaking perils to a sure footing such as uncovered roots, fallen branches, tendrils, and thorns. He stumbled on several occasions, but finally found himself in the clearing at the apex of the hill and spied the ruins; the remains of huge stone walls, some with peaked, vacant windows and also a few broken columns left standing with nothing to support.

He made a circuit of the area and behind one of the walls discovered a wooden panel, covered with fallen snow, which had been laid horizontally over a gap in the flagstone floor. Once he'd got the obstruction shifted aside, he shone his torch down into the aperture and revealed a flight of narrow stone stairs in a brickwork corridor. At the bottom of the flight was an open doorway, arched in the Gothic design. The beam of the torch could reveal nothing farther than the doorway entrance itself.

Should he descend? He was certain he could hear some sort of chanting faintly emanating from those subterranean depths. It was against all his instincts to do so. He should call for backup; but what "backup"? Headquarters was half-deserted, and the idea of a police van full of armed officers in bullet-proof vests was now as fantastic as the U.S. Cavalry coming over the hill while a triumphant bugle sounded a charge. He carried no firearm, only his aids to torture. But then again, what did that matter? He could not kill or be killed: if it all went wrong he would still return, though in a more damaged state. So he descended.

These were the catacombs; there could be no doubt. Rows of coffins in recesses lined both sides of the walls, and overhead the roof was rounded and low. The sound of the chanting was growing more distinct as he advanced down that macabre underground passageway, and he had a fearful jolt of recollection: disjointed phrases crowded his thoughts—"below there is only pain," "the things which must be fed," and "behind those eyes there is only darkness." Gray gasped for breath and felt his heart racing in his chest like a jack-hammer. He managed to walk a few more paces, made a sharp, blind turn, and was then inside some sort of lighted chamber, wherein he stepped to one side, trying to take in the enormity of the scene in front of him.

He leant back, finding support from a wall at his rear.

It was a low, vaulted crypt, adorned with grotesque plaster statues, one of which was a weeping woman veiled in blue lace from head to waist, wearing a crown of stars, standing on a crescent with a serpent crushed underfoot, and with seven silver daggers plunged into her flaming heart. Antique pews had been laid out in two sets of three with a central aisle left clear. Hundreds of candles blazed on all sides. And, lingering in the air, there was an aroma of incense having been burnt in a censer not long ago. The adherents of the cult were kneeling in the pews, facing forward, with only the backs of their mostly bald or else white-haired heads visible; the women's all covered by mantillas of black lace. An overwhelming sense of panic rose up in Gray's mind at observing the mysterious Latin rites which were being observed in these, the very bowels of the earth. He felt an unaccountable certainty that he had no right to be there, and he recalled a phrase he'd read by an author in one of the old horror fiction paperbacks which he owned about the real essence of sin being the taking of heaven by storm.

And at the far end of the crypt there stood a figure in a black robe, his back to all the adherents, his arms aloft, his hands bearing up a tiny, circular, white disc before some sort of altar on which there was a chalice of blood. High above that dreadful altar there stood the fearful "X" sign before which the adherents of the cult were so eager to prostrate themselves.

Gray heard the sound of an insistent bell from the shadows, some more words murmured in Latin, and he felt as if his world were wholly giving way.

At the last, prior to losing consciousness, Gray saw a person (whom he clearly recognised from the case file photograph as being Gregory Holder) step forwards, kneel before the altar-rail with some of the others, and make a curious sign across his chest—before they were surrounded by a nimbus of blinding light and then, unbelievably, disappeared wholly from view.

Gray awoke in his vehicle. He was slumped in the front passenger seat, miles away from "Bevelham," and the car must have been driven to—and then been dumped at—some lonely country road with him still inside the vehicle. As was the case when awakening from sleep, it was as if Gray's mind had simply turned itself back on, like a light-switch worked by an automatic timer. And he could not clearly remember what had happened; even recent events seemed as elusive as old dreams. The surgeon's kit-bag on his lap was empty. For some reason there was dirty slush on his boots, though there was no snow at all outside; only the ever-present low mist.

At headquarters, the same day, he was debriefed by Chief Inspector Mortimer, who was left exasperated by Gray's vagueness. The general malaise and memory loss had finally, it seemed, caught up with the detective inspector too.

A few hours later, however, a short handwritten note addressed to Mortimer arrived, in an envelope bearing an illegible, smeared postmark. It formally announced Cargill's resignation from the force and, bizarrely, his "firm intention to finally climb the sacred hill."

"Hmm. Well, that's that. I'm not wasting any more police time on the matter. If some damned idiot wants to throw away his career to consort with lunatics and devils, that's his affair," Mortimer said to Gray. He was staring pointedly at Gray as if he expected more information.

"Devils?" Gray vacantly replied, turning over a loose key in his jacket pocket with his long, bony fingers. He couldn't recall why such a thing was even in there.

"Hmm. One last thing. I have to advise you that we found Zachary an hour ago. Had to break down the cell door. You made quite a mess of him. Your methods are truly barbaric, especially in this enlightened day and age. You've also misled a senior officer: me. The superintendent is beside himself. Zachary fully intends to press charges, and I certainly don't blame him. You're now officially suspended for an indefinite period. It's only your current mental deficiencies and record of long service which stops me from throwing you into a gaol cell right this minute."

"Then perhaps you'd better take this, sir. It may form a useful part of the case against me," Gray said, passing the key over to him.

"Hmm. Get out of my sight, Gray. You're a bloody disgrace," Mortimer said.

One day was much like another, its half-light still leaden, the sky still overcast with low, grey clouds which continually threatened rainfall and a dank, oily, vaguely greenish ground-mist which never quite seemed to wholly disperse.

Gradually, however, and over the course of the following days, Inspector Gray began to recollect more and more of the details from his recurring dreams. He now recalled with joy, not horror, the friendly faces in an ancient inn with a blazing fire in its hearth and the snowfall in a tiny village nestled at the base of a mystic hill.

On the morning of the twelfth day he came across the flier giving directions to "Bevelham," which had been secreted in the breast pocket of his overcoat and then forgotten by him. He did not know if it would be as easy to find the mystic hill a second time, and was certain there was much for which he had to atone before it was possible.

Still, what else was there left to do?

Nothing, only to hope he would be freed from all past terrors to reach, finally cleansed, the candlelit catacombs beneath the sacred ruins wherein he might join the last of the remaining adherents of the "Old Faith" in the ages-old ceremonial rites and, with them, worship "X" in all His Glory.

The Interminable Abomination

"He asked me if I had read the stories of a certain Edgar Poe. I told him I knew them better than anyone and had good reason for doing so. Then he asked me, in a very emphatic tone, if I believed that this Edgar Poe existed. *I* of course asked him who he thought wrote all the stories. He answered: *"A club of very clever, very powerful writers, who know everything that's going on."*
—Charles Baudelaire to Auguste Poulet-Malassis, 8 January 1860

"I became *insane,* with long periods of *horrible sanity*."
—Edgar A. Poe, 4 January 1848

t is a curious thing, but despite a thirty-year career in the trade, of handling books, reading them, and selling them on at a small profit, I cannot say that my occupation ever inspired in me the desire to write anything by way of a narrative—whether fictional or autobiographical. I confined my writing activities to business correspondence, to my *Secondhand Bookshops Gazetteer,* and to my quarterly mail-order catalogue, *Vathek's Book-List.* If I were to mention that my principal London "rival" in the trade was Aloysius Condor Books—a long-established firm and member of the ABA, currently run by its founder's even more unscrupulous nephew Nicholas Condor—then the genre of literature which I bought and sold will be immediately obvious to its aficionados. How horrible, then, that I am now *under a compulsion* to write what follows hereafter and to do so in that very genre.

But I must not get ahead of myself. Let me, then, try to arrange events in their proper chronological order and reveal them as they were themselves revealed to me.

I had, for the last few years, become semi-retired in the bookselling trade: the increasing domination of the internet pushed up prices everywhere (even in high-street "charity"—a gross misnomer—shops) so that not only were fewer bargains to be found but also the traditional bricks-and-mortar secondhand bookshops began closing down. They were the prey of increasingly fiendish local business rates as London streets previously thought of as "down-market" were gentrified and diversified by the ruling Islington tyranny. My own *Secondhand Bookshops Gazetteer* halved in content as the closures gathered pace. It was becoming more difficult to obtain stock cheaply for my quarterly book-list. Although I could still rely on the occasional sale of an individual's personal library (often sold by a next-of-kin with no interest in reading, let alone an interest in books), the physical labour involved in carting hundreds of volumes by myself over uneven pavements aggravated my lower back to the extent that my occupation became akin to medieval racking.

And it was in this sad twilight of my career as a bookdealer when I received a query from a customer with whom I had not communicated for a couple of years—Colonel Archibald Dowson. Once he had been a valued, lucrative client of mine (though we had never spoken over the telephone, let alone met face-to-face, and his typed letters were always curiously unidiomatic). Another of my customers had told me this lucrative client had once been a colonel in the British Army—stationed somewhere out in Burma during the Second World War. He was notorious for his obsession with horrors; the ghastlier the better. It seemed he could not get enough of them on the printed page, even after his experiences with nightmarish, real-life horrors committed out in the Far East. And there were also strong rumours that his own military career had ended in disgrace. He had, it was said, perfected acts of hideously refined cruelty against captured soldiers of the Imperial Japanese Army. But—rather oddly in light of the above—he had, it was said, married some Oriental widow twenty years after the end of the war.

I had sold dozens upon dozens of extremely rare and expensive volumes to him (volumes which now, I had no doubt, would fetch an even greater sum when advertised and sold via *Vathek's Book-List*). In his latest typed communication, as unidiomatic as ever, he made it clear that he wished to offer for sale his entire library, since he was in dire need of funds because of his impending move to a bungalow situated out in Gallows Langley in Hertfordshire. The thought of what items he might still have in his possession (and of how cheaply they might now be obtained) flashed through my mind; I had delicious visions of row after row of shelving filled with well-kept volumes, of hundreds of choice items issued by the likes of Arkham House.

It is common practice with me to insist upon a list of at least fifty or so of the titles contained in a private library before I commit myself to making a personal visit to view and to make an offer (I loathe all time-wasting). However, the colonel had bought dozens of individual titles of the highly collectible, expensive type from me in the past in order—as he then un-grammatically put it—to "gaps fill up some in our library."

Would that I had followed my own tried-and-tested precautions!

We had arranged over the telephone for me to visit late in the morning; and I was struck by the breathless, wheezing quality of his speech and by his curt manner. He did not seem able to talk much at length, and so I had not insisted upon his giving me some verbal idea as to the current state of his book collection. I wondered if he had been a heavy smoker, and if the edges of the books in his possession were irrevocably browned by the tarry patina of decades of pipe or cigarette smoke. Sometimes even the tobacco stench takes months to dissipate from books contaminated in this inexcusable fashion.

Colonel Dowson still lived in the same flat on the second floor of one of those steep six-storeyed Victorian buildings on the Muswell Hill Broadway (the address, of course, was familiar to me), and, once I located his bell on the outside intercom in the porch (it read simply "The Colonel" in all upper-case letters but with the additional words "& Mrs." crossed out), he buzzed me in through the main front door following a brief exchange of words. It had been extremely difficult to find a spot to park my van within reasonable walking distance, and I thought—with some trepidation for the state of my lower spine—of the effort which might well lie in store for me: viz., the carrying of boxes of heavy books to my vehicle. I had already decided upon my maximum financial outlay: two thousand in banknotes and another two thousand by cheque; the latter only if absolutely necessary. I had no doubt that, in a month or two, I would recoup the investment and eventually make a reasonable profit on my bulk purchase.

As I climbed the winding staircase with its ornate iron-wrought balus-trade and marble steps, I wondered how long Colonel Dowson had been confined to this place and whether he would have adopted all the suspicious reserve which is supposed to be characteristic of the hermit. There seemed to be no lift in the building and it did not appear possible—if his breathless-ness over the telephone were a true indication of his health—that Colonel Dowson would have been capable even of descending the stairs; let alone of ascending them! He must have made arrangements for all provisions and so forth to be delivered and then carried up to him.

On the second-floor landing I saw that the door to his flat had been left slightly ajar, but nevertheless I paused on the threshold, knocked upon the peeling black paint of its panelled wood, and called out "Colonel?" through the gap. I heard the sound of something like a rusty bicycle approach the other side of the door, but there was no spoken reply to my query. Eventually, however, the door swung inwards and, beyond it, in the hallway, seated in a rickety wheelchair, was an emaciated ancient whom I supposed to be in his early eighties. A pure-white toothbrush moustache bristled above his upper lip, and his bald pate was heavily liver-spotted. He wore a pair of black rimmed NHS-issue spectacles, and the lenses were of such thickness that the eyes behind them were weirdly distorted. He must have been virtually blind. The unpleasantness of his wrinkled features was complemented by an expression of acute impatience. A long, slightly askew, hooked nose and obscenely age-enlarged ears provided the finishing touches to this ghastly portrait of death-defying decrepitude.

He was wheezing in a highly alarming manner.

"Ah, you must be the colonel," I said. "How nice to see you in the flesh. We arranged for me to come over today, just before lunchtime, so I might make an offer for your books."

Colonel Dowson did not reply, but looked me up and down with unconcealed distaste. He put a gnarled, arthritic forefinger to his lips, bumped the wheelchair around until it faced in the opposite direction, and hand-propelled his little chariot along the brown linoleum of the hallway towards the dark interior of his second-floor hermitage.

I followed after him, murmuring vapid pleasantries about the awfulness of this cold weather for the time of year. He made no response. Perhaps, I speculated, his brain was as infirm as his body and I might obtain the collection at a considerably reduced price.

I found myself in a dingy parlour with flock-red-velvet wallpaper and little furniture: always a terrible omen. There were no bookshelves in sight; nor were there any books. On a corner desk squatted an old, battered, manual typewriter. There was a lingering, persistent smell, though not born of tobacco—but as of something organic and rotten concealed close by. Two central-heating radiators continually gurgled as the hot water circulated inside them.

Colonel Dowson had positioned himself alongside an oxygen cylinder and was inhaling weakly from behind the clear plastic mask which he had placed over his nose and mouth. I heard the increased hissing of the gas whilst he adjusted a pressure valve. Finally, apparently refreshed—or re-plenished—he discovered there was now enough oxygen inside his lungs to speak to me.

"You are uncommonly tardy," he said. "I expected you ten minutes ago. You have caused me to delay my luncheon."

His speech had that peculiar combination of tone—wheedling and men-acing at the same time—which is often characteristic of the strong-willed when they are enfeebled by old age.

"I can only apologise," I said. "It was very difficult to find somewhere to park. I wonder if I might sit down? My back is playing me up."

"BLAST YOU AND YOUR STUPID BACK!" he shouted, although the rather shocking initial effect of this outburst was mitigated by its trailing off into a wheeze after the "stupid."

He coughed weakly and swallowed twice before absently waving his hand towards a frayed easy-chair to his right, impatiently motioning at me to be seated.

"Again, I apologise, Colonel," I said. "I don't wish to intrude or to take up more of your time than is necessary, so perhaps I might just see the books? I assure you I'll offer a fair price."

He utilised the oxygen cylinder again, on this occasion for a longer pe-riod. He seemed to be preparing himself for a short soliloquy, and it was finally delivered with little of the cultivation he had previously evinced. He was, I supposed, consciously getting down to business.

"A fair price? A fair price? I should think so too! It was my late wife who built up the collection. That's how she learnt our lingo. You probably don't realise what widows—or Oriental ones at least—are like. She was an obses-sive: and cruelly devious. Anyway, obsession was what killed her in the end. She read those books to me once my eyes were buggered up—that was thir-ty years ago—they started to go bad just after I married her. I should have expected it all along. Anyway, don't think I don't know about those books and their subject-matter. I demand that horror stories be realistic—and the more *informative,* the better. What I want are the facts, not imagination. I understand what real horror is, and I won't be fobbed off with the usual artsy and bohemian fictional claptrap which passes for it these days."

"Ah . . . well . . . yes . . . quite," I replied, intermittently, as he ex-pounded his personal philosophy of the horror genre. I wondered how long he had been cooped up in these rooms alone. His vapid loquaciousness indicated he had possibly not spoken to another living human being for weeks.

From what he had said I surmised that the purchases he had made in the past from *Vathek's Book-List* were made on behalf of his wife (probably, I supposed, as wedding anniversary or birthday presents). I doubted that a man like Colonel Dowson would have let his spouse anywhere near a chequebook. He probably gave her a weekly allowance which was sufficient for basic housekeeping and no more. Still, he was practically blind, so doubtless she'd managed to arrange things to her own liking on occasion.

Eventually I managed to turn matters back to the business in hand.

"And where," I said, "do you store the library now?"

"The collection's all in the 'book-room,'" he said. "I have to warn you, though, I'll want the whole amount in cash in advance. I can't be going along to the bank to cash cheques at my age and with my handicap. Too many bl—um—muggers around these days."

His head swivelled vaguely towards a doorway on the far side of the parlour, which I had assumed contained a kitchen area. The interior of this great beyond was obscured by one of those hanging screens of bead-strips which keep out flying insects, and which went out of fashion sometime in the late 1970s. Its gaudy design depicted a tropical jungle, and the idyllic scene (doubtless now unappreciated by the colonel himself) undulated gently in his overheated but draughty flat.

"It's the doorway on the left, NOT the one on the right. That one's my late wife's room," he said. It was closed off by white, heavy drapes hanging from a rail. There were several large black beetles crawling along the folds of the material.

I still harboured the hope that the "book-room" on the left would be a bibliophile's Aladdin's Cave.

The colonel took several further deep inhalations from his oxygen cylinder and then wheeled himself in the direction of the tropical barrier. I followed close behind and was soon within the *sanctum sanctorum*.

It was not a large room; scarcely more than an oversized larder, but the walls were lined on three sides with shelving—and what awaited me therein was bitter dregs and the disappointment of my recently raised hopes. A bare light bulb, suspended from a cord in the ceiling, revealed the degree of despoliation to which the "book-room" had been subjected by an earlier raider. A strong whiff of musty, decaying old books still remained to taunt me;

that odour which, to the non-reading public, is as unwelcome as halitosis at close quarters, and yet which, to a book-lover, is akin to the fragrance of roses in a summer garden.

"Nicholas Condor—perhaps you've heard of him?—came the other day," the colonel wheezed. "Still, I'm certain there's enough good stuff left to make your journey worthwhile. He assured me he didn't take very much of real worth away with him."

I tried to articulate a coherent response but managed only a half-stifled gurgle.

"Anyway, I'll leave you alone to make an estimate," he said, bumping his wheelchair around before disappearing behind the fake tropical-jungle.

I grimly surveyed what little remained upon the denuded shelves: a ratty and dusty complete set of Dornford Yates hardbacks, a few audiobook cassette editions of "Sapper," a wide selection of titles on Second World War military campaigns in the Far East, and an extensive variety of large-print biographies or memoirs, mostly of former servicemen.

Nicholas Condor had been extremely thorough.

On only the half-concealed bottom shelf was there anything of the slightest interest to me in my line of business, and these were all just extremely well-thumbed paperbacks. There were a handful of Panther editions from the 1970s by "Lovecraft & Derleth" [sic], Clark Ashton Smith, and Arthur Machen, also a few Tandem collections by Charles Birkin and R. Chetwynd-Hayes, two Sphere-issued titles by William Hope Hodgson, an inevitable early-1980s Corgi paperback reprint of Robert Bloch's *Psycho,* and half-a-dozen battered Fontana or Faber paperback horror and ghost story anthologies, including two edited by Rupert Alderman, and the only one edited by Sinclair Xavier. Lastly, however, there was an anthology edited by Victor Armstrong. At sight of the spine my breath came a little quicker. This final book bore the title *Unknown Nightmares.*

It appeared Condor had not been as thorough as I had first thought.

I fairly snatched this thick, yellowing-edged paperback off of the shelves to take a closer look at it. Published in 1996 by Maelström Books (an imprint of Jackson Publishing Ltd.), it was an item for which I had received several enquiries. The entire edition had been cancelled before it had gone to print and only a few advance reading copies had leaked into general circulation. I could not recall the exact reason for its sudden withdrawal, but it was certainly the sole item of any real value left in what remained of Colonel Dowson's—or, rather, his and Mrs. Dowson's—collection. I was still rather staggered that Condor had overlooked it. The cover (an uncredited piece of art heavily influenced by the style of Neil Harkness in his artwork for Charnel House) depicted the rotting face of a corpse with an interpenetrating background of dotted starlight in dissolving, surreal technicolour.

I turned to the contents page. It listed rarities such as "The Corpse-Brotherhood" by Edmund F. Bertrand, "The Mind of Midnight" by Ivan Gilman, "The Hideous Pleasures" by Henri Nisard, "Ego et Mater Tenebrarum Unum Sumus" by Veronica Plunkett, "Inside the Fungal Lobes" by Cesare Thodol, "The Dybbuk Pyramid" by Trefusis Vrolyck, "Teeth of White Static" by Joanna Wolski, and a tale entitled "The Interminable Abomination" by "X."

I flicked through the volume at random and arrived exactly at the page where "The Interminable Abomination" story began.

I glanced at the first line and then the next line, and then the one after that, and the words, which themselves seemed grotesquely disordered and unidiomatic, rapidly began working on my mind like an incantation. By the time I was only halfway through the initial paragraph, the page became the sole object of existence in the entire universe, blotting out all else. Reading the text was akin to falling into a night-black well of inconceivable depth—with one's own thoughts disintegrating the further one descended into its mystery.

The narrator told of being dead and buried but of slowly regaining self-awareness—and of the dreams a rotting brain is forced to dream. The tale gradually unveiled what really happens to sentience after one dies; that death is not always the end at all, but can be a doorway to the beginning of stupendously greater terrors undreamt of by the still-living. There were terrifying references to labyrinthine nests of necrophagous larvae infesting night-black coffins in the subterranean depths of cemeteries right across the globe. Here were unveiled the terrors of a larvae-riddled brain as it deliquesced in an eternal nightmare: destined, *post mortem,* to become a hopelessly insane, nightmare-tortured carcass. And the hellish cycle went on indefinitely via metempsychosis; the larvae pupated into beetles, carrying the cumulatively festering dreams inside them, emerged from underground and mated, and then burrowed back down, depositing their eggs in newly dead human brains, creating more and more larvae, and . . .

Suddenly I was dimly aware of the colonel wresting the book out from my hands and then his raised voice.

"YOU'LL PAY FOR THAT PARTICULAR BOOK BEFORE READ-ING IT!"

I was dumbfounded and still in shock after reading even that small portion of "The Interminable Abomination." My knees felt like water and a sheen of ice-cold sweat soaked my forehead. A wave of nausea swept over me and I felt a strong urge to vomit.

"Get a grip on yourself, man!" the colonel barked, indifferent to, or unaware of, my distress. "You daydream as much as an old sergeant-major of mine did—that is, until I arranged to have him chased for two miles by a saltwater crocodile through a swamp on Ramree Island!"

I staggered through into the parlour and then slumped into an armchair. My head lolled against a white lace antimacassar. The oppressive heat in the flat was overwhelming.

The colonel followed after me, apparently unsure as to how to react to my now-obvious distress. Getting no answer to his barked queries, he disappeared into another room.

A few moments later he reappeared with a dusty bottle of Hankey Bannister in his lap and fumblingly poured out a finger into a chipped, bone-china cup.

"Drink some of this," he said. "Works wonders."

After I'd drunk it there was a long pause. He took the opportunity to use his oxygen cylinder again, but his distorted, useless eyes were fixed on me the whole time. I had the distinct impression he thought I might be putting on an act.

"I must have given you quite a scare just now," he said, when he could breathe more easily again, "but the truth of the matter is that you've been daydreaming in there for well over half an hour. Couldn't make out what the devil was taking you so long. Anyway, let's get down to brass tacks. How much for the lot?"

It was still difficult to concentrate on what he was saying; however, I did feel myself recovering, at least partially. I wanted nothing more than to get out of his flat as soon as possible. My mind was in revolt against my experience in the "book-room," and I wondered whether I might in fact have been the victim of some kind of epileptic seizure. Even the thought of the value of that copy of *Unknown Nightmares* had been thrust to the back of my mind.

"I'm still not feeling well, Colonel," I said. "I'm going to have to leave now. I'll write to you about the books when I can think straight. I need to see a doctor."

"WHAT'S THAT?? LEAVE?? LEAVE!! Don't talk rot. You haven't even made an offer yet," he replied. The wheedling-cum-menacing tone was back in his voice. "Nothing wrong with you, damn it: just had a funny turn is all—a touch of the vapours. Don't be such a bloody fool. Stay and read the rest of that book if you like."

"Yet again, I can only apologise," I said. "I really must go. I'm feeling very ill."

I shakily got to my feet and wandered along the hallway towards the landing, keeping one hand against the wall to provide some support. Behind me, I could hear the colonel alternately wheezing and cursing.

"Come back here, you damn swindler! CROOK! SCOUNDREL! Don't you walk away from me while I'm talking to you! GET BACK HERE! THAT'S AN ORDER!"

I inadvertently slammed the front door behind me.

That afternoon I spent several hours in the Accident and Emergency ward of the nearest hospital—the Whittington on Highgate Hill. When I explained what had happened to me at the front desk, they seemed to think it quite possible I had suffered a kind of minor stroke, and a battery of tests was immediately performed upon me. In the end, however, they could find no evidence of brain haemorrhaging, nor any kind of microbe infection, and I was sent home with the recommendation I should have a further series of tests in a week or so to examine other possible physical or organic causes.

These further tests yielded no solutions to the mystery.

During this period I expected to be the recipient of irate, typed communications from the colonel, but he did not contact me at all.

I dismissed the sudden effect the story had had upon my health as some bizarre coincidence. But, as time passed, I was haunted each night by those dreams I was convinced a rotting, larvae-infested brain is forced to dream.

I was driven to discuss these events face-to-face, in confidence, with a young psychiatrist friend of mine (and subscriber to *Vathek's Book-List*), a certain Doctor Arnold, who recommended I start on a course of anti-depressants. He also made the following observations:

"Don't take this the wrong way," he said, "but I think it would actually be beneficial if you could locate another copy of that story. It appears to have acted as some kind of psychological trigger-mechanism. Best not to read it again, of course, at this point, but I'd like to take a look at it myself, as a preliminary measure. I might well be able to connect it, through psychoanalysis, with suppressed mental trauma from your childhood lurking deep in your unconscious mind. It should aid me in determining the exact nature of any complex. Eventually, when properly understood, the story will be divested of whatever hold you imagine it possesses over you. Tell me, were you ever locked in a cupboard under the stairs for bad behaviour as a boy?"

His last query seemed asinine, and I was reluctant to follow his other advice. But what else could I do?

Was what I had read in "The Interminable Abomination" really just a fictional account of larvae-infested corpses made aware, over and over again, *and in different bodies,* of their own dissolution—a *post mortem* insanity raising the infernal curtain to infinitely greater horrors? Did the dream spawn reality or did reality spawn the dream?

I simply had to dispel all such debilitating obsessions. No piece of fiction can have an effect like that on a reader in real life. But still I continued to ask myself the same question: *who was* its author? *Unknown Nightmares* had listed the tale only as being by "X," and I decided to contact the book's editor, Victor Armstrong.

Tracing Victor Armstrong proved to be no simple task. Maelström Books (and indeed Jackson Publishing Ltd.) had closed down almost a decade previously after its premises had mysteriously burnt to the ground following the (hastily withdrawn) publication of *Unknown Nightmares,* but I did manage to contact the publisher of Armstrong's last anthology (called *Blind Nightmares,* appropriately enough), issued merely half-a-dozen years ago by JAW Books. The publisher, Jacob Andrew Whitemoor, was extremely sympathetic (and happened to be a subscriber to *Vathek's Book-List*), but he told me the last he had heard of Armstrong was that he had decamped permanently to Mexico a few years ago and had now given up editing anthologies; furthermore, Armstrong expressly no longer wanted to have anything further whatsoever to do with weird and horror fiction, in all its various guises. Whitemoor, however, did—finally—give me the name of the hotel on La Calle de Bucareli in Mexico City which was Armstrong's last known contact address.

After three telephone calls to the hotel I finally managed to track him down to another place—the Café la Habana—which, apparently, he had made his regular haunt during afternoons and early evenings:

"Victor Armstrong?" I said.

A muffled pause, then a cry of:

"¡Señor Ingles, el telefono!"

"¿Quien es?" came the distant-sounding reply. "¿Lopez?"

"Perdón pero no lo sé señor. Un otro Ingles."

"Who is this?" a voice slightly slurred by excessive drinking eventually enquired in English.

In as concise a fashion as I was able, I explained why I wished to speak with him. After digesting the information he replied:

"No, I don't know who actually wrote the story. It was listed as being by 'X,' and therefore anonymous. Anyway, it must have been long out of copyright. The elderly woman who sent it to me at claimed she found it in some obscure Victorian periodical dating from the 1890s and transcribed it herself. Rather haphazardly."

"Who was the woman?" I asked.

"What was her name?—um—Dawson, I think."

"Not Dowson?"

"Yes, you're right, it was Dowson, not Dawson. Originally her surname was—apparently—'Mleen,' though. Some ex-pat Oriental lady. The wife of a half-mad, blind old sod of an English colonel, so I gather. He certainly was a character all right. Kept getting her to pass on complaints that my anthologies weren't gruesome or realistic enough."

"Did you read the story yourself?"

There was a pause. I heard him swallowing a drink filled with chinking ice cubes.

"Of course I read it—well, some of it: despite the fact she'd banged it out on an old manual typewriter. I don't publish stories without reading them first. Not unless they're written by Steve King."

The line was breaking up. I had another question:

"What did you make of what you'd read?"

"I was already over-budget, had a pressing deadline, desperately needed a royalty-free filler for the anthology, and I thought the idea, despite its deficiencies, was a pretty interesting one: that central conceit of a game of chess played in a nightmare between the author and the reader which————"

The line dropped out, but was re-established.

"——but anyway, publication of the book was taken out of my hands."

"That doesn't sound like the same story. The one I read was more *ghoulish* and, well, much more——I suppose——*Lovecraftian*."

I heard a distinctly audible groan down the line at my citing that particular adjective.

Then the line abruptly went dead.

Thereafter, despite numerous attempts on my part, Armstrong could never be persuaded to come back to the telephone to speak to me.

It proved impossible to obtain another copy of *Unknown Nightmares* on the open market. After making enquiries amongst all my other competitors in the book trade who specialised in weird/horror/fantasy/speculative fiction (which enquiries were met either with baffled amusement, pleas of ignorance, or a kind of 'in-the-know' disgust), I concluded that what few——if any——extant copies there were remaining of the anthology were now secreted away in private collections. I even put out a rushed "special supplement" of *Vathek's Book-List* featuring a front-page advertisement making it known I would pay the best price for a copy housed in any of the personal libraries of my subscribers. ABE Books and the other online book retailers were also consulted by me, but similarly to no avail. Finally I turned to the British Library in the hope that a file copy had been deposited (as was customary with reputable publishers) for the purposes of establishing copyright. After much to-and-froing I was advised their copy had been stolen several years earlier (or, rather, was suspected of having been stolen) by a notoriously light-fingered scholar, one they would not identify——but since insane and then deceased——who was rumoured to have had sordid connections to another older person they would not name, a sometime contributor to the *Necrophile*——that infamous, banned magazine published briefly in the United States during the 1950s.

The younger, nameless, light-fingered scholar's private library had been left to the Sternburg Institute Library in Bloomsbury. I made an appointment there on the basis of undertaking some research, but found, whilst on the premises, that they disavowed being in possession of *Unknown Nightmares*. Instead, a security guard was summoned and ushered me out after I mentioned to a librarian the likelihood that any copy of the anthology in their possession had actually been stolen from the British Library and was not, therefore, legally their property.

Since my own nightmarish experiences in reading only a fraction of the story "The Interminable Abomination," it was not difficult for me to understand how a tangled web of intrigue, evasion, denial, secrecy, and even outright fear had been weaved around the anthology in which it had last appeared.

Readers may wonder about the very first publication of the story, but my efforts to track it down via this method proved equally frustrating—though in a more prosaic fashion. Of the innumerable journals and periodicals containing fiction published during the 1890s only a percentage have survived into the modern era, and of that number an even smaller proportion have been transferred to microfilm or digitised. The tale having been published pseudonymously as "X" was a further barrier (since X was often used by printers in lieu of "anonymous"), as was the possibility that "The Interminable Abomination" may not even have been the story's original title. Certainly, I could find no trace of its existence at the Colindale Newspaper Archives or in any other such records offices.

The nightmares were getting worse. I frequently had to resort to a mixture of morphine and Dexedrine in order to keep myself going. My health, both bodily and mentally, was deteriorating at an alarming rate. Doctor Arnold wanted me to check into his private "psychiatric welfare centre," The Glanville Home, for observation and treatment, but I declined his offer.

There was nothing for it but to approach the colonel again. Now I knew his late wife had been instrumental in bringing "The Interminable Abomination" to Victor Armstrong's attention in the first instance, it seemed logical that it was actually the colonel who knew more about this whole ghastly affair than anyone else. He was also the only person who was still definitely in possession of a copy of *Unknown Nightmares*. Perhaps he even owned a copy of the original 1890s periodical in which "The Interminable Abomination" had first appeared. After all, Armstrong had told me it was the colonel's Oriental wife who had "haphazardly" transcribed the thing from its first publication.

I could trace no telephone number and therefore, in desperation, wrote him a letter of grovelling apology, asking for another opportunity to examine what remained of his book collection. This time, so I assured him, I could make a definite commitment to pay him very handsomely indeed—in cash—on the spot. I would even make an extra reimbursement to him for my "unforgivably rude behaviour" on the last occasion we had met. I hoped that a kindly friend or neighbour would read it aloud to the blind old fascist swine.

My letter must have been forwarded on by Royal Mail to the colonel, who, it transpired, had already quit his Muswell Hill eyrie in order to relocate to sheltered accommodation in Hertfordshire. The perfunctory, scarcely legible handwritten reply contained no more than instructions detailing how to find (on foot from the nearest railway station) the bungalow in which he now dwelt and the time and date at which it would be convenient to him for me to make my visit. Doubtless he had dictated the reply and had someone write it down on his behalf, as I'd hoped he would.

Two days later, just after 11 A.M., following a train journey of half-an-hour or so, I disembarked from the stopping service I had caught at London Euston and stepped out onto the platform of Gallows Langley station in the South Hertfordshire countryside. It had been continuously pouring with rain all morning in London's endless brick-and-concrete labyrinth. And now, as if the deluge had followed me here, I saw, in the western distance, lushly green, open fields rising up along the side of a valley, and Hertfordshire's wider, rural skies also churning with a Stygian mass of seething black-and-grey storm clouds. Dotted here and there one could spot flocks of dirty sheep grazing, all seemingly utterly oblivious to the elements.

I was feverish and running a temperature. I could not face the prospect of trekking on foot through dripping arcades of trees and uphill lanes, as the written directions demanded, in order to reach the colonel's bungalow.

Just outside the railway station's entrance porch and halfway up a grassy bank was a small wooden cabin. Above a front window-cum-hatch was a cheaply printed commercial sign reading "Gallows Taxies [*sic*]: We Won't Hang About." I went up to the hatch and knocked on the raindrop-splattered glass. A blurry face momentarily appeared behind the pane on which a handwritten note had been stuck up on the other side saying "back in 5 mins." Then a side door opened and the owner emerged, wearing a sou'-wester, mackintosh, and wellington boots, all of a matching shade of truly garish yellow.

"Down there!" he said, pointing to the rusting pile of metal parked up on the kerb—which deathtrap he appeared to be indicating was the taxi.

The thing was some sort of model surviving from the 1970s (I have no interest in the make of motorcars), but I wondered if he was still running this antique wreck in order to save paying the full road-tax.

Once I was ensconced in the back seat, I felt even clammier than before, and my fever had appreciably worsened. I had also developed a hideous migraine.

"Where to, mate?" the driver said without turning around.

I wordlessly passed to him, over his shoulder, the written directions which the colonel had sent to me.

He studied them momentarily and then said:

"These directions are all wrong. Whoever wrote these would have sent you on foot round the long way. But righto, I'll get you there in a jiffy."

The bungalow proved to be at the end of an unmarked but gated side-turning off a meandering country lane hemmed in on both sides by rows of dripping hornbeam trees. The lane had snaked up the entire side of the valley, and rivulets of rainwater ran down ditches on both sides of the slightly raised, puddle-pitted surface of the tarmac. The taxi had struggled to make the steep ascent, but my driver evinced not a word of protest about the hazardous driving conditions. Perhaps driving a deathtrap makes one indifferent to such lesser dangers. I dreaded to imagine the consequences had I attempted to make the journey myself on foot as the colonel had instructed. When the taxi driver dropped me off I provided a generous tip along with his stated fare, although he merely tipped his sou'-wester without ever turning around, let alone expressing thanks, and seemed eager to be on his way.

Such was my confused state of mind that I quite forgot to tell him to return in half-an-hour and wait here to collect me.

As I have said, the bungalow was situated at the end of a gated side-turning; and a single stile along the path prevented anything other than pedestrian access. There was no sign to indicate ownership or even the address.

The bungalow itself was a red-brick construction of no great distinctiveness, save for an enormous mass of ivy which had been allowed to engulf almost the whole of the exterior apart from the windows. Dotted around on the vast, overgrown front lawn were a multitude of stone objects which, in the gloom, and at first glance, I took to be the remaining foundations of a former extensive construction, one imperfectly razed at ground-level.

My feverishness was turning into a palsy. My head seemed to be splitting.

I looked for a doorbell or knocker and discovered instead an old hand-bell fixed and mounted vertically on the adjacent right-hand wall, with a length of string attached to the clapper.

I rang the bell several times, the noise piercing through the background hiss of the heavy rain which still continued to fall.

The door to the bungalow swung open and I nearly fell through it, staggering inside.

When next I was fully conscious of my surroundings I found myself slumped in the same armchair—with its white lace antimacassar—from the colonel's flat in Muswell Hill. So, too, the same oppressive heat and foul background smell; as of something rotten having been concealed somewhere close at hand. Momentarily I wondered if I might actually be back in his previous residence, and if all the intervening events since had been nothing but a nightmare brought on by "The Interminable Abomination." But I *was* inside a bungalow; of that there could be no doubt. The colonel was sitting in his wheelchair facing me, drawing heavily from the oxygen mask on his face and adjusting the pressure valve on the cylinder. Behind him was a door to another room. It was closed off by the familiar white drapes hanging from a rail—and the black beetles which I had seen upon it the last time had now considerably multiplied in number. The interior of the bungalow had become dark and the colonel had lit table lamps on opposite sides of his living quarters; for my benefit rather than his, I supposed. There were a number of cardboard boxes still unpacked, a couple of bulky, unpacked tea-chests, and, atop a small corner desk, there lurked the same old manual typewriter with a sheet of blank paper already inserted.

"Awake, are you?" he said, after taking off the mask. "But still feeling poorly, I suppose? Don't have another attack of the vapours. We've yet to conclude our unfinished business. I know why you're here—and it's not to buy my remaining books; it's because you want that particular story. And I want you to have it."

I felt worse than ever at the realisation that he knew, as well as I, the cause of my physical and mental deterioration.

"I'll give you six thousand pounds—cash," I said, taking out a hefty, somewhat damp packet from my raincoat. "For both *Unknown Nightmares* and for the magazine in which the original version appeared."

He rolled his wheelchair across the carpet, paused at one of the tea-chests, fumbled around inside, and drew out from its depths a mouldering

Victorian periodical enclosed in a bright-yellow plastic folder and the bulky copy of *Unknown Nightmares*.

We exchanged goods.

He really couldn't tell the difference. What I had given him was not six thousand pounds; it was fake—Monopoly money.

But then, one by one, he began tearing up the false banknotes with his arthritic and gnarled fingers, chuckling obscenely as he did so.

"I imagine that you'd like to sit here and read through both of those things, but—all in good time," he said.

His words seemed to be coming from a great distance away. His voice was little more than a dim echo. And had the room become appreciably darker? It could not still be early afternoon; it must now be the middle of the night.

"Yes, it was the missus who rediscovered that damned thing by 'X' in that old Victorian magazine, and, yes, she sent it to Armstrong after 'transcribing' it herself. But it's never the same story when read twice: it changes constantly and takes more and more of the life from its readers. You know, by the end the doctors told me her brain was so rotted and so acidic that parts of it actually began leaking from her skull, dribbling in a yellow putrescence out of her ears and her nostrils. Nevertheless, it was amazing how lucid she appeared to be at the very end. The doctors said that's often the way in the final hours before death with patients who've suffered massive brain-damage and the like—terminal lucidity, they call it. Finally, I told them to turn off the damn life-support: and that was the only thing still keeping her alive. Not that that was the end of it. Not by a long chalk."

"But WHO was the original author, this 'X'?" I managed to gasp. "Someone struck entirely from the records?"

"How the devil would I know? Maybe it's 'The Interminable Abomination' that's the author—*or the authors*. The last thing my wife would say to me on that point—though she must have gone insane by then, despite her apparent lucidity—was to babble some fanciful rot about *an irresistibly horrible, aeons-old continuum*. And she still babbles on about it even now. Useless."

The following phrase came back to haunt me: *"he was notorious for his obsession with horrors; the ghastlier the better. It seemed he could not get enough of them."*

Had he himself been mentally and physically damaged after hearing the story read aloud and yet had escaped the worst of its effects through not being able to read it for himself? Although the room was beginning to turn on its axis, my thoughts felt clearer than they had ever been; as if I had finally recovered my sanity—but a sanity which was now infinitely horrible.

Something warm and slimy began oozing out of my nose and ears, and I found myself looking over at the corner desk to the manual typewriter with its waiting sheet of blank paper. I felt compelled towards the machine in order to write.

"Read the stuff I've given you first," he said. "That's what you came for. Then whisper to me, one page at a time, as you write your own version. Start at the beginning. Type it up just as it really happened. First-person singular is always best. And you must give me only the facts. I don't want any products of your imagination. It's cowardice to create a horror which avoids stark reality."

The Ominous Revival
of Certain Old Customs

n the far reaches of Thool Valley, some five miles distant from the more southerly town of Gallows Langley, lies the ancient hamlet of Reapers End. The place is a collection of two dozen mediaeval cottages flanked on the east side by cornfields and turnip patches gradually sloping uphill, and on the west side by a meandering, sluggish tributary of the River Thool. Although both the 1962 discovery (made during roadworks that year) of a Roman villa just outside Reapers End—and the site's subsequent excavation a year later—drew considerable archaeological interest, on only one other occasion has the hamlet received much attention: in July 1986, during the course of some interior renovations, there was another such chance, important discovery. It was made in one of the houses in a row of gabled buildings, constructed a few years before the Reformation.

The man who owned this house, Antony Harwood, a professional electronics engineer, had accidentally discovered a curious series of long-forgotten wall-paintings hidden therein. It was not long after he had inherited the property from a recently deceased elderly aunt. The disinterment of the pre-Reformation wall-paintings occurred while Harwood was undertaking DIY work during the course of a two-week annual holiday. The old building was in constant need of close attention, given its great age, and, rather than go to the expense of hiring workmen, Harwood boldly decided to tackle the job himself. The major part of the work was the removal of a section of wooden wall-panelling afflicted with dry-rot and which must have stood for centuries. He had found this surprisingly easy to achieve, having familiarised himself with the procedure beforehand. He already possessed most of the tools required for the purpose and had no qualms about damaging the wood-panelling. Dry-rot had affected it to the extent that it was almost worthless, and useful only for firewood.

It was when he had removed the panelling and stripped away several layers of wallpaper that he discovered an innermost protective linen sheet: behind this final barrier were the paintings, directly wrought upon white plaster covering the walls. Crude in their execution, with their strange colours greatly faded, the paintings depicted what the one expert (from the British Museum, no less) who was briefly allowed to examine them interpreted as "symbolic representations detailing scenes from some witchcraft rite associated with a sacrificial harvest associated with the faerie folk." This expert also professed himself perplexed by the anachronistic depiction of certain figures in the tableaux; several of them appeared to belong to a period postdating that during which the paintings had been first created. Although they must surely have been later "pastiche" interpolations, such was the similar technique that all the renderings could easily have been regarded as the work of the same hand.

In the days following this discovery, Harwood's (at first) merely bemused interest in the long-hidden wall-paintings appeared to escalate to the level of some kind of obsessive mania. Although due to return in less than a week to his employment as an electronics engineer at Broadcasting House in London, he instead abruptly resigned his position. The expert from the British Museum, who was eager to photograph the wall-paintings and to bring in other experts to assist in his research, was curtly rebuffed in all his attempts to communicate with Harwood further concerning the matter, culminating in the latter even disconnecting his telephone.

Harwood would spend hours sitting in front of the paintings, unable to remove his gaze from the nebulous tableaux depicted on the walls and mesmerised by its greatly faded yet still unearthly colours. When daylight ended, he took to lighting candles in order to continue his vigil. During this period he became a complete recluse. It was rumoured that he had become quite ill. Delivery vans were occasionally seen supplying groceries and other essentials on a weekly basis, though these also eventually included one or two additional deliveries of electrical goods, which seemed to indicate Harwood had not lost all interest in some of the technical aspects of his former profession.

Only on two subsequent occasions was he seen outside the house, and both times on the 28th of September. During the afternoon of that day, he was noticed awkwardly erecting a six- or seven-foot-high transmission mast upon the roof of his house; he was easily recognisable by his mane of silver hair and spectacles. He was then spotted putting up handwritten fliers on each of the telephone poles lining the high street of Reapers End, zigzagging his way around in a seemingly drunken fashion.

I have previously stated that Reapers End rarely garnered much attention; and the claim is essentially true—when taken in its wider sense. Locally, however, the hamlet had long been the subject of fearful rumours and persistent innuendo, particularly amongst the traditionalist-minded residents of Hallam Hardwick, the old Victorian market-town on the hill, scarcely a mile distant, where mistrust of those who dwelt in Reapers End had been faithfully handed down from generation to generation on account of the hamlet's residents reputedly having the power of second sight. Perhaps this mistrust had its roots in the claim that, during the nine days of 1553, when the country was divided over the struggle between Lady Jane Grey and Queen Mary Tudor for the Crown, the people of Reapers End had bewilderingly declared themselves the loyal subjects of "Albions olde trew Mothere, the longe-fyngr'd Quene of Faeries."

One can easily imagine how the elder residents of Hallam Hardwick regarded the 1986 discovery of the bizarre wall-paintings in Reapers End, and the matter was the talk for days of all the greybeards who cluster together in one of Hallam's centuries-old quartet of taverns in order to quaff their evening ale, to smoke their pipes or cigarettes, and to chuckle at the scientific ignorance of their grandsons and granddaughters. In Reapers End, so it was said by the Hallam folk, the secretive residents spent night after night stuck in front of their television sets; probably watching those notorious "video nasties" which sensible Christian folk like Mary Whitehouse had tried to ban. Old Bert, one of the greybeards, swore that, on the very night of the 30th of September, after a pint or two too many, he'd been confused trying to find his way home from the pub, had taken a wrong turn, wound up staggering through the hamlet close to midnight and, with "no word of a lie" as he put it, saw the eerie flickering lights of television screens through the lace-curtained windows and heard what he was absolutely sure was the sound of crazed screaming hailing from within each and every one of those damned cottages.

Two days after Old Bert had found himself wandering in a drunken stupor through Reapers End, an amateur television enthusiast, Priam Stanhope, had moored his narrowboat, named the *Beagle,* alongside the bank which sloped down to the River Thool from the imposing Georgian structure of the Egremont Arms pub situated on the outskirts of the hamlet. While travelling along the Grand Union Canal, he had picked up a bizarre signal from the mast antenna perched atop the roof of his narrowboat. The broadcast was initially grainy and indistinct, but appeared to be the UHF test pattern of some pirate television station operating somewhere in the region. Stanhope had travelled over a great extent of the inland waterways network, and when he slipped from one regional broadcast area into another he eagerly consulted the latest television guides in order to note variations in the scheduled programming.

During breaks to his journey, at locks, or to moor up, he would endeavour to fine-tune the frequency (located at around 721 MHz) on which this freshly discovered pirate station was broadcast. He twiddled the dial back and forth on his small portable television set in order to improve the reception and went up top to adjust the outside aerial mast. The farther north he travelled up the canal, the greater the improvement in the picture being transmitted, until, after an hour or so, to his disappointment, it had disappeared abruptly, presumably shut off at source, to be replaced by the buzzing snow of electronic static.

Eventually, he found himself motoring along the calm, shallow, narrow waters of the almost impassable Thool River, beneath the iron-wrought Victorian Thool Bridge, until he was forced to come to a final halt at an improvised mooring beside a mass of willows. It would have been perilous to attempt to proceed farther; the hull had already bumped against the river bed several times and the profusion of weeds threatened to tangle up his propeller. This stretch of the river was clearly impassable.

The test card, thought Stanhope, had been freakishly strange. Far from the usual Phillips PM5544 pattern, this one displayed, in vertical strips, what seemed to be genuinely negative, impossible colours—not merely their complementary equivalents. A horizontal bar across the middle read "Experimental Test Transmission." The test card appeared to have been purposely designed in order to ensnare the curious; for, after just a few moments, Stanhope felt hypnotised. Even the music accompanying the test card had been outlandish and mesmeric; a sort of high-pitched tune repeated on a cycle every thirty seconds or so—more akin to chimes than anything else.

Stanhope was intensely intrigued by the unexplained broadcast, and resolved to spend some time moored in Reapers End in order to investigate the matter further and to see whether he might pick up the broadcast once again on his portable television set. He was one of those enthusiasts who, having retired from employment, allow their hobby to occupy all their attention thereafter. He did not see the irony that, despite cruising along the canals of the beautiful English countryside, he was still much more interested in watching television than in observing the landscape around him. He also did not see that he might just as well have remained in his lonely one-bedroom flat up in Hampstead Village, doing what he had done every single night for those same thirty years after coming home from the office: rotting in front of a television screen.

If he was, he thought, to moor at this spot he would have to seek permission from the owner of the stretch of property adjoining the canal; presumably the landlord of the Egremont Arms pub. He made his way up the grassy bank to the imposing whitewashed Georgian edifice—its long terrace festooned with small corn dollies—only to discover, when reaching the entrance, that it closed for the afternoon at 3 P.M. sharp. It was now 4 P.M. Stanhope had failed to reckon with the licensing laws. However, a sign indicated the pub would welcome customers again from 6 P.M. onwards. He tried knocking anyway, but there was no answer, and so he returned to the narrowboat, jotted down a brief note explaining his having moored at the bottom of the pub's garden due to a "mechanical emergency," went back up the bank, and slipped the piece of paper into the letterbox on the entrance door. Satisfied he had done all he could reasonably be expected to do in the circumstances, he decided to stroll around the hamlet of Reapers End. He had been confined to his narrowboat for most of the last few days, save for those occasions when he'd worked the locks, and welcomed the chance to take some exercise.

What first struck him about the hamlet was the preponderance of ravens cawing from its trees. It seemed as if almost every one of these trees harboured nests cobbled together by the ravens from branches and twigs— large, strangely grotesque constructions in the shape of inverted cones. The birds fluttered from tree to tree, the black shadows of their wings standing out starkly against the whitish and dull expanse of low cloud which blanketed the late afternoon sky. He had the unnerving impression that they were keeping tabs on him as he slowly made his way along the single street which ran the length of Reapers End.

Between the mediaeval cottages dotted along the road, he caught sight of the cornfields beyond, consisting mostly of farmland. In the far distance there were several child-sized figures wearing straw hats standing in the open, none of them more than five feet tall, but all perfectly still; again, Stanhope had the impression he was being watched. One of the figures was slightly slumped over to one side, as if its back were crooked. Stanhope stood there for several moments, raised his arm, and waved at one of them, hoping for a response. None of them moved at all. Shrugging his shoulders, he wandered farther along the street until he came to a cottage with a large front garden and, peering through the slated wooden gate, the mystery of his being ignored was solved.

Standing in the middle of the garden, propped up by a wooden pole, was a particularly ugly-looking, shrunken scarecrow. The thing had been dressed in old clothes, gloves, muddy boots, and a dirt-speckled tweed cap. A tightly fitting linen bag covered its oval-shaped, flattened head.

Stanhope could not look at the ghastly apparition without feeling a sense of revulsion, and he was glad that the similar figures he'd seen in the field—which he supposed also to be scarecrows—had been too far away for him to discern quite as clearly as those which were close to hand. What was the purpose of these things? To keep the ravens off at harvest time? But weren't ravens carrion birds?

It did not take him long, however, as he passed more deeply into the hamlet of Reapers End, to discover that every single garden boasted one of these child-sized scarecrows: of course they differed somewhat in their construction and apparel but, nevertheless, each were gloved and each had linen bags over their misshapen heads.

Such was Stanhope's unease at the repeated sight of those alarming scarecrows in the gardens that he passed several telephone poles before eventually noticing one of the handwritten fliers which had been tacked with a pin to all of them.

"Reclaim your Heritage. Return of the Horkey Festival. Tune your Telly at Midnight to 721.25 MHz. Friday the 30th of September," it urged in a clumsily written script.

Two days ago!

Stanhope stuffed the flier into his jacket pocket. Would the broadcast be repeated? What did it contain? As he mulled over these questions, he caught sight of someone watching him from the attic window of the last house in a row of gabled buildings. Whoever it was wore a wide-brimmed

straw hat, frayed at the edges and with several gaping holes in its woven surface. The face was not visible, being entirely lost in shadow. Stanhope stood
there for a while, mimicking the scrutiny of the faceless watcher, and the
thing's small stature and complete stillness convinced him that it, too, was
one of the half-sized scarecrows. Stanhope waved as he had done before—
though expecting no response—and, of course, none was forthcoming. Curiosity was now beginning to blunt the sharp edge of the growing trepidation which he felt and, when he saw that the front door to the house had
been left open, he began to advance up the pathway across the garden towards the entrance. He had not gone more than three paces when a little,
grey-furred, mongrel dog appeared, slowly advanced towards him as if to
block his advance, and then began barking in a curiously strangled tone. After a few moments more of this stand-off, the dog raced towards him,
changed direction at the last instant, rounded Stanhope, and then ran off
across the street, making its way towards a nearby wooden footbridge
which spanned the narrow, weed-infested tributary.

Stanhope proceeded up the path, stood in the doorway, and called out:

"Hello, anyone at home? The door's open. I require assistance."

Then he cried out:

"Your pet dog's escaped, you know. The fellow seems to have run off."

No answer was forthcoming. From somewhere deeper within the house
he could hear the stately ticking of a grandfather clock as its pendulum se-
dately swung back and forth.

After a minute or so, Stanhope slowly wandered along the short hallway and found himself gazing into the front parlour. He could not tell if it
were in a state of unusual disarray or whether the owner simply happened
to be extremely untidy. The sight of the condition of the television set gave
him cause for alarm. Its screen had been broken; someone had smashed the
device and then stuffed the insides with sheaves of corn. The perpetrator
must have cut himself in the process, for the sheaves were dappled with
what looked like dried blood. Beneath the broken television set, on a lower
shelf of the same cabinet, Stanhope spotted an undamaged Panasonic VHS
front-loading video recorder. A possibility occurred to him and, unable to
resist its prompting, he crossed the room and pushed the eject button. With
a loud mechanical whir, the machine disgorged a videocassette. Written in
Biro, on the tape's side-label, was scrawled the following: "Horkey Time,
30/9/86."

He had the absurd idea that he would next hear a noise coming from upstairs, the clump of boots attached to fake legs which were not familiar with the act of walking, and then the rustling of straw or hay stuffed into old clothes shifting in lieu of bone, muscle, and flesh, as if something were clumsily descending the flight of stairs in the hallway: but all that Stanhope actually heard was the continued, slow, metronomic rhythm of the unseen grandfather clock.

This thought, however, was enough to hasten his departure, even if it was not enough to cause him to leave the videocassette behind.

He tried knocking on doors and ringing the doorbells of several cottages and houses situated alongside the single street which wound through Reapers End, but all his summonses went unanswered. Perhaps, he thought, he might learn more when the Egremont Arms reopened. It was now only ten minutes before six, and not long to wait. In any case, there seemed to be an excellent chance that the tape he had in his possession would offer some insight into the nature of the pirate broadcast which had been transmitted two days earlier.

As Stanhope walked back the way he'd came, the cawing of the ravens appeared even more frantic than before, and when he passed by the farmlands he was half-convinced that the shrunken scarecrows with linen bags over their heads were not in exactly the same place as when he had glimpsed them previously; surely someone had been moving them around as a prank, uprooting their frames, and then repositioning them closer to the hamlet itself? Even those lolling in deck chairs in the gardens did not seem to be in precisely their former attitudes; it was as if their limbs had been subtly adjusted. Some person, or more likely a group of persons, perhaps a pack of local children, doubtless enjoyed playing tricks upon visitors to the hamlet. Perhaps it was all part of the "Horkey Time" mentioned in the flier, whatever the devil that might be, but, in any case, it was definitely high time that the ominous revival of certain old customs was stamped out. Once he gained entrance to the pub, he would use its public payphone and advise the local constabulary. If a pack of children were responsible, then their larks had tipped over into vandalising private property; and if grown adults were responsible, they needed to be caught and locked up.

*   *   *

The Egremont Arms had been opened on time, for Stanhope's wristwatch showed it to be just after 6 P.M., and the entrance door had been left ajar. However, when he wandered inside he found the whole pub deserted. Rather than any human customers, there were instead half-a-dozen of the same type of dwarfish scarecrows he'd seen previously, complete with the same linen bags over their oval-shaped heads, and all propped up in various positions; some seated at the bar counter and some seated at tables. He discovered the note he'd left earlier on one of these tables; someone had torn it into pieces and then deposited the fragments into an empty pint glass. He found the public payphone easily enough, but a sign had been hung onto it stating "Out of Order"; and when he lifted the receiver and put it to his ear there was no dial tone.

"I tell you, the police didn't want to know," said Old Bert, who was already into his third pint despite his arriving half an hour ago and it being only just after 7 P.M. As he was a pensioner, he kept to a strict budget when it came to his boozing, but tonight he seemed determined to drink a skinful as quickly as he was able. The other ancients sitting at the table behind the larger of the two bowed front windows of the Olde Queen's Arms in the high street of Hallam Hardwick's old quarter smirked to themselves and nudged one another in the ribs. It was a picturesque location; across the way there loomed the towering spire of St. Margaret's church, rising high above the red-tiled rooftops.

Ever since his peculiar experience two days earlier, Old Bert had refused to let the matter drop; he'd had to come out tonight to the pub to hold court—his wife had threatened to brain him with a saucepan unless he cleared off and gave her a little peace and quiet. Her "nerves," she said, couldn't stand it. Well, he thought, if she drove him out, he'd jolly well have a good time.

"And what happened, then, Bert? Didn't they investigate?" said Charlie-Boy (a mere lad of fifty-seven) as he rolled a Rizla paper around a slim core of Golden Virginia tobacco and made a cigarette.

Old Bert pulled at the grey-white whiskers below the left side of his mouth, adjusted the bulldog pipe hanging from the other side, took another gulp of his ale, and exclaimed:

"Did they hell! They told me I shouldn't get mixed up with Reapers End business; told me it's Degabaston-owned land and that during Horkey Time harmless japes are to be expected!"

Three or four of the other customers in the pub, overhearing mention of the name "Degabaston," seemed to shift uneasily in their chairs, for the now-derelict Thool Abbey in Gallows Langley lies scarcely five miles from Hallam Hardwick, and Hallam folk possess long memories of Thool Abbey's rumoured association with witchcraft **and** its evil reputation had cast a long, not-yet-vanished shadow across the whole of the valley.

"Well, what are you going to do about it, eh, Bert?" said Charlie-Boy, puffing away on his roll-up.

"I've a pocket camera, here, see? A Canon Sure Shot. Built-in flashbulb. There are ten frames still left on the roll of film. Soon as I've had a few more pints, I'll go down to bloody Reapers, take some photos, and sell them to the *Thool Gazette*. An exclusive, like. They should be worth a fair few bob, I reckon. What do you all think of that?" Old Bert chuckled.

"Wasn't that rag owned by a Yank, Lord Zeb De Gabiston—and wasn't he related to that same *Degabaston* lot?" enquired Rob-the-Gob, who scarcely ever said anything at all; hence his nickname.

One of the other customers, who had shifted uneasily at the first mention of that name, now sank his pint at the second mention, got up, and made for the exit, mumbling something about having a previous engagement.

"Come off it. That was all of thirty years ago. I'll 'ave another pint over here, thanks," said Old Bert, gesturing to the barmaid.

Two more pints of ale later, around an hour after sunset, and Old Bert was wending his way alone down the hill which runs for around half-a-mile from the old quarter of Hallam Hardwick to the outskirts of Reapers End. In the darkness to his left, beyond the low stone wall, he could just about make out the expanse of Thoolbridge Park, the gloom punctuated by pools of yellow light emitted from the old Victorian streetlamps which periodically lined its leafy footpaths. The closer, however, he drew to the hamlet, the less effective seemed to be the Dutch courage which had led to his boastfulness back at the Olde Queen's Arms. The others had attempted to talk him out of his plan, but Old Bert had felt bound to carry the thing through so as not to lose face, though when he finally found himself standing in front of the old, rotten wooden sign marking the boundary of the hamlet—the sign which read "Reapers End"—he found himself much less inclined to go any farther.

He didn't doubt personally that the screaming he had heard two days earlier had been real—or had seemed to be real—but, after all, it was true he'd drunk more than his usual limit that evening. If the police were inclined to make nothing of his concerns, why should he interfere again? Blimey, he thought, he was also a little muddled tonight. Perhaps he would think it over again while squeezing in another pint at the Egremont Arms; though, of course, he'd not be able to breathe a word of his having paid that hostelry a visit if he ever wanted to hold his head up in any of the quartet of familiar pubs up in Old Hallam.

When Old Bert reached the entrance to the place he was confused as to whether it was actually open for business. The lights were not on, but he could make out what he thought were a handful of oddly immobile figures both seated at tables and seated at the bar counter within the premises. They looked oddly undersized, not like any of the usual scarecrows Old Bert had seen in these parts. This peculiar sight was, in itself, more than enough to deter him and give him an excuse to retreat back whence he'd came, especially during Horkey Time, and he was on the verge of fleeing when he heard a sound coming from his left, originating farther down the grassy slope which terminated at the waters of the Thool River tributary. It was a weird sort of high-pitched chiming. From what he could see in the murk, there seemed to be a narrowboat moored up alongside the bank; the lights were on in the cabin and the strange noise was coming from there.

Old Bert, despite his better judgement, found the sound curiously hypnotic and found himself wandering down the slope towards its source.

"Who's there?" said Priam Stanhope as he heard two footsteps on the standing deck outside. He paused the playback of the video cassette which he earlier taken from the old gabled house, leaving the television set displaying the flickering image of the pirate test card pattern and stilling the accompanying, high-pitched tune on the soundtrack. Damn! He'd scarcely put the tape marked "Horkey Time 30/9/86" into his video player and had seen no more than the prelude to the actual midnight broadcast itself, when he had been rudely interrupted.

Perhaps, he thought, it was the owner of the tape coming to reclaim his stolen property. The memory of that horrid attic-dweller came back to him;

the thing of rags and straw with the linen head and blank face—was it now able to stalk abroad in the absence of daylight? For a moment he held his breath.

"Who's there? Who's there, I said!" Stanhope exclaimed.

"It's only Old Bert, sir," a somewhat slurred voice replied. "Down from Hallam."

Stanhope opened the small aft door leading to the standing deck.

Outside was a wizened old fellow, most of whose facial features were obscured by a bushy grey-white beard. A frayed tweed cap was perched on his head. In one hand he clutched a pocket camera.

"Sorry to trouble you, sir," Old Bert said. "Having a bit of trouble finding the landlord up at the pub. Not from around here, are you? Just visiting?"

"No, I'm not from 'around here,' as you put it," Stanhope replied, "and I'm extremely busy, so kindly state your business or leave me alone."

Typical London-type, Old Bert thought, a toffee-nosed, wealthy, "superior" snob. Not that Old Bert was prejudiced—not all London-types, he knew, were born-and-bred Londoners. Often, countryfolk who spent too much time there gave themselves the same airs. Alas, they were now to be found across the whole English countryside. Ruining it, for the most part, with their continual "improvements" to things which didn't need fixing in the first place. Old Bert grunted, turned on his heels—somewhat unsteadily, it must be said—and made to leave.

"Wait a minute," Stanhope said. "Come back here. What do you know about all those horrible child-sized scarecrows? Is it some sort of prank? If so, it's gone too far. Someone's even been going inside people's homes and committing acts of vandalism. You're not involved with all that, are you?"

Old Bert snapped. London-types! he thought. Always accusing!

"Get stuffed. We have nowt to do with Horkey Time up at Hallam, Mr. Hoity-Toity—so don't ask me," Old Bert mumbled over his shoulder as he stepped from the rear of the narrowboat onto the grass verge and made his up along the bank as quickly as his aged legs would carry him.

"Damned idiot," Stanhope said, slamming the aft cabin door and returning to his folding canvas chair in front of the portable television set.

He pressed play on the video cassette machine and the frozen picture on the television screen started into life, as did the high-pitched chimes of its soundtrack. As he watched the impossible-colours test card and listened to the accompanying hypnotic noise, Stanhope's eyes became glassy, his jaw slackened, and he forgot all about the person from Hallam who had so impudently interrupted him.

Meanwhile, Old Bert discovered that it was not going to be as easy to leave Reapers End as it had been to arrive. Someone, it seemed, had been moving the shrunken scarecrows around again, if scarecrows they were, and several of them had been propped upright and deliberately placed so as to block off the narrow lane leading up to the sanctuary of Hallam. Old Bert, even in his beer-befuddled state, thought better of trying to ignore and breach this grotesque, ragged line of dismal, faceless sentinels. He knew an alternative route which began around the rear of one of the cottages, cut across a stretch of farmland, and then ran up through the turnip patches. As he hurriedly set off on his diversion, he could not help noting, with fearful astonishment, that the ravens were cawing frenziedly. It was, surely, a dreadful omen for them to be doing so during the hours of darkness.

Back on the narrowboat, the sight of the test card and its accompanying tune which so strangely entranced its audience finally gave way to the actual programme which had been broadcast on the night of the 30th of September, was then recorded on this video cassette, and which Stanhope now saw and heard for himself two days after the event.

It began with an (at first) simply rendered animated title screen in which jagged lightning-like rays emanated from a mast attached to the roof of an old house—these rays doubtless representing the television signals it broadcast. Floating in the sky above the house there then appeared a dancing, slender, raven-haired female fairy draped in flowing robes, complete with gossamer, sharp-pointed butterfly-wings and waving a magic wand—like some tribute to that Cottingley business, thought Stanhope, as he chuckled to himself.

The picture reverted to pure static for about five seconds, and then there was a jarring adjustment as the next segment began. It was clear to Stanhope that what he was watching were pre-recorded 8mm tapes produced on a camcorder; each one being, in turn, inserted manually into a VHS video player which was hooked up directly to a UHF transmitter.

It was a recording of a late-middle-aged man, with a striking mane of silver hair and black-rimmed spectacles, sitting facing the camera. It looked as if he had not slept for days; the salt-and-pepper stubble, the exhausted, anxious expression, and the bloodshot eyes told the tale. Behind him the viewer could see the nebulous tableaux in the background, painted directly on the walls, with greatly faded yet still unearthly colours. Stanhope could not help but think the colours used in the wall-painting, despite their deterioration, had once matched those used in the test card. The lighting was poor; candles appeared to be the only source of illumination, albeit dozens and dozens of them.

There was another jarring interruption of static before the next cassette had been presumably inserted into the video player and the subsequent part of the playback had been broadcast on the pirate station's UHF transmitter.

This one was a recording made within the confines of a series of labyrinthine, wood-panelled corridors lit solely by tapers in wall-mounted candelabra. These corridors appeared to have been constructed in a disorientating, off-kilter design, their floors noticeably askew, their walls slanting so that the flame of the tapers were not always vertically parallel to them, and the low, beamed ceilings scarcely seemed horizontal at all. It appeared to be the same individual as in the previous segment who was rapidly making his way through this interminable mad-house; but this time there was a sound of laboured breathing, grunts, and gasping.

After several minutes of such footage there was another burst of interrupting static before the next video cassette had been inserted and transmitted.

There came the now-familiar noise of laboured breathing, grunts, and gasping, as was heard in the previous segment, but on this occasion the picture remained completely black. Eventually these sounds were accompanied by the noise of the agitated rustling of straw or hay very close by, until finally the set-up of the first scene was repeated, with the background of the candles and the tableaux of wall-paintings. What had previously been badly faded colours, however, were now restored to the full potency of their original state; completely overwhelming and hallucinogenic in their intensity, even by candlelight.

And the figure in the foreground, that of the silver-haired man with the eyeglasses, was also radically altered. The figure was much smaller in stature and was wearing a linen-covering over his face, a covering with no holes for either the eyes or mouth.

Stanhope at last began to think of actually switching off the recording, for his pulse was racing and he was now more terrified than intrigued. Then the figure tore off its linen head-covering, revealing the features of the man who had appeared before—the former pallor of his face had become a pasty-white complexion with an unearthly purple mottling and a corn-yellow hue around the neck, his silver hair had turned raven-black, while his strained, anxious expression had become a malevolent, fixed smile.

It was all too unnerving for Stanhope and he finally made to switch off the VCR.

As he did so, however, the background tableaux, with its series of impossible colours, leapt to the foreground, and then streamed beyond the confines of the television screen—like the beam of a searchlight—filling the whole cabin of the narrowboat with a kaleidoscopic, dazzling radiance.

"HORKEY TIME," a rustling, disembodied voice boomed.

Stanhope felt that his physical form was being drawn into the colours being broadcast and was becoming a part of the tableaux, whilst his place in the real world was usurped by an ancient, intelligent symbol, one much older than humanity, and a closer participant in the endless cycle of nature.

And at the same moment as he screamed in protest, the screen exploded violently, scattering broken glass across the confines of the narrowboat's cabin, and sheaves of bloodied corn spilt out from the inside of the television set.

Up in the Olde Queen's Arms pub at Hallam Hardwick, a couple of weeks later, Charlie-Boy was explaining to the assembled band of greybeards the reason for Old Bert's absence. It was not like Old Bert to have foregone having his daily pint or two in the snug for such a length of time, not like him at all. Rumours began to circulate that he had found religion and taken the temperance pledge, but, then again, he had not even been seen picking up his regular half-ounce of Clan pipe tobacco from the local newsagent's.

"No," said Charlie-Boy, after taking his first swig of Double-Diamond and wiping the foam from his moustache with the back of his hand, "it's like this, see. I know for a fact that Old Bert has gone and left his wife."

"Deserted his wife! I can't believe it," said one of the greybeards, shaking his head solemnly. "They've been married over thirty years."

"It's true. But even worse than that he now lives down in the hamlet. He dosses in some rickety old shed around the back of one of the farms, out in a cornfield. Refuses to see or talk to anyone. Happens that way with folk who move into Reapers End."

Rob-the-Gob again broke his Trappist-like habit of merely nodding in reply and added:

"That's not the worst of it. I found a camera, a Canon Sure Shot, just the other day, lying there all muddy in a ditch. You know, it was the one Old Bert told us he took with him that night. Got the roll of film developed at the chemist's. Turns out it was nothing but flash-photography of small turnip-headed figures—nine frames taken close up in the dark, one after the other, and the last one, taken by accident it looks to me, of Old Bert himself stuck in front of the telly and watching what looked like some video nasty. Here, have a look for yourselves."

He laid the photographs on the counter for everyone else to see.

Charlie-Boy frowned. He disliked being upstaged.

"Well, I been to a bookshop and done some research of my own—now listen to this," he said, taking a dog-eared 1960 paperback from his pocket, its cover painting depicting a valley with a half-ruined abbey in the far distance, titled *The Ancient Mysteries of Thool Valley,* and written by Roderick Carden. Charlie-Boy thumbed through it until he came to the place he'd marked by turning down one of the page edges, and read aloud the following passage:

"The last celebration of the ancient 'Horkey Time' in the Thool Valley occurred at the hamlet of Reapers End, just outside the town of Hallam Hardwick, in late September 1874. There is anecdotal evidence that the origin of this particular festival (which is lost in antiquity and which formed a prelude to the *Samani* or 'Samhain' festival) lies with a sect of recrudescent Druids attached to a local Celtic tribe. These people worshipped and offered sacrifices to the faerie-folk whom they believed to be all that remained of the degenerated and unknown multitudes of the old Celtic gods. It is said this cult was responsible for the disappearance of the inhabitants of a Roman villa (reputed to have existed in the north of the valley close to Reapers End), who were replaced by large, turnip-headed corn dollies representing the faerie-folk."

During the first few weeks which followed these events, disturbing talk up at Hallam Hardwick concerning the folk down in Reapers End increased, and not only amongst the greybeards. A handful of the residents of the feared hamlet were sometimes glimpsed going about their business. They seemed to have shrunk in size, with none of them being more than five feet tall at most; their skulls seemed somewhat squat like turnips, and they had acquired a bizarrely archaic idiom in their turn of expression, "like acting in a Shakespeare play," as one shopkeeper on Hallam High Street put it. Also, "they have horrible wrinkled skin; the colour of corn—except for funny-shaped heads coloured pasty-white and purplish," as another said. The whispers continued. Although the folk from Reapers End were perfectly capable of recognising the purpose of many modern contrivances, such as motorcars and telephone boxes, they exhibited an ill-disguised astonishment at the existence of these objects, as if they were encountering them for the first time. Almost all the newspapers and periodicals in the old quarter were snapped up by them at the Hallam newsagents, leaving only the likes of the *Racing Post* left on the shelves.

However, these factors aside, it was the sight of their constant, inane grinning which most grated upon Hallam folk and which worked to their disadvantage. This behaviour had led to several of the visitors from the hamlet being knocked down in the street, since many of the Hallam roughs did not take kindly to being stared at, and grinned at, for no discernible reason at all. Rather than having the stuffing knocked out of them, however, these assaults always left the victims completely unharmed—and their absurd mode of behaviour was not altered in the slightest.

Perhaps it was the sudden appearance, on the morning of the 31st of October, of handwritten fliers (which must have been pasted during the early hours of the previous night) upon pillar boxes, telephone boxes, and the shop windows of Hallam which proved to be the final straw. Its text ran as follows:

"Witnesse that Greate Hallow's Eve Mysterie Drama—as will bee Sette forthe in the Box Under the Formulae 721.25 at Close on Mid-Nighte. Squire Harewoode hath Increas'd the Pow'r of the Maste."

The greybeards gathered early that Hallowe'en evening at the Olde Queen's Arms.

Whether or not the subsequent conflagration later that night was started deliberately is purely a matter for conjecture. It was seen for miles around and consumed most of the cottages in Reapers End, but centred upon the Tudor-era house with the transmission mast wherein the wall-paintings had originally been discovered. Certainly, the local police constabulary seemed disinclined to attribute the destruction to wilful arson and soon terminated their perfunctory enquiries. It is, however, difficult to understand how the flames could have leapt from one separate cottage to another, let alone to account for the fact that only the interiors of a distant old shed in the middle of a cornfield, and also of a narrowboat called the *Beagle,* moored on the outskirts of the hamlet, had been reduced to blackened husks. Then again, no human remains had been found in any of the ruins, even though the preponderance of burnt masses of corn sheaves so arranged as to form parodies of the human form, with turnips for heads, was certainly a uniquely curious feature of the general destruction. But this aspect of the general mayhem was also dismissed as insignificant. The loss of the wall-paintings was, however, much lamented by an expert in Tudor history at the British Museum.

And the greybeards up at the Olde Queen's Arms in the old quarter of Hallam Hardwick will now mutter evasively if asked for their opinion concerning the destruction-by-fire of most of Reapers End. Charlie-Boy and Rob-the-Gob, in particular, will shrug their shoulders, smile enigmatically, and take another self-satisfied swig from pints of foaming English ale raised in tribute to absent friends like Old Bert—the likes of whom were not to be forgotten and who had even been, perhaps, avenged.

Dedicated to the Weird

Excerpts from certain letters attributed to Henri Nisard, Author, and translated from the French into English.

17th March.

Ma Chérie Beatrice,

I do hope you receive this letter. I shall continue to write even though it is not possible to receive a reply from you.

Please make no attempt to try and locate me. I have had quite enough of everything (you alone know why) and must recover some proper sense of perspective. I am boarding in an establishment in a coastal town, far across the marshes, with one lonely track in and the same lonely track back out again. The nearest other town is some twenty miles distant. There is no railway line or station, simply an omnibus service which runs but once a week.

I can stay here, nurse my wounds, and try to regain some of my old confidence. It is a strange, unearthly region upon which I have stumbled! And the people here . . . !

But I shall divulge further (astounding!) details next time. I merely wish now to assure you of my being in good health and my attempting to remain cheerful of spirit.

Affectionately yours,
Henri

19th March.

Ma Chérie Beatrice,

Doubtless you think I am behaving like a veritable bohemian of *La Rive Gauche!*

Do you know (but of course you do not) that you are the only person to whom I am writing? Surely that fact alone is a measure of my continued esteem?

If you could see this town! It is like something conjured from a nightmare poem by the master, Baudelaire. Tiers of clustered-together old houses hanging on the side of a cliff leading down to a tempestuous sea. No one has erected a new building in over a hundred years: the roofs are sagging and a grey lichen infests all the brickwork. There is a multitude of stairways with hollowed steps and crooked archways.

But what of the town's residents?! I hesitate to be uncharitable, and yet it cannot be denied that they are all—to put it plainly—imbeciles. Each one possesses a mindless expression, a slack, gaping-open mouth, and, worst of all, whitish-glazed eyes which appear to have no intelligence working behind them. There must be some ocular disease abroad which has long been endemic in this district and which, when left untreated, spreads its contagion into the brain!

My concierge is a typical example. When I arrived here and enquired about a room (after all, there *was* a sign in the downstairs window grandly declaring *"L' Hôtel,"* albeit only *just* legibly) she gazed at me as if contemplating a blank wall and muttered her few replies. When a room was finally found for me (after much prevarication) she then neglected to ask me about payment. So I merely left some banknotes in an envelope downstairs on the hall table, sufficient for the first week of my stay. Nearly every question of mine was answered with the dull, monosyllabic response, "I don't know"!

Those eyes. Fagh! Like those of boiled fish.

There is no one else residing at *"L' Hôtel,"* and enquiries have determined that there are no alternative lodgings available. Nevertheless, I cannot understand how Madame Maillat (so I shall call my concierge) occupies her time, for her activities certainly do not entail cleaning, or even the organisation thereof, for *"L' Hôtel"* is quite filthy and disgusting. It is a gross exploitation of her monopoly on all the local accommodation for visitors.

Affectionately yours,

Henri

26th March.

Ma Chérie Beatrice,

You doubtless wonder about the illegible postmark on my letters and, having now had two of them returned to me (which I simply reposted, but with the address rewritten plainly in block capitals upon a new envelope), I declare I cannot account for it. But such an illegible postmark certainly serves a purpose; it conceals my exact whereabouts. Doubtless it is nothing more than the consequence of some long worn-out rubber stamp still in use in the office of a doddering postmaster.

It is a four-mile hike just to reach the nearest pillar-box in the locality.

And this is the only one I have discovered anywhere hereabouts. When I last asked Mme Maillat about the nearest post-office (I wanted to telegram my bank for funds) she replied, again: "I don't know about such things"!

I do wish she would clean her filthy establishment. I have already complained, but as yet to no avail. The profusion of dust is agitating my throat and lungs. In the hallway there is also a mass of cobwebs in every angle betwixt wall and ceiling and each of these natural insect-traps is invariably dotted with huge, dead (or else dying) bluebottle flies.

This morning I was thinking yet again about [illegible]'s remarks upon my tale *"De Terribles Plaisirs,"* in which (you surely recall the review as well as I do) the said pernicious "critic-oaf" stated:

> Mons. Nisard's work is in a creative dead-end and he would be well-advised to cease writing altogether. The putrid literary reign of such decadents with their weird, unhealthy obsessions is now, mercifully, over.

(His customary impudence! *Mons.,* indeed!)

Well, contrary to that "sagely" advice, I know you will be interested to learn that I have already begun work on a new tale. I am still just preparing a synopsis, but this strange town itself furnishes a strong impetus to one's imagination. The more I see of its inhabitants the more I am reminded of certain organic derangements delineated in Lautréamont's *Les Chants de Maldoror.*

Affectionately yours,
Henri

28th March.

Ma Chérie Beatrice,

I undertook an extended constitutional around the town yesterday. It was pouring with rain and, apart from a few local *pasty-grey* phantom-cretins wandering around aimlessly, I virtually had the streets to myself. I sought to locate a bookshop or stationers, but could not find one. And then, out of curiosity, I walked rather closer to the walls of the houses so that I could glance more easily through the window panes.

Like those outside, the inhabitants within were just wandering around aimlessly, staring into space with those dead, fishy eyes. Beatrice, it was as if they were dreaming but still awake. They are all in the same communal trance. What is the correct term? Collective somnambulism? I believe so.

I do not think that the people here present any physical threat to my person, but I appear to have acquired the troubling, persistent notion that they might be somehow conspiring in secret against me. I know how that suggestion must sound to you. But why do I never see them talking to one another? In fact, I cannot recall that I have ever heard them speak except when prompted, and even then the sole response has been those repetitive words (always muttered in the same hollow monotone): "I don't know."

Surely something truly *outré* has occurred in this town. Perhaps the water supply was contaminated with cholera, for some calamity must have produced this outpost of simpletons! No, I withdraw that last observation: even the likes of simpletons talk to one another, if only in gibberish!

Still, apropos of nothing, the story is progressing well. I have already written a few pages of the first draft (whether you want to or not, yours shall be the first eyes to see it! Your opinion ranks more highly in my estimation than any other I could name). It is the only thing keeping me from abject despair. Naturally I am certainly trying to work some aspects of this town into the narrative. How could I fail to do so? It constitutes more than half the reason it is now absolutely essential I remain here!

Affectionately yours,

Henri

30th March.

Ma Chérie Beatrice,

I must here affirm that I have not been drinking to excess. Half a bottle of *vin ordinaire* a day at the very most, but no more. It is not simply alcohol which has conjured this place from out of the depths of a brain already overtaxed with misery, Beatrice. When the worst of all this is over, when I have completed *"La Fête de la Mort"* (I have now formulated a title), I shall prove every word which I have written is stark truth. I concede, however, that if I had not seen such spectral wonders with my own eyes then perhaps I might also harbour doubts as to the state of mind of a person making such wild claims. I wish I could have sight of a letter from you: but it is impossible! The thought that *you* might entertain the notion my letters to you are an imposture almost maddens me to distraction in itself!

I should not care for it to be made public that I have any contact with the world outside this locality. And now I hear Mme Maillat's tread upon the stairs and so must quickly cease from writing.

Affectionately yours,

Henri

4th April.

Ma Chérie Beatrice,

Have I mentioned the bluebottle flies before? They seem to turn up everywhere. The streets here attract endless swarms of them (though we are barely out of this year's harsh winter!). One can spot them crawling up lampposts and over the clammy lichen on the external walls of the houses. Now I can partially understand why Mme Maillat doesn't get rid of the cobwebs in this place. (I am assuming, of course, that she acts deliberately rather than it being a case of sin by omission. But perhaps I am being overly charitable to her.)

Apropos of said personage, she still has not asked me for payment: and when she sees me upon the stairs continues to regard me with a dull lack of recognition.

I have been suffering from horrible dreams about staring eyes. I awake in a cold sweat and in the grip of absolute terror. I have filled a page of my notebook with such dream-images (which have proved inspirational for *"La Fête de la Mort"*): they are truly terrifying visions.

Accordingly, I thought it advisable that I spend a little time away from this town and that I should pass at least an afternoon elsewhere, somewhere inland across the marshes. My only route of escape proves to be the once-weekly horse-drawn omnibus service to Champavert (no, this is not the real name, but I can't have you checking up on these things, my dear). This excursion of mine is therefore scheduled for tomorrow at noon. The service returns here at dusk on the return leg of the journey.

I caught sight of my first "tourist" yesterday! He was creeping around the town like some escaped criminal, apparently trying not to be noticed. A young fellow, not more than twenty-four years of age I should think, with a shock of bright red hair and carrying a knapsack. He must have come in on the last omnibus service and thus have already been here a week. But when I called out to him he fled, like a lunatic, down the promenade steps and then ran along the beach-front. Astonishingly churlish behaviour! One would think he would have been more courteous to a fellow exile from the common round of life!

Affectionately yours,

Henri

6th April.

Ma Chérie Beatrice,

I did not manage to depart from the town after all. I arrived at the terminus in the central square some fifteen minutes before the omnibus was due. I just sat there, fortified by a small amount of wine, and watching the waves break on the shore in the distance. The seagulls were making an awful row. Most of them seemed clustered around the burial ground at the top of Lourps Hill (for future reference none of the names I provide will be genuine, so I shall stop mentioning the fact). It is a huge old church with two enormous spires. Parts of it are in disrepair, but I have noticed that Masses are extremely well attended. In fact, the entire populace seems to make its way up to that place whenever Mass is held. Anyway, there I was looking up at the wheeling, screeching gulls and watching the foaming sea, when the fabled omnibus finally trundled into the square!

I remind you, Beatrice, that this particular conveyance is the sole means of public transport. Well, I am afraid it was a wreck of a carriage drawn by a pair of sorry-looking nags. Doubtless it has been in continuous use for decades. An open-mouthed dullard of a coachman sat up in front and seemed to take no interest in avoiding obstacles in his path. I had to step out in front of the horses to make the vehicle halt, and it was a pretty close thing as to whether or not I were slowly trampled under their hooves.

Before I climbed aboard I had asked the peasant coachman what the price of the fare to Champavert was and he simply grinned like an imbecile, flashing broken teeth. I was repulsed: greenish drool fairly oozed down his chin. His dead, fish-like eyes stared back at me until I took my seat towards the rear of the omnibus. And then we were off on our journey, the carriage creaking and groaning like a flimsy wooden barge tossed around in a sea-storm.

The interior was deserted, save for a young lady seated opposite me upon the facing bench. When I had boarded the omnibus her head was turned away; for she was gazing out of the window towards the sea on her side. But as soon as the vehicle shuddered into life she turned back and addressed me (and no one in this town has spontaneously done such a thing!). Rather a forward gesture for a young lady, you might think, and I was, for my own part, certainly taken aback by it.

The young lady introduced herself as Mademoiselle Juliette Marles and was actually quite charming. Her hair was long, raven-black, and shoulder-length, whilst her skin was of alabaster translucence rather than the local pasty-grey complexion; but her eyes, exactly like all the others I have seen in the town, bore the selfsame repellent, "boiled-carp" appearance. Although she had an air of distraction and seemed to make a pronounced effort to concentrate on what I was saying, she was nevertheless quite lucid. How unlike her fellow townsfolk!

Our conversation was stimulating and she evinced such a wide vocabulary as to lead me to surmise she was self-taught, and to a remarkable degree of accomplishment. However, her mispronunciation of certain words betrayed her humble station in life. The volume in her lap (Charles Robert Maturin's *Melmoth ou l'Homme errant*) drew an admiring aside from me. But when, in answer to a further enquiry, I owned that I was indeed myself an author, she sounded perturbed, as if I had committed some nebulous *faux pas*.

Alas, the omnibus ceased operation only two miles from town on a steep rise that curved over to the beginning of the vast marshlands. One of the pitiable old horses had collapsed; and it was soon apparent that the other could not possibly do the work required of two. The coachman had sat there as inanimate as a discarded Grand Guignol dummy for several moments but then finally jumped into life and climbed down to examine the fallen, panting beast.

Mlle Marles and I tried to converse upon general topics, such as the weather, while the coachman crudely attempted to thrash the poor beast into action by means of a horsewhip. It was at this juncture that I ventured a joke (purely to try and lighten what had become a truly distressing turn of events!) concerning the probability that he would, when asked what was wrong with the animal, merely reply, "I don't know." And in response to this *jeu d'espirit*, her smile had a peculiar crooked shape to it, as if strained and artificial.

But that, of course, was exactly the remark the coachman finally made.

And so we were forced to wend our way on foot back into the town. The next omnibus is scheduled for a week from today. I wonder if it will actually reappear. In the interim, it appears that I am trapped here. Still, perhaps I may take consolation from the possibility of having made a new acquaintance, or—in good time—perhaps even of having gained a new friend.

Affectionately yours,

Henri

10th April.

Ma Chérie Beatrice,

I have so much to tell you: so much that is quite horrible and unbelievable.

I had to cease momentarily from writing. The room was under assault from several bluebottles. How they annoy me! I have opened the window and managed to gesture them outside. Do you recall the old trick which I showed you once—to spread your arms wide and move from side to side until you force them to retreat? I remember your mother coming in upon me unawares once, whilst my attention was wholly engaged in just such an attempt!

How we all laughed together over my folly later.

And I wonder whether you might think my letters form part of *"La Fête de la Mort."* As I have already intimated to you, I am using only *elements* of my experiences.

Mlle Marles (you remember the young lady I told you about, the one on the omnibus?) "ran" into me whilst I was tramping the streets a few days ago. In fact, I am sure that it was no coincidence. I have seen her loitering around *"L'Hôtel"* of late. But there is no need for you to be jealous, my dear! I imagine that she is lonely and obviously the prospect of any stimulating conversation in this town is extremely limited.

She tried to make me promise to accompany her to Mass at the church on Lourps Hill, declaring that it was unlike other *bourgeois* (so she said) churches and I would find myself very much relishing the experience. Of course, I declined her invitation: she then became rather peevish at this unexpected rebuff.

And, although I outwardly evinced no interest, I confess that my curiosity was piqued. I had been thinking of incorporating the church (the structure is a true Gothic nightmare and the twin spires are simply magnificent) into *"La Fête de la Mort"*: I was of a mind to explore its interior when a Mass was not in progress. I reasoned that if I examined the inside during early afternoon I should be unmolested by worshippers. It would also be a good opportunity to look around the burial ground. Although the yard was walled in, I suspected that entry could be gained through some linking door within the church itself.

Now what follows is strange and rather horrible, Beatrice, but it is not fiction. I have to admit, though, given my own literary proclivities, part of my imagination was exhilarated by the *implications* of what I discovered in the church and in the burial ground.

The sky was a grey and miserable void that Saturday afternoon when I found myself climbing up the hollowed steps towards the church on Lourps Hill. Its huge soot-blackened spires loomed over the sagging roofs of the rows of high, terraced houses and cast twin shadows over the vista, shadows which seemed to be possessed of a wholly independent existence.

(Observe how easily I conjure up the literary shade of Edgar Poe!)

I found the church door had been left ajar. It is obviously not unusual to find churches in small towns, or villages, left unlocked, but I admit I myself found the fact suggestive; as if my visit had been anticipated in advance. The interior proved to be dilapidated (despite the large congregation that must frequently gather here), with multiple fissures scarring the vaulted roof. The central nave, transepts, presbytery, and altar were depressing in the extreme. A few burning candles formed oases of light in the gloom and I could see that the pews had been in continuous use for centuries, even though many were now in shocking states of disrepair. It was just after I had entered that I first heard an unnerving sound. High up, just below the vaulted roof, were thousands of huge bluebottles, all buzzing, and moving as one, like some murky cloud. The noise they created was abominably disgusting. I could discern no sign of Christian iconography upon the walls or even upon the altar—a fact which perturbed me, though I am, as you know, no regular churchgoer.

Upon the flagstones were scattered certain discarded objects, in some profusion, which looked like chalices, though their filthy state was surely sacrilegious. They may have once been used for communion wine but the sheer number of them baffled me.

Well, Beatrice, this is not even the end of the hideous episode.

For I discovered that another door in the north transept indeed led directly into the walled burial ground. Though I was delighted to have quit the gloomy interior and to be outside, the irritating noise of the bluebottles was merely exchanged for the deafening screeches of gulls; dozens of them hovering and swooping towards the gravestones. The birds were of enormous size, and I had to step carefully in order to avoid those that fluttered their wings imperiously upon the weather-beaten and crumbling monuments to the dead. The creatures concentrated around a particular area and I made my way towards it, through long and untended grass, until I was crawling on my hands and knees, so as not to be seen by any of the townsfolk who might be lurking inside the confines of the burial ground.

And then I saw what it was the gulls had so eagerly sought. A sexton stood over an open grave. All the birds appeared desperate to get at the mournful cavity. He was actually beating them off with a mud-, gore-, and feather-caked shovel. He was grey of skin and dead of eyes and he lashed out with mechanical strokes at the gulls, as if he were some kind of automaton. Suddenly, another personage—and an even more curious individual than he—joined him.

This second individual came striding through the long grass: but his limbs seemed to bend outlandishly, as if he were an invertebrate in human form. That this apparent anatomical freakishness must have been the result of a queer trick of the poor light and of my own overworked imagination seemed obvious, but, nevertheless, the impression remained terrifying. He was a priest, incredibly aged, with a skeletal face and long streaks of white hair scraped across his bald pate. Although his eyes (thank God he did not see me!) resembled those of all the other townsfolk, they possessed additionally, at their centre, black spots like drops of Indian ink, and these radiated a monstrous inhumanity. The intensity of the gaze was a thousand times more nightmarish than any I had hitherto seen.

Beatrice, I swear that they were the original of those eyes which have long haunted my dreams!

With the appearance of this demon in a cassock, the gulls scattered instantly and before he and the sexton quit the grave they covered it with a heavy tarpaulin.

Do not mistake me for a fool, Beatrice. I realise I should have crept silently away from the place. Yes, a part of me, a very great part in fact, wanted to flee from the town altogether. But I thought of [illegible]'s sneering comment and I thought of my tale *"La Fête de la Mort"* and I thought of how I desired to make my writing truly authentic! To experience *absolute fear,* so that I could myself *communicate* it to others, would be incontrovertible proof of continued dedication to my own dark Muse!

And so I crawled over to the tarpaulin and drew the sheet back just far enough to see what lay below.

Beatrice, what was down there was this: a grave that had been dug up, a coffin which had been breached, and the corpse of a young man with the lips of its mouth crudely sewn together.

The features were distorted but, Beatrice, the worst of it is that he had a shock of bright red hair . . .

You have to believe me.

I cannot write any more at present.

Affectionately yours,

Henri

18th April.

Ma Chérie Beatrice,

I swear I am not going mad. I am, however, in something of a daze after recent events and also afraid to sleep because of those dreams about the eyes of the "priest."

Yes, I confess I have been drinking in greater quantities; any reasonable man would if forced to exist under the strain and the unearthly horror of these circumstances. But I am writing—and it is the best material I have ever produced. *"La Fête de la Mort"* will rank alongside the supreme literary achievements of Edgar Poe. The weird occurrences transpiring all around me are bringing my own tale to life!

I sit here, writing by candlelight, and I think of the vast distance between us. I think how strange it is that these words will only make their way towards you in Paris tomorrow after I have sealed them up and posted my letter in the lonely pillar-box six miles distant across the lonely marshes. (I do see townsfolk when undertaking this particular journey, but they are invariably some way off in the distance.)

I am entirely shut off from a world that is wholly ignorant of me and of this cryptic town with all its strange horrors.

Yes, I must leave soon—I realise that now—and do so before it is too late. But Beatrice, I *cannot leave* until I have finished *"La Fête de la Mort."* Once it is complete (no more than a fortnight hence, I swear it!) I shall post the manuscript to you, just in case—and, again, I emphasise: *just in case*—I cannot make good my escape. But I shan't let anyone know where I am until my work is finished.

Two more weeks. Then all this will be over and the ordeal will have surely proven itself to be the making of me as an author.

Two more weeks.

Do not despair. The omnibus will surely resume its services by then!

Affectionately yours,

Henri

25th April.

Ma Chérie Beatrice,

Mlle Marles has taken to loitering outside *"L'Hôtel"* again. I have been purposefully avoiding her: there remains far too much work left for me to complete, not least upon my story. She has been maddeningly insistent that I go with her to one of the Masses held up at the church, and she hinted that it was only a matter of time—that I would go in the end, *and whether I cared to do so or not.*

But after what I have seen and experienced, I would have to be forcibly dragged up there! The poor young lady must be suffering from derangement, like all the others, and what I misinterpreted as unique lucidity on her part might instead form a carefully calculated, wider plot to violate my seclusion.

Four days ago, in middle of the central square, I saw the burnt-out shell of the omnibus. The inside of the vehicle was completely gutted and a few charred pages (of course, they were from *Melmoth*) fluttered across the square, carried on the wind. I cannot tell what happened to the imbecile coachman.

The bluebottles are in greater numbers today than ever before.

I do wish the weather here were not always so terrible. The town seems forever to be surrounded by storms or impending storms! Oh, it is the right atmosphere for my work, but at least I would have the option of escaping on foot along the track across the marshlands if they would only let up. Six miles in such weather to a pillar-box is one thing, but twenty miles to the nearest town is quite another.

Now I must return to working on my story.

Affectionately yours,

Henri

26th April.

Ma Chérie Beatrice,

I am almost overcome with tiredness—I scarcely slept at all yesterday.

Mme Maillat keeps pacing back and forth along the corridor outside my room like some warden in a gaol. This is the first time she has taken any apparent interest in either myself or my activities. I certainly have to be more careful about my comings and goings in future. If it were discovered I have any contact whatsoever with the outside world then what has been general indifference towards me might be replaced by outright malignity.

And Mlle Marles has taken to following me everywhere I go when I am in the open air, as if she also is keeping watch: though now always at a careful distance. It seems imperative that I should question her here in the privacy and close confines of my room. If I were to make certain promises in advance (please do not be shocked by my candour, Beatrice!) then, with the assistance of a copious supply of *vin ordinaire,* I might obtain precious information. I need to know the full extent of the horror, not only for my own, but for *literature's sake!* My now-dwindling supply of wine is only sufficient for one bold attempt to breach her defences. I have spent far too much of my time, when not writing, in alcoholic stupor.

But all is not hopeless: I have almost completed *"La Fête de la Mort"!*

A few more days of exertion are all that are required. Did I claim that it would rank with the literary achievements of Poe? If I did, then I was being unduly modest. The atmosphere and sinister fear of this town have lent the tale a dramatic authenticity which cannot be underestimated. Poe conjured all his horrors from the brilliance of his own imagination, but mine is an objective, waking universe of terror vouchsafed to me alone! Imagine, if you will, what Poe might have written had he actually *dwelt* in the House of Usher or had he experienced *first-hand* what it was to *be* his Monsieur Valdemar. Imagine that, Beatrice!! *Then* you will have some inkling of what I mean to achieve! I must be on the verge of finishing the greatest weird tale ever written. And this prospect is all that sustains me, through the hangovers, through the despair, through the horrors of isolation: for I have always been dedicated to the weird.

Despite the perils I might be courting (and even if a portion of you still suspects that there is an element of embellishment in my letters) my long, terrible ordeal has been worth it. And its consummation is now almost upon me.

Three days hence and I shall depart. Yes, on foot across twenty treacherous miles of marshland if necessary. And what a glorious account I shall render of my adventures!

Affectionately yours,
Henri

27th April.

Ma Chérie Beatrice,

The gulls were frantic last night. There were stupendous numbers of them swooping and wheeling around the burial ground and the twin spires of the church up on Lourps Hill. I could not sleep again (the same recurring dreams) and I watched the white birds for hours, like aerial ghosts fluttering in the night sky. What gulls are these which feed even during the hours of darkness?

Yet I cannot help thinking of that gutted omnibus. And of the fate of the man with red hair. I am not really myself of late.

Henri

29th April.

Ma Chérie Beatrice,

Tomorrow will be my last day here.

I can scarcely write down what I must here confess, but I am compelled to do so by my eternally binding promise that there never be any secrets kept between us.

The young lady, Mlle Marles, kept the rendezvous with me which I had carefully planned for last night. For once, the miserable Mme Maillat absented herself from pacing up and down my corridor. I wish that I had not kept the rendezvous, for the experience was horrible, but I was under some sort of inner compulsion and I had been drinking heavily beforehand. What was meant to be an interrogation . . . [illegible]

When I awoke after dawn Mlle Marles was gone. The morning light streamed through the open window and made my eyes smart, so I raised a hand to shield them from the sun's glare.

Caught between my fingers were several long strands of white hair. The bedsheets were smeared with traces of lipstick and fairly reeked with the distinctive, clammy musk exuded by the bodies of the extremely elderly.

Later, the room was assailed by bluebottles, and for hours thereafter I suffered from a horrible choking sensation.

Forgive me. I have made a terrible, terrible mistake.

Henri

30th April.

Ma Chérie Beatrice,

This will be my final letter. As soon as I have completed it I shall make my escape attempt. I have no choice now other than to directly attempt the twenty-mile trek across the treacherous marshes. I shall post this last communication in the pillar-box six miles away.

There is nothing left of my *magnum opus*. My room has been ransacked. They have taken the manuscript of *"La Fête de la Mort"* along with all my notebooks.

There is something inside me now, Beatrice. I can feel it moving under my skin, wriggling around, and I know what it is.

(God, there are bluebottles *everywhere!*)

While I am still able to think and write coherently I have to tell you what happened before they finally discover where I am hiding.

And I must try to do so in the correct order.

Earlier this evening I found myself wandering up to the church on Lourps Hill. It was as if I were in a trance and not fully in control of my own actions. I seemed to be a passenger in my own body. I climbed the staircase, hollowed by centuries of footsteps, up the hill to the church, moving amongst all the rest of the muttering townsfolk. Cracked bells were ringing from the twin steeples and summoning the damned to worship. Those hideous crowds! They were more rotten and mindless than ever, and they half stumbled up the interminable series of steps, like the legendary zombies of Haiti, with their dead, fish-like eyes staring up at the spectral church. I swear that, amongst their number, I saw the youthful, living— *though still cadaverous*—body of the man with the bright red hair who had been interred in the burial ground.

The doors to the church had been flung wide open. The thronging press of the vile masses carried me into its dim interior. The bluebottles had vanished, probably having escaped through the various holes that riddle the vaulted ceiling. The townsfolk took up their places in their pews and the rows of mostly bald, white or grey-haired heads lolled vaguely in the flickering pools of candlelight.

Then the hideously aged "priest" with the skeletal face appeared at the altar, clad in his black cassock.

The eyes of this squalid priest! How false they seemed in the setting of a human face.

What inconceivable horrors had they seen?

Such was the unnatural perversity of their filthy rites that I cannot bring myself to detail them to you, Beatrice; even those notoriously abominable passages in J.-K Huysmans's *Là-Bas* or those in Arthur Machen's truly frightful *Le Grand Dieu Pan*—over which we both shuddered as I attempted to translate it—are no more than a pale shadow of the ultimate cosmic foulness which, I alone, *of living men,* have now personally witnessed.

Rooted to the spot, still in a stupefying trance of supreme horror, I was quite incapable of independent motion; even though my very soul cried out for surcease from terror.

When the monstrous ceremony was completed and the worshippers slowly, gravely filed away, the squalid priest himself advanced towards me, accompanied by an ancient crone. At first I saw only his eyes—those horrible eyes, all white, but with a pin-drop of black at their centre—the eyes that stare without blinking, even in dreams, and which bind one irrevocably to him. But it was the crone who addressed me and I forced myself to turn my attention to her: it was Mlle Marles. Her face was withered and leathery; long white hair, ravaged by alopecia, hung down over her naked shoulders—what remained of her was surely far more dead than alive.

"He speaks no French," she whispered confidentially, "but he wishes me to advise you that, soon, all your old thoughts will be gone."

The squalid priest said something in Latin to her.

"Exsurge, de Vermis, adjuva nos: et libera nos propter nomen tuum ..."

Then she spoke again to me:

"He knows many languages but they are all dead and half-forgotten. He has lived a very, very, very long time. He is their avatar and came to us half a century ago from a great plateau in central Asia. He has buried himself amongst the lost mysteries of occult antiquity.

"The Red Worm speaks through him—"

She grinned, revealing a rotten set of decayed teeth.

"Soon you will die, and then, just as soon, you will return. I myself will again be young soon. There is everlasting youth in the caress of the Red Worm."

The squalid priest began to laugh and I saw huge bluebottles crawling around in his toothless mouth.

"The Red Worm will wax strong inside you," she said, even as I turned and stumbled away, the trance-like spell momentarily broken. "You are a perfect host—"

[Later]

[illegible] sewn my mouth shut [illegible] and eventually there is scarcely any power of reason left in its victims—there remain only the visions;

surely visions dreamed by the damned in hell.

His . . . its . . . memories are becoming my own. I see him . . . it . . . in the hidden, ancient monasteries of Mongolia, in half-ruined vaults of forbidden scrolls, the key to eternal existence. Despoiler of [illegible] tombs [illegible] writhing in corpses as part of some necromantic rite. I see him . . . it . . . driven out of country after country, until [illegible] our Republic, [illegible] infesting. *Olgoi-khorkhoi*. What scourge [illegible]

Something [illegible] black spaces on the outside that we damnable scribblers have not even [illegible] walks with its foul companions.

[illegible] destroys thought; no brain [illegible] coiling beneath the skull.

Beatrice, my eyes do not belong to me any more. I cannot see this world.

[illegible] for me. The [illegible]

Advise the authorities, [illegible] razed and the ground sowed with salt.

Goodbye forever, I have always loved you.

Keep away—the town's real name is [illegible] in the county of [illegible] Will try to make it to the pillar-box somehow [illegible] to cease here.

1st May.

Ma Chérie Beatrice,

Doubtless the manifold absurdities of my recent letters will have already been an indication to you that I have been subject to extreme mental turmoil, and the sheer fertility of an *outré* imagination has led me, unintentionally, into the realms of (inadvertent) literary hoax. Ignore all the ravings written therein. You will recall my telling you once that my idol Edgar Poe was not himself averse from using a similar technique, though he did so consciously, in order to generate a willing suspension of disbelief— Please try to find it in your heart to excuse my having subjected you to such a strange epistolary ordeal, my own Beatrice.

I can readily reassure you that all the ridiculous claims in my previous communications were a consequence of the strange delusional malady which has lately affected me, but which has now altogether passed; just as the sudden breaking of a high fever results in fully-returned sanity. I shall never return to my old habits, and, in fact, I shall give up forever the "art of literature" (not to mention drinking wine!). I wish us to be married at once—without any further needless prevarication on my part. Our destinies are entwined and we must be together always!

Please come to me at once, *and in secret,* for now that you know the name and location of the town wherein I reside, we shall be separated no more.

Absolute discretion is vital.

I now possess an unexpected inheritance, and poverty, as you well know, has been the only real obstacle to our happiness. Repletion shall prove to be its bridge! I shall explain everything in detail when you arrive here.

You will find this marvellous old town quite delightful and *so* full of wonders—but only when you finally see it through your own eyes!

And we shall laugh together, as we did of old, over all my past follies!

Please do not fail me! Come at once, my dearest love, speak of this to no one, *as you value your life,* and hasten to my embrace!

Monsieur Henri is waiting for his Mlle Beatrice—*and he is crying tears of blood.*

Devotedly yours,
Henri

Acknowledgments

"Dedicated to the Weird." Original version first published in *The Derelict and Other Stories,* ed. John B. Ford and Steve Lines (Rainfall Books, 2003). The present revised version is previously unpublished.

"Duxford's Blackberry Wine." Original to this volume.

"An Elemental Infestation." First published in *Black Wings VII,* ed. S. T. Joshi (PS Publishing, 2023).

"The End of Death." First published as two chapbooks by Zagava, 2021.

"If Destiny Still Reigns." First published in *Penumbra* No. 1 (2020).

"The Interminable Abomination." First published in *Penumbra* No. 2 (2021).

"A Letter from Jack." Original to this volume.

"The Ominous Revival of Certain Old Customs." Original to this volume.

"Posterity." First published as a chapbook by Zagava, 2020.

"A Universe of Charnel Glamour." First published in *Disintegration,* ed. Darren Speegle (PS Publishing, 2023).

www.ingramcontent.com/pod-product-compliance
Lightning Source LLC
Chambersburg PA
CBHW051526050726
47503CB00014B/1983